THE DAM

THE DAM

Robert Byrne

ATHENEUM   NEW YORK

For Russell Byrne

Contents

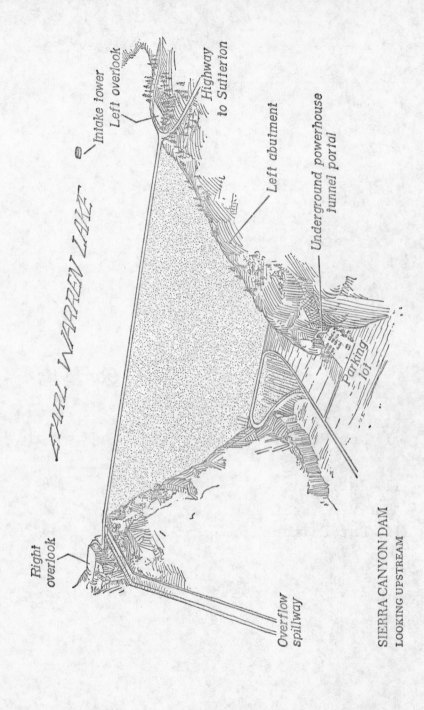

EARL WARREN LAKE

Intake tower
Left overlook

Highway to Sutterion

Left abutment

Underground powerhouse tunnel portal

Parking lot

Right overlook

Overflow spillway

SIERRA CANYON DAM
LOOKING UPSTREAM

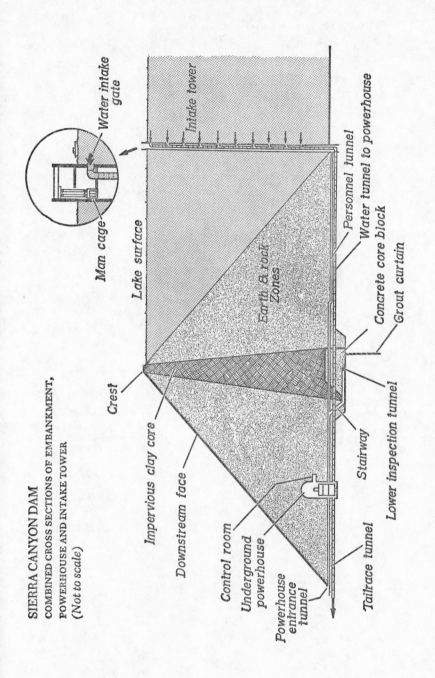

SIERRA CANYON DAM
COMBINED CROSS SECTIONS OF EMBANKMENT,
POWERHOUSE AND INTAKE TOWER
(Not to scale)

Water intake gate

Intake tower

Man cage

Lake surface

Crest

Impervious clay core

Downstream face

Control room

Underground powerhouse

Powerhouse entrance tunnel

Earth & rock zones

Personnel tunnel

Water tunnel to powerhouse

Concrete core block

Grout curtain

Lower inspection tunnel

Stairway

Tailrace tunnel

I

The Fear

1

FIVE YEARS AFTER ITS COMPLETION, SIERRA CANYON DAM, AT EIGHT hundred and twenty-five feet, the highest dam in the United States and the highest earth and rock dam in the world, was subjected to a series of minor earthquakes. Seismograph needles in northern California trembled at 8:20 A.M., when the first of twenty-nine foreshocks was recorded. The main tremor, which struck five hours later, had a magnitude of 5.5 on the Richter scale and rattled dishes over an area of two hundred square miles. The rolling motion lasted for seven seconds and was disconcerting mainly to people who were indoors at the time. Most of those outdoors ascribed the quiver to the passing of trains or trucks. Fishermen and water skiers on Earl Warren Lake behind the dam noticed nothing.

The only terror was experienced by a hiker crossing a hillside meadow five miles southwest of the dam, the epicenter of the quake. He was thrown off his feet by the heaving ground and grabbed handfuls of grass to keep from rolling down the slope. "It was like trying to hang on to a raft in rough water," he told a reporter from the Sacramento *Bee*, "and wondering if there was a waterfall ahead. A crack opened up in the ground and I could see the sides rubbing together. I heard limbs falling off trees and rocks rolling downhill."

The crack in the meadow delineated a previously unknown rift in the surface rock, now called Parker's Fault after the hiker who first saw it. The fault ran in a northeasterly direction and could be

traced on the surface for nearly half a mile. Geologists found that
the ground had shifted six inches horizontally and three inches vertically. According to a study made by the United States Geological
Survey, there was a possibility that Parker's Fault ran under Sierra
Canyon Dam.

Large reservoirs that fluctuate in size have been known to cause
seismic disturbances. The USGS study included a graph on which
was plotted every earthquake detected in the vicinity of the dam
since its construction, along with the surface elevation of the lake,
which was at its lowest in the fall and highest in the spring. No
correlation was found; that is, the earthquake that endangered the
dam was not caused by the dam.

Despite the scarcity of measurable property damage, the earthquake made headlines in Caspar, Butte, Sutter, and Yuba counties.
Hard-digging reporters described the orchards outside Wheatland,
where fruit was shaken from trees. A thousand turkeys panicked in
a pen at Rio Oso, and three hundred were so seriously wounded in
the back-and-forth stampedes that they had to be slaughtered.

Only two people suffered injuries requiring medical care. An
electrician kneeling on a kitchen floor in Grass Valley took six
stitches in the cheek after being hit by a falling wall clock. A
woman in a Roseville supermarket had a toe broken when her feet
were engulfed by a collapsing display of canned peaches. With so
little hard news to go on, newspapers had to run editorials on what
might have happened had the quake been bigger or in a different
place. The Yuba City–Marysville *Valley Herald* observed that
modern civilization exists at the whim of the forces of nature, compared to which the works of man are puny.

One thing that might have happened was a failure of the dam, a
thought that crossed the mind of Wilson Hartley, Chief of Police of
Sutterton, a town of 6,500 on the Sierra Canyon River downstream
from the dam. Hartley was the local officer in charge of public
safety, which meant that it was up to him rather than the county
Sheriff to supervise the evacuation of Suttertonians in case of a disaster or a threatened disaster. In his files was an Inundation Map
furnished to him under state law by the Office of Emergency Planning in Sacramento. It was required of the owner of every large
dam to confront the possibility of instantaneous failure and to make
estimates of the resulting flood. The map showed how high the flood
crest would be and how long it would take to reach key points

downstream. Such information was valuable to communities with time to react, but in the case of Sutterton it was good only for morbid jokes around the office. The flood Hartley and his staff would be faced with would be five hundred feet deep and would be upon them in minutes. They would hardly have time to reach for their rosaries.

When the quake hit, Hartley was sitting at his desk. He put his pen down and stared at the office window, which had begun shaking noisily. A small vase of cut flowers his secretary had put on his desk that morning wobbled from side to side and fell over. He picked it up with his left hand and with his right rescued a sheaf of papers before they were soaked by the spreading puddle of water. The first thought that entered his head was that Mitchell Brothers had set off a particularly illegal blast at their quarry, but when the window and floor continued to tremble he knew it was more than that. He rose to his feet trying not to imagine the worst.

A policeman appeared in his doorway. "Did you feel that? We just had an earthquake."

"I think you're right," Hartley answered. "Now we might get a bath."

They moved to the window. Even though the dam was almost half a mile away, they had to look upward to see it looming above the trees of an intervening hill. The dam was almost unimaginably massive, higher than an eighty-story building, more voluminous than Grand Coulee and Boulder dams combined. Only the knifelike straightness of its mile-and-a-half-long crest, outlined sharply against the sky, identified it as man-made. Its vast downstream face was like a prairie tilted at thirty degrees.

The two men studied the dam. "It's still there," Hartley said. "Looks tight as a drum."

"The mountains will cave in before the dam goes. When they built that sucker, they built it to last."

"That's what the engineers say, anyway. All the same, if I could do it without making the town nervous I'd drag my office to higher ground."

As they turned away from the window, the overhead light flickered and went out.

Four days after the earthquake, a Pan American flight from London landed at Los Angeles. Among those waiting for the passengers was a newspaper reporter with a notebook in his hand and a tape recorder suspended from his shoulder. "He's a crusty bastard," the city editor had told him when making the assignment, "but he's sharp and he speaks his mind. Ignore his insults and you'll get some quotes we can use." The reporter watched with interest as the man he was after appeared in the doorway of the plane. Shrugging off the assistance of a stewardess and wielding his aluminum crutches expertly, he swung his legs across the step between the fuselage and the movable corridor and maneuvered himself into a wheelchair. Theodore Roshek, president of the international engineering firm of Roshek, Bolen & Benedetz, Inc., was easy to recognize, and not just because of his handicap. His thin, angular face was always topped by a gray felt hat with an unfashionably wide brim. Full black eyebrows, which contrasted with his white hair, gave his deep-set blue eyes an unnerving intensity. He sat erect in the chair, leaning slightly forward, as if he were a commander at the bridge of a warship. It occurred to the reporter that if Roshek could walk it would be with the stride of a man crossing a room to poke someone in the nose.

The interview was conducted as the wheelchair was pushed by an aide from the concourse gate to the street, where a limousine was waiting.

"Excuse me, Mr. Roshek, I'm Jim Oliver of the Los Angeles *Times.*"

"My deepest sympathy," Roshek said, not turning his head. "I read the *Herald-Examiner* myself. Now there is a hell of a paper."

"I hope you don't mind a few questions. May I use my tape recorder?"

"Please do. It might cut down on errors."

"Your firm designed Sierra Canyon Dam. . . ."

"Right. We also supervised construction. We have a twenty year contract to provide inspection and monitor performance. Not that it needs inspection. It's probably the safest dam ever built."

Oliver, a short man, had to walk as fast as he could to keep up with the wheelchair. He explained that the *Times* was doing a background piece on the earthquake and was soliciting comments from a number of authorities.

For the first time, Roshek looked at him. "The earthquake? Are you just getting around to that? Newspapers dealt with news when

I was your age. I'd rather talk about something more current, wouldn't you? Do you think the Dodgers will ever score again?"

"We tried to reach you in London."

Roshek turned away. "I was busy. I thought you were calling about a subscription."

"Did the earthquake cause you any concern?"

"Yes. I have a summer place below the dam. The fireplace may be cracked."

"The designer of the dam has a place downstream," the reporter said, scrawling a few words in a notebook. "That's an interesting point."

"I always sleep like a baby when I'm there. Must be the mountain air."

"Then you don't think the public was in danger."

"No. Well, yes. The public is always in danger. Did you get here by car? Have you no regard at all for your safety? Fifty thousand people were killed last year in the United States by cars. I just took a ride in a plane . . . that probably wasn't too smart, either."

"The fact remains that an earthquake took place next to the world's highest dam."

"The fact remains, and so does the dam. It's not the world's highest. It's the world's highest earth and rock embankment. Several concrete arches are higher. Grand Dixence in Switzerland is nine hundred and thirty-two feet. Nurek, if the Russians ever get around to finishing it, will be over a thousand. A scrupulous regard for accuracy, that's what I like about the daily press."

"Is Sierra Canyon Dam earthquake-proof?"

"Earthquake-resistant. Nothing is earthquake-proof. You get as much safety as you're willing to pay for, but never perfect safety. The little shake we had last week was five point five on the Richter, hardly enough to set a coop full of chickens clucking, and was centered five miles from the dam. The dam is designed to take six point five at five miles. There hasn't been a quake that big in that neck of the woods for a hundred thousand years."

"The little shake, as you call it, shut the power plant down for forty-five minutes."

"That was the result of too much of a good thing. There are hundreds of sensors of one kind and another in the dam and power plant. The rotating shafts of the turbine generators are three feet in diameter, and if they quiver more than a couple of millimeters in any direction, everything shuts down automatically until the situation can be assessed. You don't take chances with million-dollar generators, nor with dams."

"You say you designed the dam to stand up against an earthquake of a certain size at a certain distance. It may be that way on paper, but isn't it true that the contractors who built it may not have followed the plans and specifications in every detail?"

"Who gave you that question, the Sierra Club? A great bunch. I'm a member myself. Don't look so surprised . . . they're not all bad. My wife is a big fan of their weekend hikes. The dam was built as designed. I made sure of it by spending three years of my life on the site watching every move the contractor made. I needed only canes then and got around fairly well. I wasn't quite the physical wreck you see before you now. That was six, seven, eight years ago. I took a personal interest in the design because I wanted to prove that embankment dams of that height are perfectly safe as well as practical, and I took a personal interest in the construction because I wanted to make sure the thing would never help you sell papers by falling apart. If anything, the design is conservative. This is my car, so I'm going to say goodbye. It's been a pleasure! Sorry I didn't give you a better story. If you are bound and determined to write about the threat to the public from dams, you'll have to go outside California. California has a whole department that does nothing but worry about dams and another one that figures out what to do in case one fails. Most states have no inspection system at all. Once dams are built, they forget about them. I'm telling you God's truth! It is a scandal, my boy, that deserves the attention of your fine paper. March right into Otis Chandler's office and dump it in his lap. And tell him he'll be getting an announcement next week of my thirty-fifth wedding anniversary. We expect a gift that reflects his net worth. Goodbye! Drive carefully!"

The six water districts that jointly owned Sierra Canyon Dam, responding to a directive from the California State Division of the Safety of Dams, convened a panel of engineering consultants to determine if the earthquake "had in any way compromised the structural integrity of the dam or its appurtenances." While no structural damage was found, almost a third of the measuring and recording devices that had been implanted during construction were put out of service by the tremor. This was not considered serious by the panel because the remainder still left the dam the most extensively instrumented in the world. It was found not to be practical to try to replace the severed wires and plastic tubing that led from sensors in the embankment to the banks of dials in the drainage and inspection galleries beneath the dam. However, so that the behavior of the dam in future earthquakes could be studied more profitably, the board recommended the installation of five additional strong-motion accelerographs, two force-balance accelerometers, three pore-pressure sensors, and ten soil-stress cells.

Inspection and drainage tunnels were contained within a concrete core block that ran like a spine through the heart of the embankment at foundation level. The shocks sustained by the dam opened construction joints in the core block, allowing brown water to flow into the tunnels in the weeks following the earthquake. This caused considerable concern, but a program of grouting—involving the injection through drilled holes of a mixture of sand, water, and quick-setting cement—reduced the flow and eventually eliminated it entirely. The temporary crisis was not made public.

As a safety precaution during the following spring, the reservoir was filled at a slow, controlled rate and its highest elevation held to twenty feet below maximum. It was not until the fifth year after the quake that the lake reached capacity. On May 19, for only the second time in the ten-year life of the dam, water poured over the concrete spillway on the right abutment, providing a sensational display for tourists. A three-inch-deep sheet of water flowed in shimmering waves down the thousand-foot-long concrete chute, ending in an explosion of spray. No one who heard the roar, who felt the cold wind and mist, or who photographed the rainbows will ever forget it.

On May 22, the water gliding ponderously into the spillway to begin the long plunge reached a depth of eleven inches, a historic high. Water also reached a historic high in the drainage and inspection tunnels that were buried like intestines deep within the embankment. It was particularly wet in the lowermost tunnels, which rested on bedrock eight hundred and twenty-five feet below the crest of the dam. Water stood an inch deep on the walkways, the most inspector Chuck Duncan ever had to wade through in making his weekly rounds. Water was trickling, dripping, and flowing from every drainage hole, crack, and crevice and running down the endlessly descending flights of concrete stairs in a series of miniature waterfalls. There was more water than usual, but not so much more that Duncan was moved to make a note of it. The tunnels were al-

ways sloppy when the lake was high, and the form he had to fill out
with meter readings provided no space for editorial comments from
a beginning-level technician.

Duncan hated the eerie lower tunnels, which were so small he
could almost touch both walls at once. He hated the long climb and
the stale air, the dampness, and the tomblike silence. The light
bulbs on the crown were too widely spaced to alleviate the gloom
and had shorted out more than once, forcing him to depend on a
flashlight. How in the hell was a person with just two hands supposed to write on a clipboard while holding a flashlight? Worst of
all was knowing that the full weight of the dam and the lake was
directly overhead—thinking about that sometimes made sweat form
on his back and stomach despite the coldness of the air. There was
no point in looking for another job, not if he wanted to go on living
at home. Sutterton offered nothing that paid as well year round for
somebody only two years out of high school. If he could stick it out
long enough to build up some seniority, the dirty job of taking
readings in the lower tunnels could be dumped onto somebody
else.

A heavy steel door marked the entrance to Gallery D, a hundred-
foot-long side tunnel that housed almost half of the dam's monitoring instruments. It was hard to open because differential settlement
had twisted the jamb out of alignment. With his clipboard tucked
under his arm, Duncan used both hands to wrench the door free.
He swung it against the wall and fastened it with a length of wire
so it couldn't close behind him with a clang of doom the way it had
once before.

Standing before the bank of dials at the end of Gallery D was
like standing in a rainstorm. Grinding his teeth and shivering as
water dripped on his head and shoulders, Duncan quickly jotted
down figures for the dials he could see and made educated guesses
for a few that were obscured by falling water. What the heavy
seepage and the meter readings revealed about the condition of the
dam was for other people to decide. His only concern was filling in
all the blanks on the form and getting the hell out. Once back on
the surface, he would take a break, light a cigarette, and think
about his upcoming Friday-night date with Carla, now just a week
away. Carla of the gyrating hips and flickering tongue, who had
put him off on his first try on the grounds of indigestion. Next time,
with the help of a joint or two, he would score with her for sure.

2

AFTER ONLY THREE WEEKS IN SOUTHERN CALIFORNIA, THE NEWEST employee of Roshek, Bolen & Benedetz, Inc., found himself in a position that struck him as wholly extraordinary—naked on a shag rug in Santa Monica. A month earlier, Phil Kramer was mowing a lawn in Wichita, Kansas. "Just because you finally got your degree," his mother had said, "doesn't mean you don't have to take out the garbage and cut the grass." Each time he pushed the clattering machine past the front porch, he stopped to read the framed document propped against the steps:

The Regents of
THE UNIVERSITY OF KANSAS
have conferred upon
PHILIP JAMES KRAMER
the degree of
DOCTOR OF PHILOSOPHY
CIVIL ENGINEERING

How he loved that piece of paper! Invested in it were seven years of canned food, examinations, and lecturers with speech impediments. He had thought those years would never end, and now, miraculously, he was lying on the floor of a young woman's apartment two blocks from the Pacific Ocean. Better yet, he was without the protection of his clothes. He wasn't exactly sure what was going to happen when Janet came out of the bathroom, but whatever it was, it was bound to be good. He had a sneaking suspicion that he was going to get laid. What she *said* was going to happen was a massage.

"You've taken me to two expensive restaurants," she said, "you fixed my car, and you moved my sofa. Now I'm going to do something for you. I'm going to give you my Class A deluxe total body massage."

"Here? At the dining-room table?"

"No. There, on the living-room floor. On the shag rug in front of the fire. Take off your clothes and lie down while I heat some oil and change into my masseuse outfit."

He walked to the rug and hesitated. What if she was kidding?

"Don't be bashful," she said. "You will love it."

To get him started, she reached up to his neck and slipped the knot of his tie. Deftly she unbuttoned his shirt from top to bottom. He frowned, slowly pulling his shirttails out of his slacks. "Isn't this a little strange?" he asked. "I mean, we haven't—"

"Just do as I say." Before disappearing into the bathroom she tossed him a towel. "Here. This is for your modesty."

He waited face down on the rug, resting his chin on the backs of his hands, feeling the glow of the fire on his skin, the towel draped over his posterior. What struck him as so extraordinary was that they had not yet made love. This was only their third evening together, and while the urgent nature of recent kisses and caresses suggested that they would soon be lovers, he didn't think that when the moment came he would be relegated to such passivity. Not that he was naturally aggressive. He was in fact shy, especially in crowds and with women. As a youth, his premature height and unmanageable hair had made him feel ungainly and even absurd. That self-image plus a religious mother and a touch of acne had conspired to safeguard his virginity until he was a sophomore in college. Said the freshman girl who helped him seduce her: "He's only shy at first. In bed he talks your leg off." Five years and eight girls later, he was still unsure of himself. He knew he wasn't a sex object, even naked on a rug. Too tall and nervous. His hair looked too much like a shock of hay that had been hit by a tractor and not quite knocked all the way over. A sprinkling of freckles across his nose undermined his credibility. He had learned to live with the harsh truth that he was cerebral rather than physical and that any girl who went for him would probably be known for her brains.

He had met Janet Sandifer at a weekend seminar sponsored by IBM on new computer languages. He glanced at her several times during coffee breaks, but he didn't have the courage to start a conversation until she smiled at him. She had a trim, compact figure and a face that held his eyes like a magnet. She was three years out of UCLA, she told him when they were trading facts about each other, where she had earned a dual degree in computer science and mathematics, and now worked as a computer systems analyst for a firm in Torrance that designed and manufactured scientific instruments. Three raises and two promotions made her feel that it was no longer important or inevitable that she become somebody's mother.

Phil closed his eyes and smiled. Things certainly were going well for him. It was a wonderful feeling to be finished with school at last, and lingering in his ears were the words of praise he had received from the faculty for his dissertation on computer prediction of dam failures. He had landed exactly the job he wanted with one of the world's most highly regarded engineering firms, and he was fast learning how much he didn't know about hydro-electric design.

The only thing that had gone wrong in Phil's life recently was the crazy response that the Roshek, Bolen & Benedetz computer had made when he tried his failure prediction program on Theodore Roshek's most famous structure, Sierra Canyon Dam. The readouts on the cathode ray tube plainly indicated that the dam was about to burst like a water-filled balloon, which meant that there was something wrong with the computers, the dam, or the program. The computers were in robust health; the dam was a universally revered example of exquisite design. So the disease had to be in the program. He would describe it to Janet when they had finished ravishing each other. She might be able to spot some flaws in the premises or the logic.

She was kneeling beside him, dressed in a kind of short Japanese robe, spreading warm oil on his back. Phil put an arm around her waist, but she pushed it away. "There is something you have to understand," she said. "I'm not trying to seduce you. I'm just trying to give you a massage. It's one of the nicest things one person can do for another, but it doesn't necessarily involve sex. Your only role is to enjoy it. Close your eyes."

She pressed her fingers into the muscles of his neck and shoulders, using a combination of kneading and stroking motions. She urged him several times to relax. "My God, you're as tight as a coiled spring. Haven't you ever been massaged before?"

"Massage isn't too large in Kansas. Neither is public nudity."

"This is private. The door is locked and the drapes are drawn."

"Alone is private. Two is public."

He lifted his head to look at her. She pushed it down. "You're a square, did you know that? Are all engineers like you?"

"I don't know. I never massaged an engineer. The only girl in engineering school weighed two hundred pounds and wore steel-toed work shoes. We called her Puss in Boots."

She scratched his scalp with ten fingertips at once, molded his shoulders with pressure from the palms and heels of her hands, tightened her fingers around his biceps and forearms, drew her fingernails down the length of his arms, made circles on his palms. She inserted her fingers between his, caressed them, rolled them, and wiggled them. When she finished with his arms, she returned to his back, straddling his legs for better leverage. Pressing hard, she slowly pushed her fingertips from the small of his back to his neck.

"It feels unbelievably good," Phil said. "Where did you learn how to do it?"

"When I was very young, I went with a creep who thought massage was the end of the world . . . instead of merely unbelievably good. I was still in undergraduate school. Once he took me to a place in Malibu where everybody took off their clothes and practiced on each other. The instructor was a guru type who said that through massage you could get in tune with the Universal Oneness, or some such shit. That's when I bailed out."

Phil wondered what she would do when she worked her way down to the towel. Would she skip over it discreetly and proceed directly to his legs out of respect for his puritanical upbringing, or would she cast it rudely aside as the creep and the guru would have done? She cast it aside and attacked his buttocks as if they were two mounds of bread dough. But she was so expert at what she was doing, so matter-of-fact, that he never felt the feared flush of embarrassment.

Her fingers stroked his upper legs and the sensitive areas behind the knees. Tenderly she pinched his flesh, squeezed it in her fists, pummeled it with the edges of her hands, and drew long lines on it with a touch so light that her fingertips contacted only the hair and not the skin.

"I don't know how much more of this pleasure I can take," Phil said. "I want to reciprocate. I feel selfish just lying here. I want to caress *you.*"

"That's not the idea. The idea is that I am giving you a gift. You are supposed to accept it and enjoy it. Concentrate on the feeling and keep your mouth shut."

He found out how pleasurable a foot massage can be. She pressed her thumbs against his instep and arch, manipulated each toe lovingly in turn, rubbed her palms and fingers across his heels and soles, first lightly, then firmly. Finally another question that was growing in his mind was answered.

"Roll over," she said.

He did. She didn't cover him with the towel. She massaged his scalp again, this time from the front. With the touch of a butterfly she traced lines across his eyelids, his lips, his cheeks, and his neck. His chest was next, then his stomach, then his abdomen. Her hands brushed his genitals on their way to his upper legs, and after they had worked their way down to his ankles they returned up the inside of his legs to the top, where they closed gently around him. Her hands left him for a moment, and he could hear the rustle of cloth. He felt her hair against his forehead and her lips on his.

He slipped an arm around her and drew her body close.

"I've changed my mind," she whispered. "Now I'm trying to seduce you."

It was easy.

3

THE LOS ANGELES HEADQUARTERS OF ROSHEK, BOLEN & BENEDETZ occupied three floors of the 500 Tishman Tower on Wilshire Boulevard. Most of the senior company officers were on the top floor,
where also were located the advance planning and project development departments. On the middle floor were sections specializing in
highways, structures, and tunnels. The lower floor was devoted to
computer services, hydroelectric, nuclear, and mining. There were
over a hundred employees on each floor, more than half of them engineers, who worked at desks or drafting tables in a central area
surrounded by a ring of offices. Departments working on pet-
rochemical developments, pipelines, ocean facilities, and foundations were in other buildings in the Los Angeles area, and one of
the proposals being evaluated on the upper floor was the construction of an office tower that would consolidate all operations
under one roof.

On Tuesday morning, May 26, Phil Kramer was at work an hour
early, sitting at a terminal feeding his remodeled dam failure program into a computer. The revision was the result of five evenings
of collaboration with Janet. She knew nothing about dams, but she
knew how to forge a chain of logic and she knew how to ask questions that made him alter some of his numerical assumptions. It
was she who suggested that the original mathematical model was
too small and too simple to be applicable to Sierra Canyon. The
model had to be expanded to accommodate the sheer size of the

structure and the greater-than-average volume of data the instrumentation provided. The work they had done together had resulted in a program that was no longer appropriate for an "average" dam. It was tailor-made for Sierra Canyon.

When he had completed the required preliminary operations, Phil typed "List Gallery D meter points." A touch of the Execute key brought a column of two dozen code letters onto the screen. By touching the four Cursor control keys in a certain sequence, he brought the green indicator line to the top of the column. Phil opened a copy of the latest inspector's report from Sierra Canyon. The readings had been taken three weeks earlier, when the surface of the reservoir was still five feet below the lip of the spillway at the crest of the dam. With his left hand holding the report open and his right working the keyboard, he entered a number after each of the letters on the screen. When the column was completed, another appeared.

Thirty minutes later, all of the available data had been fed into the system. Phil instructed the computer to make estimates of the dam's condition under his "best case" assumptions. Four minutes later, columns of figures appeared relating to ten-thousand-cubic-yard blocks of the dam. Since there were ninety million cubic yards of material in the dam, there were nine thousand coded blocks, but the instructions were such that only those with an above-normal seepage, pressure, settlement, or shift were identified. Twenty blocks came on the screen under the heading "Exceed Values Predicted in Design." Five were labeled "Critical." "Conduct Visual Inspection," the computer suggested. Touching another sequence of keys brought to the screen code letters for the dam cross-sections containing the critical blocks.

Phil pursed his lips and shook his head, wondering if he should junk the program and start from scratch. Apparently it was even more skewed than before. First he wanted to see just how far off it was. He asked the computer to calculate the "worst case." This time forty-seven blocks appeared under the "Exceed Values" heading, and twelve were called "Critical." The characters faded and were replaced with the command "Take Immediate Action." Phil asked for successive displays of the critical cross-sections. As the triangular images came on the screen, dotted lines moved from right to left indicating the plane of maximum weakness—in each case it was at the lowest elevation, apparently the interface between the embankment and the foundation rock.

A new message appeared on the screen: "Garbage coming out? Don't cry. Recheck garbage going in."

It was one of the phrases Phil had included in the program to relieve the tedium.

Janet greeted him cheerfully when he phoned her at work. "How is everything over at Colossal Engineering?"

"Wonderful. According to the giant brain, our finest dam is dissolving in forty-seven places at once. I'm calling to advise you to dump any shares of Colossal that might be in your portfolio."

"You know I can't afford a portfolio. I keep my shares in a drawer."

"Janet, the results are worse than before. I don't think anything's wrong with the logic. My initial assumptions, the arbitrary coefficients, must be too pessimistic."

"I can't help you there. Until you dropped this dam on me, the biggest thing I ever analyzed was a silicon chip. Why don't you explain it to old what's-his-name—Roshek? He could probably spot the flaw in a second."

Phil laughed. "You must want to get me killed. That guy scares me to death. You should see the way he swings through here in the morning on his crutches. You can hear him coming down the hall from the elevators like something out of a monster movie. It's funny, the way everybody stops talking and starts working. That old man, I swear, can look around the room and just with a glance knock a man right off his stool."

"You've got to talk to somebody. You can't just sit there worrying about it."

"Should I call the senior partners together and tell them that according to my calculations Sierra Canyon Dam is on its way to Sacramento? They would fall on the floor laughing. They would say, 'Gee, those must be swell calculations.' I'm fresh out of college. I'm not supposed to act as if I know anything. My eyes and ears are supposed to be open and my trap shut."

"You're too bashful. You've got an ingenious program and you should feel more confident about it. Don't you have a boss you could talk to?"

"Two. One doesn't know enough about computers and the other

doesn't know enough about dams. I suppose I could go to Herman Bolen, who interviewed me before I was hired. A pretty nice guy, I think, but a little on the pompous side."

"Talk to Bolen. If the dam collapses tomorrow, you don't want to have to say that you knew it was going to but were too embarrassed to mention it. Oh-oh, I've got to hang up—here comes my supervisor looking at her watch. You think you've got a movie monster at *your* place. . . ."

Phil spent the rest of the morning as well as his lunch break trying to summon up enough courage to ask Bolen's secretary to make an appointment. Twice he put his hand on his desk phone and withdrew it in the face of dreadful visions. "Are you crazy?" Bolen might rage at him. "I have better things to do than talk to children about their hallucinations. Do you seriously think I give a good goddamn about your old school project?" No, Phil corrected himself, Bolen wasn't the type to rage. He was more likely to belittle him with paternalism. "Your little computer program is very nice. You should look at it again in a few years when you've had some experience. Now if you'll excuse me, I'm expecting the Chancellor of West Germany." Another possibility was that Bolen would fire him on the spot for wasting valuable computer time and for not devoting a hundred percent of his attention to his assigned work. He certainly didn't want to risk losing his job.

Phil was part of a four-man team designing a rock-fill dam for an agricultural development in Brazil. Most of his time was spent double-checking the drawings and computations of others, which was educational and to which he didn't object. He was sure that if he applied himself and avoided serious mistakes he would be given more responsibility and original work to do. Already there was a possibility that he would be asked to accompany the team leader on a trip to the jobsite later in the year. A junket to Brazil! There would have been no chance of that had he taken his father's advice and joined one of Wichita's small consulting firms. He would be stuck laying out sewer connections for tract homes and hoping for a driveway design job as a change of pace. He was glad he had decided to take a crack at a big firm in California. As the days went by, the danger receded that he would make a fool of himself and have to slink back home in disgrace. Quit worrying, he scolded himself. You've got a good brain, a decent education, and a willingness to work. Bolen is the type who puts a high value on things like that. You're not nearly as tongue-tied as you used to be. So *what* if you look too young to be taken seriously? Time would correct that condition.

He put his hand on the phone again. Bolen was nothing to fear. He might be impressed with a new employee who looked beyond his immediate assignment, and would think of him when a promotion was to be made. Phil thought of the various pieces of advice his father had given him on how to succeed in the business world. Present yourself as a person who solves problems rather than causes them, but if you have a problem you can't solve, take it to someone who can, and make sure your facts are right. Phil frowned. His facts were three weeks old. He'd better call the dam and get the latest meter readings. Another thing his father believed was that the higher a person is on the ladder the easier he is to deal with. Bolen was certainly high enough: the second rung from the top.

Phil picked up the phone and put in a call to Sierra Canyon.

Herman Bolen had the second largest and second best equipped office in the company. There was all-wool carpeting, a private bathroom, and floor-to-ceiling walnut paneling—the real McCoy, not plastic or veneer. The left side of his desk resembled the instrument panel of his private plane. At the touch of a button he could summon his secretary, ring fifty phones around the world, get a weather forecast or a stock quote, rotate the louvers outside the windows, light a cigar, heat a cup of coffee, or manipulate numbers in every manner known to mathematics.

He didn't mind being number two when number one was Theodore Roshek. Roshek was a brilliant engineer with an inhuman capacity for work; he deserved his prestige and his larger share of the profits. Herman Bolen wasn't envious at all. He was, in fact, grateful to the older man. If Roshek hadn't taken a chance on him years ago, he would probably still be lost in the Bureau of Reclamation labyrinth, a federal drudge nobody ever heard of. As it was, thanks to Roshek, his own hard work, and a run of luck in the form of illnesses that had struck down rivals inside the firm, he was now enjoying considerable power and prestige. He was making more than he ever dreamed he would—more than a hundred thousand dollars after taxes in the previous year. He had played a role in some of the twentieth century's most notable engineering achievements, as could be gathered from the framed photographs and artist's renderings on the walls: Mangla Dam, the Manapouri Power Scheme, the Iraqi Integrated Refineries, the Alaska Pipeline, the Sinai Canal, Sierra Canyon Dam.

He worked well with Roshek. Roshek could turn on the charm when he had to, but his normal manner was harsh and cutting. Bolen's was soft and fatherly. He smoothed the feathers that Roshek ruffled. Not that life was perfect. Bolen mourned the retreat of his hair and the advance of his waistline. His body, pear-shaped and high in fat content, was gaining weight relentlessly—the current rate, according to his desk-top calculator, was approximately 0.897 pounds per month. *Reading* about exercising and dieting was, obviously, not enough. He touched a button. Instantly appearing on a small glass screen was the time to a hundredth of a second in twelve time zones. In Los Angeles it was 5:06.34 P.M. Time to call it a day.

There was a light knock on his door, followed by the gray head of his secretary. "Mr. Kramer is here to see you," she said.

"Who?"

"Mr. Kramer, the young man from downstairs. He asked early this afternoon for an appointment. Tall, with the reddish hair? The hydro design section? Computers?"

"Oh, oh, oh, yes. Send him in."

For some preposterous reason he thought she meant that Jack Kramer, the old-time tennis pro, was in the outer office. He had once seen Kramer play a very fine match against Pancho Segura . . . good grief, over thirty years ago! *Phil* Kramer was the lad who had just come aboard. Bolen had interviewed him himself, recruited him, recommended that he be hired. Likable young fellow, and well mannered. Presentable. Bright future if he applied himself. Just the kind of raw material that Bolen, Roshek & Benedetz was looking for. *Bolen,* Roshek & Benedetz? *Roshek,* Bolen & Benedetz . . .

Kramer was thanking him for his time with a trace of awkwardness as he sat down on the edge of a chair. "You said that if I ever had any trouble I should feel free to come to you."

Bolen smiled in a friendly fashion. The boy was nervous and had to be put at ease. "I said that and I meant it. I know how hard it is to come right out of college into a huge organization. It's a kind of cultural shock. The shock of the real world, eh? When I graduated from St. Norbert's, I enlisted in the Seabees! There was a shock for you!" He chuckled at the memory, mirth that wasn't shared by his young visitor, who sat staring at him, frowning. Bolen joined his hands and leaned forward, lowering his voice. "Now, then, what seems to be the problem? We are both engineers. If you can state the problem in specific terms, we'll solve it."

"Well, Mr. Bolen, yes, there is a problem. I think that one of the firm's structures . . . that is, according to some computer modeling I've been doing . . . Sir, I think that Sierra Canyon Dam is, or *could* be, and I might be completely wrong, probably *am* completely wrong, and I'm hoping you can show that I'm off base in thinking that the dam is . . . well, is . . . I hate to go over people's heads, but I thought before mentioning this to anybody I would talk it over with somebody who . . ."

"Mr. Kramer, just lay out the problem in an orderly manner. Sierra Canyon Dam is what?"

Phil composed his thoughts before beginning again. "In graduate school I worked out a computer program to analyze the performance of embankment dams with the goal of being able to detect conditions that might precede . . . um, failures. It's a mathematical model built up of data from ten dams on pore pressure, settlement rates, seismic response, seepage under various hydrostatic loads, and so on. There's a built-in comparison with conditions that prevail when dams fail, which I got from studying Baldwin Hills and Teton."

"I remember reading about it on your résumé. We chatted briefly about it during our interview. Nice piece of work for a student. Imaginative. But as for its *practical* value . . ." What was he working up to?

"I use a three-dimensional matrix that has been very productive in the chemical process field. Not just the *amount* of pressure, seepage, settlement, and movement in different parts of the embankment, but their *relationship* to each other, how each one affects the others, and, most important, the *rate of change* of the values as the reservoir rises."

Bolen nodded and tried to adopt an expression that would convey both sympathy and a slight impatience. "I like the general concept, but there are too many unknowns to get the solution you want. Baldwin Hills and Teton dams weren't well monitored before they failed. The trouble with your approach would lie, it seems to me, in assigning meaningful numerical values to such things as relationships and rates of change."

"I made a lot of assumptions."

"Ah . . ."

"Mr. Bolen, on my own time I've been trying my program on Sierra Canyon. What happens is that . . ." He paused. "The dam, according to the model, is not . . . is not doing too well."

Bolen shook his head and smiled faintly. "Now, really, Mr. Kramer . . ."

"It sounds ridiculous, I know, and that's how it struck me at first. When I made this appointment to see you, I was intending to ask your advice on revising the program. But this afternoon I began to wonder if maybe I'm not onto something."

"Oh?" Bolen was beginning to regard the young engineer in a new and less flattering light. He was clever, but there was something immature about him. He seemed to lack a sense of propriety and proportion. Bolen couldn't help thinking back to the beginnings of his own career and how impossible it would have been for him to approach a senior officer with such a wild tale. Times change and not always for the better.

"I had been using readings from three weeks ago, when the lake was five feet from the top. This afternoon I used values from last Friday, May 22, when the water was eleven inches deep going over the spillway. The computer showed that . . . that . . ."

"That the dam is failing."

Phil exhaled. "All the way from the maximum transverse section to the right abutment."

While Bolen searched for a remark that was suitably sarcastic without being contemptuous, he asked how Phil got Friday's figures.

"I called the dam," Phil said.

"You *what?*"

"I called the dam and talked to the man in charge of maintenance and inspection. A Mr. Jeffers. I wanted to have all the facts I could when I saw you. The lake is higher right now than it's ever been—eleven inches deep going over the spillway."

"You called Jeffers? And told him you were with R. B. & B.?"

"Yes, sir. I asked him if there was excess seepage in Gallery D. He said the inspector hadn't mentioned anything. I asked him about the meters that weren't registering and—"

"I hope to God you didn't tell him that the dam was failing."

"No, sir. I was surprised to learn from him that in the earthquake five years ago—"

"I've heard enough." Bolen raised his voice slightly and lifted his hand for silence. He could be firm and decisive when he had to be. "This is a serious matter. Something must be done and I'm not sure what."

"Well, the spillway gates could be opened to start lowering the reservoir and a special inspection could be made of—"

"I don't mean the dam," Bolen said, practically shouting. "I mean *you!* I don't know what should be done about *you.*" Surprised at his own vehemence, he lowered his voice to a whisper. He didn't want Charlene sticking her head in again. "I hired you and so I feel a special responsibility. The failure lies with you, not with the dam."

"I was only trying to—"

"You are behaving like a partner in the firm without putting in the required twenty years of hard work. The only failure we need concern ourselves with is a loss of perspective. Have you ever *seen* Sierra Canyon Dam? Have you ever worked on the design or construction of a dam of any kind, even in the summer months? I thought not." Bolen studied the young man seated across from him, whose eyes were round in shock and whose cheeks were turning red. He couldn't help feeling sympathy for him. There was something affecting about his naïveté. He was sincere. He was open. He probably expected to be complimented for his efforts instead of bawled out. Kramer had talent and could become an asset if brought along properly. Bolen adopted his well-practiced soothing manner and said, "I want you to attend to the duties for which you were hired. Don't use the computers for anything not authorized by Mr. Filippi or myself. Don't mention what you've done to anybody or, I can assure you, you'll be the butt of jokes for years to come. Years from now, you and I can have a private laugh about it. Above all, don't call the site again. Leave the dam in the hands of those of us who have lived with it since the day it was conceived. You have a lot to learn, Mr. Kramer, before you can think about telling us how to run the company. All right? Agreed?"

Kramer gestured with his hands, then let them fall helplessly to his lap. "The readouts scared me," he said in a soft voice. Now he was having trouble meeting Bolen's eyes. "I still think an inspector should be sent down to Gallery D. The readings there are high by anybody's standards."

"You have the courage of your convictions, I'll give you that, even if they are wrong." Bolen waved vaguely toward the door to indicate that the meeting was over. He watched Kramer struggle to his feet like a man who had been flogged. The poor kid was obviously one of those people who couldn't hide their emotions, a trick he'd have to learn if he wanted to go very far in the engineering profession. Bolen stopped him at the door with a final comment designed to cheer him up. "I won't mention this to Mr. Roshek. He would take a dim view of one of his own employees, especially one without experience, raising doubts about a dam that happens to be one of his special favorites. This will just be between the two of us."

Kramer nodded and closed the door behind him.

Thirty minutes later, after checking the Sierra Canyon report himself, Bolen touched a button on his console. A phone rang five hundred miles away in an underground powerhouse.

"Jeffers."

"Herman Bolen. I was afraid you'd be gone for the day."

"Hello, Herman! Hey, we work day and night up here in the mountains. Not like you city slickers."

"I'll trade places with you anytime. You breathe this air for a while."

"It's a deal. You ought to pay us a visit, at least, to see the water spilling over the top. It's quite a show. Makes Niagara look like a leaky faucet. I shot a roll of film today; I'll send you some prints if they turn out."

"Do that. Larry, did you get a call from our Mr. Kramer this afternoon?"

"Yeah, what was that about? He seemed all excited, especially when he found out that a lot of the instruments haven't worked since the quake."

"You volunteered that?"

"I sort of mentioned it in passing. I figured a man in the company would already know. I called Roshek to find out what was up, and damned if the girl didn't put my call through to him in Washington! I didn't mean to bother him there. He didn't know Kramer or what he was up to, and seemed a little pissed about the whole thing."

Bolen had been doodling on a scratch pad. The lead broke when he heard about the call to Roshek. Now he would have to try to reach the old man himself so he wouldn't think something was being hidden from him. "Thanks for getting him riled up," Bolen said. "He's difficult enough when he's happy."

Jeffers laughed. "Sorry about that. Did he call you?"

"No, but I'm sure he will. Kramer is a young engineer we just hired . . . green, right out of college. I prefer a man with a little experience, myself. We gave him a research job to do, checking some hydro stuff in our files. We didn't intend for him to start phoning around the country. God knows what kind of bill he ran up!" He chuckled to give the impression that the affair was trivial. "But in looking at some of the figures he rounded up, I see that drainage in Gallery D is a little on the high side. Wouldn't you say?"

"Up from last year, maybe, but not much. We're going to have plenty of water all year to run through the turbines, if that's what you're worried about. The reservoir isn't leaking away."

"My thought is that the dam is under maximum stress for the first time in years. A lot can be learned that would help in some other designs we're working on. I want you to do me a favor, Larry. Make a visual check of Gallery D. Personally."

Jeffers moaned. "Jesus, Herman, do you know what a drag it is to go down there? Two hundred steps! Like climbing down the stairwell of a fifteen-story building. Duncan was down there last Friday, anyway. . . ."

"I'm sure Duncan is a very fine inspector, but he can't bring your wealth of experience to the task. Go yourself, Larry, and report back to me. I don't mean a written report, just phone and describe what you see. You might as well record the instrument readings while you're at it to make sure Duncan is doing his job."

"You mean tonight? I had three Chinese engineers in here today with some guy from the State Department and they wanted to climb around on every fucking thing. I'm bushed."

"Yes, I'm afraid I mean tonight. If there is anything down below that needs attention it should be tended to right away, the reservoir elevation being what it is. If by some miracle our young Mr. Kramer has hit on something, we don't want him coming around later saying 'I told you so.'"

Jeffers sighed. "I'll check it out later. First I'm going to have some dinner and read the paper. I'll phone you tomorrow if I see anything unusual."

"Phone me in any case. I want direct confirmation."

"Okay, boss, whatever you say. Hello to the wife."

4

BARRY CLAMPETT INTRODUCED HIMSELF TO ROSHEK AND APOLOGIZED for the short notice and the inconvenient hour. "When the President heard you were in town for the engineering convention," Clampett said, "he thought it would be a good idea to call you and arrange a meeting. First let me relay his regrets at his inability to be here. I'll have to speak for him."

"When the President of the United States issues an invitation," Roshek said, settling into a chair and leaning his crutches against the desk, "a man doesn't think about whether it comes at a convenient hour."

"You'd be surprised," Clampett said, "how many men there are who think about exactly that." He lit a cigarette.

It was nine o'clock and the sky was dark. Through the windows Roshek could see lights burning in other government buildings. Either the federal bureaucracy worked long hours or it forgot to turn the lights out when it went home. The Washington Monument, gleaming under floodlights, could be made out through the leaves of trees. Roshek eyed the man opposite him. Bland. Slick. An unblinking gaze that was probably taught to him by a consulting psychologist. Inoffensive and menacing at the same time. But wishy-washy at bottom, the kind of man who can't tell the difference between how he feels on an issue and how he is expected to feel.

"What's up?" Roshek asked. "I know you've been running a security check on me. Friends and neighbors have told me they've been questioned by FBI agents, those guys you apparently stamp out with cookie cutters." Clampett fit the pattern himself.

"I hope they haven't been too obtrusive."

"I just wonder if it's necessary. My firm has done a lot of design work for the military over the years. I must have every kind of clearance in the book."

"Except one. The kind required for a man who may enter the public eye."

The public eye? Roshek had heard rumors that he was being considered for an appointment, but had dismissed them as poppycock.

Clampett opened a folder on his desk. "What we need to know has little to do with national defense or patriotism. It has to do with things of a . . . of a personal nature. Things that could embarrass the Administration if unearthed by the opposition." He removed a sheet from the folder and studied it. "Theodore Richard Roshek. Born May 22, 1919. Graduated maxima cum laude MIT 1939. Worked for Bureau of Reclamation on design and construction of Shasta Dam and Fort Peck Dam. Served with distinction in World War II with the Army Engineers. Married Stella Robinson 1946. No children. Formed own consulting firm 1947, now ranked by *Engineering News-Record* as the twelfth largest in the country. Partial use of legs due to misdiagnosed polio in 1953."

"I hope you didn't pay too much for that information. Most of it is in *Who's Who in Engineering*."

Clampett smiled briefly, then asked, "Do you have a personal bank account of more than a thousand dollars in any foreign country?"

"I wish I did."

"Have you ever taken a loan from or made a loan to a person or company with connections to organized crime?"

"Of course not! What are you driving at?"

Clampett snubbed out his cigarette and fixed his gaze on the man seated across from him. "The President is exploring the advisability of forming a Department of Technology. This would require a major reorganization. The Bureau of Reclamation, the civilian functions of the Corps of Engineers, Transportation, Environment, Energy, and so on, a dozen different scientific and industrial research-funding programs, all would be put under one umbrella. The way federal funds are allocated now among competing needs is chaotic, I don't need to tell you. Setting priorities based on reason rather than politics is the underlying philosophy of the new approach. It's a philosophy the President believes voters will like. Now the key to the viability of the concept may be to present it along with the man we want to put in charge. You, Mr. Roshek, are one of a small handful of engineers and scientists being considered for the job. The title would be Secretary of Technology."

Roshek listened to the statement with growing astonishment. A Cabinet post! He had never seriously considered such a possibility. Chief Engineer of the Bureau of Reclamation, that's what he thought he was going to be offered. His voice broke slightly when he tried to reply: "I—I'm flattered, of course . . . this is quite a surprise. I'm honored that the President—"

"The proposal is still in the trial-balloon stage. Other candidates will be interviewed."

Roshek's mind was racing. Being in charge of federal grants and funding for science and technology, supervising the setting of policy and priorities would give him tremendous power. The nation would bear the stamp of his ideas and beliefs for years to come. . . .

"Your corporation," Clampett went on, "would have to be turned over to your partners for a period of time, with your shares held in trust to avoid overt conflict of interest."

"I beg your pardon? Oh, yes, of course." Bolen struck Roshek at times as a man who always finished second. Benedetz was a money man, a paper-shuffler with the outlook of a bookkeeper. But the two of them could probably be left in charge for a while without doing irreparable damage.

"Your technical qualifications are superb," Clampett said in a flat tone of voice. "You have a reputation as a man of imagination at the conceptual stage, conservatism at the execution stage. Your designs, our sources tell us, are noted for strength as well as aesthetics. These things can be sold."

"Sold?"

"To voters. To Congress. Your public image as it would be presented through the media would be of an experienced, decisive man of backbone and integrity. Now that I've met you, I would say that you could be presented as a kind of pillar of rectitude that perhaps"—here he permitted himself another small smile—"even the Washington *Post* would shrink from challenging. You see, Mr. Roshek, in matters like these image is as important as substance if you are to survive the Senate confirmation hearings. A number of people are as qualified as you. We will select the one we can most easily merchandise as ideal for the job."

As Clampett talked, Roshek considered the financial implications. Putting his shares in the corporation in a temporary trust was a cosmetic measure that would cost him nothing. Foreign governments would love to do business with a firm whose de facto head was a key member of the United States Cabinet. When his term was over, the lines of influence he would have established would give him the inside track on military contracts beyond counting. Within five years Roshek, Bolen & Benedetz would be ranked with the biggest consulting firms in the world, right up there with Bechtel, Fluor, Parsons. . . .

"To avoid misunderstandings," Clampett said, "we see you as a gray eminence with the vision and strength of will to forge a great new division of government; then in two or three years you step down for personal reasons. We bring on a much younger man who can be presented as forward-looking, dynamic, full of fresh ideas. In the 1984 elections the new man will be immune to criticism because he will not yet have had a fair chance. You see? To reduce points of attack, a certain amount of stagecraft is required. Do you gamble, Mr. Roshek? In Las Vegas?"

"An occasional game of poker with friends. Small stakes."

"Have you ever been drunk?"

"Not since V-J Day."

"Do you visit prostitutes?"

"For God's sake . . ."

"These are the areas our great free press will dig into once your name is brought forward. We have no moral interest in your secret vices, may I make clear, unless they can't be *kept* secret."

Roshek tightened his lips, surprised that he was submitting himself to such a line of questioning. He had a sudden notion to tell Clampett to shove the whole thing up his ass and the President along with it.

"I tried a whore once in my life," he said after some consideration, "between my sophomore and junior years in college. It was the worst two bucks I ever spent."

"Is your marriage solid?"

"Is my marriage solid! Now that makes me laugh! How long have I been married to Stella? A hundred and fifty years?"

"Thirty-five."

"Stella is the perfect corporate wife. She would love a few years as a Washington hostess." They hadn't slept together in four years, but Roshek couldn't see that that was any concern of Clampett's.

"Have you ever struck anyone in anger?"

"No, but a lot of people have deserved it."

Clampett closed the folder and pushed it to one side. "Is there anything else we should know about? Anything at all that might be used against us . . . and you? Think hard. There are a lot of muckrakers in the country and they never sleep."

"Is that so? I always have the feeling that they sleep too much. Let's see . . . no, I believe we've covered everything." Eleanor hadn't been mentioned. Surely the snoops had found out about her, but in case they hadn't he wasn't going to volunteer her name.

Clampett drummed his fingers several times as if waiting for a confession. He fastened his unwavering gaze on Roshek. Roshek stared back.

"In the past year," Clampett said, "you have been seeing quite a bit of a Miss Eleanor James in San Francisco."

"That's none of your business."

"It is if you want your name to remain in nomination for one of the most important positions ever created in the federal government."

"Jesus. What about you, Clampett? Do you fool around at all?"

Another small smile. "I like your spirit. Your combativeness. One of your business associates"—he gestured toward the folder—"described you as 'a tough old buzzard.' The President feels that's the kind of man we need."

"That was probably Steve Bechtel. He calls me that to my face. All right, I'll tell you about Eleanor James. I've developed quite an interest in ballet in the last five or ten years, maybe because I can't stand up myself without falling on my face. I contribute money to the San Francisco Ballet and I know the dancers and the staff. In my opinion it's one of the best companies of its kind in the world. Eleanor James is a dancer. She wants to start her own studio in Marin County but needs financing. I've met her several times to discuss the possibility of making her a loan. End of story."

"I see. The meetings take place at such San Francisco restaurants as The Blue Fox, the St. Tropez, and La Bourgogne, followed by further discussions, no doubt of a technical nature, at her apartment that sometimes last till dawn."

"Your French needs help. Listen, this girl is the most wonderful thing that ever happened to me. I'm not giving her up."

"We are not suggesting abstinence, merely discretion. You are sixty-two, she is thirty-two. Public restaurants are hardly the place for a married man under consideration for high government office to conduct business meetings with an attractive, unmarried woman thirty years his junior. Don't you agree? All right, enough." Clampett rose and extended his hand. "I can tell the President that you will accept the nomination if it's offered? Good. You'll be hearing from us soon."

5

THE TWISTING, TWENTY-MILE-LONG GROOVE THAT THE SIERRA CANYON
River has worn through the foothills northeast of Sacramento is too
narrow for most of its length for more than a county road and a
loose string of cabins and cottages. Twelve miles upstream from the
mouth of the canyon, the valley widens enough to accommodate
the tree-lined streets of Sutterton. Before the dam, Sutterton was a
quietly aging village with a population of less than a thousand.
Named after John Sutter, whose sawmill a few dozen miles away
was the scene of the gold strike in 1848, the town flourished and
floundered under successive waves of prospectors, miners, loggers,
railroad builders, and pensioners. By the 1930s it had subsided into
little more than a point of departure for fishermen and hunters.

Architecturally the town offers little. There is a gargoyle on the
Catholic church. The wooden tower atop City Hall is a curious example of carpenter Gothic, and the cracked bell that hangs therein
was shipped around the Horn from a Belgian foundry, now de-
funct. Three buildings with foundations dating from the 1870s are
California State Historical Landmarks, which means that their
owners can be strangled in red tape should they try to upgrade
them. What is now the Wagon Wheel Saloon began as a brothel
where, according to a widely believed local legend that is almost
certainly false, Mark Twain and Bret Harte once knocked each
other's teeth out.

In the 1960s the town was assaulted by a new wave of invaders:

geologists, surveyors, soil analysts, hydrographers, and civil engineers looking for the best possible site for a dam of record-breaking size. Close on their heels, as enabling legislation was enacted, permits obtained, and court challenges beaten back, came representatives of the Corps of Engineers, the Bureau of Reclamation, the Bureau of Land Management, the Department of Agriculture, the Forestry Service, the California Division of Water Resources, the State Department of Fish and Game, the California Division of Highways, and thirty-seven other local, county, regional, state, and federal agencies that claimed an interest in or jurisdiction over one part of the project or another.

Preparation of plans and specifications and supervision of construction were assigned by the owners of the project, the Combined Water Districts, to its engineering consultant, Roshek, Bolen & Benedetz, Inc. A year before the design of the dam was completed and final authorizations received from the regulatory agencies, R. B. & B. awarded two preliminary contracts that had to be started early if they were to be completed on time: the driving of a diversion tunnel to carry the river around the site and the excavation of a cavern in which the powerhouse would be built.

The fifteen-foot-diameter diversion tunnel entered the mountainside at river level and emerged four thousand feet downstream. Workmen experienced in underground drilling, blasting, and rock removal started from both ends and worked toward each other. Temporary barriers—cofferdams—of earth were built to keep the river away from the tunnel portals while work was under way. Diverting the river into the finished tunnel was a well-publicized event that was witnessed by hundreds of people from the overlooks and by thousands on Sacramento television. The feat was accomplished in September, when the river flow was seven thousand cubic feet per second, a tenth of what it reached during the annual spring flood. At a signal from a flagman, a fleet of thirty trucks and bulldozers dumped load after load of rock into the river, building the banks on each side toward each other until the channel was pinched off. The water rose quickly, but before it could overtop the barrier and wash it away, it found the opening of the diversion tunnel. Cheers were heard in the canyon when the water first entered the tunnel and again when it emerged from the downstream portal.

In the year following the award of the two-hundred-million-dollar contract for construction of the dam, the population of Sutterton doubled, and it doubled again in the second year. The newcomers were specialists in such things as heavy-equipment operation and maintenance, concrete production and placing, steel erection, and earthmoving. They were part of a nationwide fraternity of men whose skills and temperaments led them from one big construction job to another and whose children were used to being strangers in suddenly overcrowded small-town schools.

After the river was diverted, scrapers, power shovels, loaders, and bulldozers stripped away the topsoil along the axis of the dam from one side of the canyon to the other. Exposing bedrock required excavating a trench two thousand feet long, five hundred feet wide, and a hundred and fifty feet deep. Cracks in the foundation rock were sealed by pumping grout under pressure into hundred-foot-deep drilled holes. A solid concrete core block eighty feet high and a hundred and fifty feet wide was built along the bottom of the trench. Inside the core block were drainage and inspection tunnels, access to which was by stairs leading downward from the underground powerhouse.

When foundation work was finished, the dam took shape rapidly. Fifty scrapers and trucks shuttled twenty hours a day between the site and nearby quarries and borrow pits. Impervious clay was placed in the center while earth and rock, in precisely specified zones, were placed on either side. The material was spread into foot-deep layers by bulldozers and graders and packed down by rollers.

For nearly four years the residents of Sutterton were jolted by explosions, vibrated by passing trucks, and coated with dust. Few complained. The dam was putting the town on the map, and people were crowding in with money practically falling out of their pockets. New gas stations, car lots, realty offices, souvenir shops, and trailer parks sprang up like weeds. The highway south of town eventually was lined with every fast-food franchise known to man, plus one that was invented on the spot: Dorothy's Damburgers.

A popular form of entertainment was watching construction operations from the overlooks on the hillsides, one of which was equipped with bleachers, loudspeakers, and chemical toilets. According to a statement broadcast every hour whether anyone was listening or not, the dam required placement of ninety million cubic yards of material, enough to duplicate the Pyramid of Cheops thirty times over or to fill two cereal bowls for every human being in the world.

"Although Sierra Canyon is not a concrete dam," the voice intoned, "enough concrete is required for the core block, the powerhouse foundations, the spillway, the intake and outlet works, and a highway across the top—a million cubic yards in all—to build a sidewalk from San Francisco to New York and back with enough left over to continue it to the vicinity of Milpitas. The lake that will form behind the dam will at its maximum elevation have an area equal to eighteen thousand seven hundred and seventy-five football fields.

"The chimney-like structure you see under construction directly beneath you is located just upstream from the upstream toe of the dam and will be eight hundred and forty-five feet high, with its top twenty feet above the surface of the lake. It is the ventilation-intake tower, which among other things will provide a means of emergency ingress and egress for powerhouse personnel. Inside will be a massive vertical pipe leading to the powerhouse turbines. Water will be admitted through remotely controlled gates at ten elevations.

"The Combined Water Districts hope you enjoy your visit and ask you not to throw garbage over the guardrails. Keep children and pets under control at all times. This message will repeat in fifty-five minutes or upon the insertion of a quarter."

Sidewalk superintendents in the bleachers who took their duties seriously became familiar with a certain blue pickup truck. The driver was the chief designer of the dam and the project's resident engineer, Theodore Roshek, who had taken it upon himself to make sure the contractor followed every line of fine print in the specifications. Construction crews learned that it was useless to try to cut even the smallest corner, because Roshek would wave his canes, turn red, and threaten to shut the job down. Was a small mistake already buried under the fast-growing embankment? Dig it up. Was faulty concrete poured and set? Break it out and pour it again. He was constantly on the move, either in his pickup or on foot, despite the discomfort he felt when walking over rough ground. Each week he spent three days in Los Angeles tending to the affairs of his consulting firm and four days at the dam. During those four days, it was agreed by the project's seventeen hundred and sixty workmen, he succeeded in making life miserable for everybody.

When the dam was completed, a platform draped with bunting was set up in front of City Hall and a dedication ceremony was held featuring oratory, six massed high-school bands, barbecued chicken, German potato salad, and Popsicles. Several of the speakers mentioned Roshek. The contractor's project manager said that the engineer's nit-picking and hairsplitting, his policy of never giving the contractor the benefit of the doubt, and his refusal to negotiate even trivial points had resulted in an overall loss of four million dollars for his company over the life of the job. The audience laughed. Contractors were always claiming to lose money, even when they were driving to their private planes in their Cadillacs. The laughter changed to applause when he added that the result of "that s.o.b.'s meanness" was the best-built dam in the history of the world.

The Mayor of Sutterton, an overweight, perspiring man with a penetrating voice and the largest hardware store within fifty miles, read from a script written by his wife, who had once studied journalism at Chico State. Before describing how Sutterton intended to march bravely forward into a future garnished by economic benefits, he thanked "a great engineer for his unstinting efforts. Theodore Roshek leaves behind more than a dam that is justly famous. He leaves behind more than a legacy of dedication and personal integrity. No, my friends, he leaves behind a good deal more. Those of you who have come to know him as I do realize that he navigates on what my grandfather used to call 'gimpy' legs. His labors over the past four years haven't done those gimpy legs any good. In fact, he told me this morning at breakfast that they are a hell of a lot worse than when he arrived amongst us, you should pardon my French. Now maybe you can see what he is leaving behind. Invested in the great dam that rises behind me like the very aspirations of civilization itself are not just the best years of Theodore Roshek's life, not just the essence of his audacious and unquenchable genius, but a big chunk of his health as well."

6

LAWRENCE JEFFERS WAS A HAPPY SOUL, GIVEN TO WHISTLING WHILE HE worked and talking to himself. Chief of Maintenance at Sierra Canyon Dam was a job that suited him perfectly. He wasn't stuck in an office where his personal habits would drive other people crazy. He was alone most of the time, talking and whistling to electrical equipment and uncomplaining trees. He loved the friendly foothills of the Mother Lode country, he loved fishing in the lake behind the dam from the houseboat he had built himself, and, yes, he loved the dam. His boat was *The Blonde Beauty,* which is what he called his only daughter, Julie. In two weeks he would join the girl's mother, whom he hadn't seen in the two years since their separation, to watch their beautiful daughter graduate from college. It would be a ceremony he was sure would make him cry. He hated to see a grown man cry, especially when it was himself, but tears, of late, had a way of leaking out whether he wanted them to or not.

It was after 10 P.M. when Jeffers carefully nosed his car into the powerhouse access tunnel at the foot of the dam. Lights strung on the utility lines on each side outlined the constant left curvature of the roadway as it descended into the mountainside. Jeffers honked his horn every few seconds in case a vehicle was coming up the slope, but at this hour a control-room engineer and possibly one technician were likely the only ones on duty. He would say hello to them on the way out, but first he wanted to get the damned trip to Gallery D over and done with.

Three hundred feet from the portal, the tunnel opened into the Sierra Canyon powerhouse, a cavern carved out of solid rock that was big enough—in the words of the leaflet that was handed out to tourists—to house the State Capitol Building. Jeffers didn't drive onto the generator deck, but rather turned his car down a steep ramp that led to the floor below. He had a lot of walking to do, and wanted to get as close as he could to the drainage galleries. At the bottom his headlights fell on the six massive turbines, each one taking the thrust of three thousand cubic feet of water per second. At the center of each was a constantly rotating three-foot-diameter steel shaft that led to a generator one floor above. The generators turned out a hundred and forty thousand kilowatts each, and together could meet the peak demands of a city of more than a million people. The specific facts came readily to Jeffers's mind—he had been reciting them for years to visitors ranging from Senators to busloads of school kids.

Above the sound of his engine as he drove slowly across the steel decking alongside the turbines, he could hear the muffled thunder of the torrents hurtling through the penstocks, spinning the blades of the turbines, and surging through the tailrace tunnel to the river below the dam. There was an electrical hum as well, but so perfectly were the massive rotors balanced there was no detectable vibration.

He parked behind the sixth turbine at the end of the chamber, put on his mud-splattered hard hat, went up a flight of steel steps and pulled open a steel door marked "DANGER, NO ADMITTANCE." Inside was a rack of flashlights. He picked one, checked to make sure it worked, and set out through an eight-foot-diameter tunnel that seemed to recede into infinity. The sixty-watt bulbs at twenty-foot intervals on the crown might have been enough for a young man who didn't need glasses, but not for Jeffers. He kept his flashlight on, and the beam danced ahead of him as he walked. Thank God he had worn his boots, he thought, for there was water everywhere, seeping through hairline cracks in the concrete tunnel lining, falling in misty veils from construction joints, running freely out of drainage holes drilled through the concrete to keep pressure from building up. The trough alongside the walkway was full of water running swiftly toward the next catch basin, where pumps would lift it

into the dam's network of drainage pipes for discharge downstream. Jeffers pulled his jacket tightly around him and fastened
the top two buttons; the stale air was cold as well as damp.

Soon he was so far from the powerhouse he could no longer hear
the electrical hum of the generators. The only sounds were the soft
dripping and trickling of seepage water and his own footsteps. Now
and then he stopped and cast his beam on a dial or down a side
passage. The side passages turned the drainage galleries into a
maze, where in case of a power failure a man without a flashlight
would have a terrible time finding his way out. It had happened
once to Chuck Duncan, who spent two nightmarish hours groping
his way through blackness.

Jeffers didn't give a thought to the lake over his head, a lake that
constantly probed for points of weakness in the dam that blocked
the canyon, that tried to find ways through it, around it, and under
it, that pushed against it relentlessly and with crushing force in an
effort to push it downstream, to roll it over, and to split it apart.
Neither did he worry about the water that was percolating into the
tunnel on every side. All dams leaked, and Sierra Canyon was only
slightly wetter than others of comparable size. Seepage water was
no threat to safety . . . unless it suddenly increased, or was muddy,
or was coming in under pressure. It was simply a nuisance that had
to be pumped or drained away. It represented an economic loss as
well—water that leaked out of a reservoir was water that couldn't
be sent through a turbine to generate electricity.

What Jeffers was thinking about was an article he had read in
the Sacramento *Bee* during dinner about electric cars. Oh, how the
public loved the idea of electric cars—or was it only the newspapers? Drive an electric car a hundred miles at forty miles an
hour, then plug it in for twelve hours. While you sit on a curb and
read a book! Yes, but it doesn't pollute the air, the posy-pluckers
say. Like hell it doesn't! To recharge it, there has to be a generating
plant somewhere burning all that nice Arab oil. What you're doing
with electric cars is moving the pollution from tailpipes to a smoke-
stack. In the meantime you waste a whole shitpot full of energy
lugging those heavy fucking batteries around. God, people can be
stupid.

The tunnel took a sharp bend downward. Jeffers stood at the top
of the long flight of stairs and probed ahead with his flashlight.
Two hundred steps without a single landing to break the monot-

ony, steps that merged at a distant point far below with the overhead lights and the gray tunnel walls. "Let's go," he muttered, beginning the descent, "you need the exercise."

California was headed for a terrible energy crunch, Jeffers said to himself, imagining a microphone in front of him, and not ten years down the pike, either. Right now! The state needs more nukes, no two ways about it. And here was our loony Governor making love to solar. Solar! Jesus Christ! Solar might be all right to heat a few swimming pools, but what California needs is *power!* Lots of power! Nukes are the only way to go and to hell with Jane Fonda. Here was the President of the United States—*the President of the United States!*—wanting more nukes and a snot-nose of a rich-bitch actress not wanting any, and what happens? No nukes! The world is standing on its head and the public is paying the price.

He stopped and examined the tunnel walls, streaked where seepage flows had left mineral deposits. The top of a fuse box was carrying a four-inch-deep buildup of rust-colored sludge. He turned and resumed the downward trek. A soreness was beginning to grow in his upper legs. The climb back out was going to be murder.

"Hydro power is best, you don't have to be a genius to see that." He talked out loud to dispel a feeling of isolation. Around him was a sea of faces from the Chamber of Commerce and the Rotary Club, nodding in agreement. "It's cheap, it's clean, it doesn't use anything up, and it gives you flood control as well as water for irrigation and recreation. So why aren't we building a hundred dams at this point in time? I'll tell you why, my friends, my fellow Americans. Because the fucking Sierra Club and the fucking Friends of the Earth and the fucking Environmental Defense Fund don't want us to, that's why. Don't flood the valley, they say, crying tears as big as horse turds as they build summer homes along the river. Why not? If we don't flood the valley, nature will do it herself every year. Don't spoil the wild river, which the elitist snobs might someday want to look at and write a poem about. Now, my friends, I like wild rivers. I do! But I like electricity, too. And I hate Arabs. Look out for the snail darter, an endangered species, and the three-toed wart frog, and some other fucking thing nobody but a Harvard bone dome ever heard of. What is more important, snails and frogs . . . or people? That, ladies and gentlemen, is the choice that must be made."

He had reached the bottom. He looked at his boots and saw that he was standing in six inches of water. Jesus, why hadn't Duncan reported this? There must be a pump out of commission. In a side chamber were three electric pumps, and two of them weren't working. Jeffers opened the metal door of an electrical wall box. Two circuit breakers had tripped and cut the current. Probably overheated, he reasoned as he clicked them back into position and heard the motors hum to life. They have to work around the clock when the lake is high; maybe a couple of more should be put in. Anyway, the gallery should be dry again in a day or two . . . unless water was coming in faster than he realized. He pushed deeper into the tunnel toward a bank of instruments fifty feet farther along.

He imagined himself surrounded by reporters who bent their heads and scribbled on pads as he spoke. He used a loud voice and gestured broadly to emphasize his points. "Take Earl Warren Lake. Every weekend people come in droves in their campers, gas guzzlers, RVs, and powerboats as if there is no tomorrow. Where the hell do they think the fuel is coming from—the tooth fairy? Without nukes and hydro we need that fuel to generate electricity, but they have bumper stickers like 'No More Nukes' and 'Block Auburn Dam' and then they break out the aluminum tent poles and dig caviar sandwiches out of aluminum foil. Don't they realize that aluminum is like solid electricity? Ladies and gentlemen of the press, what the fuck are the schools teaching?"

He stopped before an array of dials, positioned the flashlight so the beam helped light them up, and began jotting numbers into a notebook. Water was falling from the crown of the tunnel almost like rain, and he had to give some attention to where he held the notebook to keep it from getting drenched. He noticed a piece of plywood that Duncan must have jammed behind several pipes to shelter some of the meters and provide a dry place to stand. There was a hell of a lot of water coming in, Jeffers had to admit, and several of the readings were higher than he ever remembered seeing them. Some new cracks must have opened up—another grouting operation might be needed to seal them.

Fully a third of the meters were out of order, most of them victims of the earthquake five years earlier. The plastic tubes that led to sensors in the embankment had been pinched off or split by settlement, or the meters themselves had corroded, been mucked up by mineral deposits, or just plain worn out. Some of them never worked in the first place, or gave readings that couldn't be trusted.

What a waste of the fucking taxpayers' money! He smiled at the thought of the kid who called from Los Angeles and how excited he got when he found out that the monitoring system wasn't as neat and clean as it was when the dam was built. As if a few meters on the fritz meant something. He acted as if he had stumbled onto some big deal! In the old days, Jeffers thought, we didn't need piezometers and strain gauges and stress cells and all the rest of that shit, and the dams we built then are still standing all over the country like so many Rocks of Gibraltar. Sorry, sonny, but Sierra Canyon Dam ain't going nowhere.

Sure was wet, though. Duncan should have said something. The trouble with Duncan is that he went too much by the book. Fill in the numbers, that's all he cared about, and never mind what they meant. If a boat full of fishermen somehow got sucked into one of these tunnels Duncan probably would ignore it if there wasn't a blank for it on his form. Awful wet. It was going to be interesting to see what the situation was at the end of Gallery D. If it was as bad in there as it was here, he would have to tell Bolen that corrective measures should be taken.

He tried to open the Gallery D door. The knob wouldn't turn.

"Ralph Nader," he announced to the gloom. "Oh, God, don't get me started on him. That sanctimonious pisspot really drives me wild." He dried his hands with his handkerchief. "Saint Ralph. Always looking out for the other guy, never for himself. It doesn't make sense. It isn't human. He must have an angle."

He grabbed the knob with both hands and applied his full strength to it. By hunching his shoulders and squeezing with all his might, he managed to turn the knob slowly all the way to the right.

"You . . . can . . . be . . . sure," he said, straining, "that good old Mr. Nader . . . is looking out . . . for . . . number . . . one—"

The steel door exploded open with the force of a cannon, sending Jeffers sprawling backward to the floor. Instantly tons of water landed on him, rolling him over and sweeping him down the tunnel in a flood of wild brown water. Over and over he tumbled, groping desperately for something to grab on to, his knees and elbows and head knocking against the walkway and walls as the boiling torrent rushed over him. With growing speed the water leaped two hundred feet down the bore until it struck the concrete stairs. A wave surged fifty feet up the slope before washing back down. Jeffers, unconscious and three feet below the surface, opened his mouth spasmodically and inhaled. . . .

On a rocky slope twenty miles away, far above the timberline on a ridge of the Sierra Nevadas and under a blinding sun, a drop of water had formed from melting snow. Down the slope it ran, joining with a million others to form a shimmering sheet on an immense tilted slab of granite, then into a freshet coursing between two shoulders of the mountain; gathering strength, fed by a hundred tiny tributaries, the freshet became a brook, entering the upper forests over rapids and waterfalls lined by wild flowers and green meadows. A growing stream, swollen with spring rains and a melting snowpack, rushing down the mountain, surging over boulders and around enormous logs, carrying a certain drop of water, adding its energy to Middle Reno Creek, from whose rippling surface were reflected the clouds of the sky and the pines. Down, a powerful river, crashing over granite ledges and through a dozen secret canyons, until, in one of the arms of Earl Warren Lake, in deep green water, its fury disappeared.

A single drop of water, now an infinitesimal part of a lake with a shoreline two hundred miles long, a surface area of twenty thousand acres, and a volume of more than a cubic mile, was almost imperceptibly drawn toward the intake gates of the Sierra Canyon powerhouse ten miles away—a drop of water sometimes so deep it touched the rocky bottom, sometimes so close to the surface it was caught by the propellers of powerboats and tossed into the sunlight. At the dam it was swung in an eddy away from the intake gates to the right, where six hundred feet below the surface it entered the graded rock and gravel of the upstream embankment zones. Forced by the pressure of the lake it found its way to the impervious face of the clay core, then down to the foundation rock, into a sliver-like fissure, through a twisting passageway, along the lower edge of the concrete core block, and into a hairline crack. A single drop of water entered drainage Gallery D, hung for a moment from the crown before dropping to the surface of the accumulated seepage that nearly filled the tunnel, then shot forward when the door burst open.

A minute later a particular drop of water, after three weeks of constant motion, came to rest at last . . . in the lungs of Lawrence Jeffers.

7

THEODORE ROSHEK REMOVED TWO FOLDED NEWSPAPER CLIPPINGS FROM his breast pockets and flicked on the overhead light of the White House limousine that was returning him to his hotel. The public-relations man at the convention had handed them to him earlier, and this was his first chance to take a look at them.

ENGINEER CALLS FOR
MORE SCIENCE EDUCATION
IN CONVENTION ADDRESS

(Special to the *New York Times*)

Washington D.C.–Delegates to the national convention of the American Society of Civil Engineers heard the nation's colleges called upon to add more science courses to their liberal arts curricula.

Theodore Roshek of Los Angeles, president of an international engineering firm and incoming president of the 77,000-member, 129-year-old technical society, made the plea at the convention's opening session on Tuesday.

"Engineers and scientists," Roshek said, "are commonly supposed to be too narrowly educated. In fact, it is the liberal arts graduates who suffer that handicap. Many universities permit arts students to escape all science courses after the freshman year. Men and women are getting diplomas and thinking of themselves as educated with only the dimmest understanding of the technological society in which they will spend their lives. They don't even know how their kitchen appliances work, much less the electrical, water supply, sewerage and fuel delivery systems upon which their lives depend.

"Ask the average liberal arts graduate how his car works and you will get an explanation suitable only for use by comedians.

"Students who are never exposed effectively to the drama of science, to the challenge of scientific work, to the power and pleasure of mathematics are being tragically shortchanged by this nation's educational system. The nation is being shortchanged as well."

Roshek, 62, also urged his listeners to take a more active role in local, state, and national politics, pointing out that the great majority of political decisions involve technical matters.

"Engineers," Roshek said, "can no longer afford to be only servants of the public. We must strive to play leadership roles as well. If we don't step forward to help make the decisions that affect the future of the greatest technological power the world has ever seen, then people less qualified will do it for us, as they have been.

"This nation is too important to freedom, democracy and peace to be left entirely in the hands of lawyers."

Following the keynote address, delegates attended a wide variety of technical sessions. . . .

The second clipping was an editorial from that morning's edition of the Washington *Star:*

AN OLD-FASHIONED KIND OF MAN

Theodore Roshek uses crutches to cross a room and for longer trips a wheelchair. But save your sympathy. He regards his polio-damaged legs as merely "a damned nuisance" rather than as an excuse to "slow down or sit on the porch swing." He has ignored the damned nuisance in the course of building one of the world's great engineering firms. The bridges, dams and buildings that bear his imprint are known for their strength as well as their beauty—it's as if he were striving for structures that lack the mortality he must be reminded of every time he moves.

He has a direct manner that is refreshing in these days of federalese, gobbledegook and psychobabble. He'll tell you what's right and wrong and how people should act for the good of all.

An old-fashioned kind of man.

Rumor has it that he's in line for a government appointment. Last week Jack Anderson guessed that Theodore Roshek would be the next Secretary of the Interior.

We hope the Administration has the wisdom to ask him.
If asked, we hope he serves.

The limousine driver refused Roshek's offer of a five-dollar bill,
but the hotel doorman accepted it with a grin. Inside the lobby an
alert bell captain was at his service with a wheelchair. Good old
Jack Anderson, Roshek thought as he was trundled into an elevator,
wrong again. Not Secretary of the tired old Interior, but of a brand
new department, one Anderson apparently hadn't yet got wind of.
Roshek had to smile at the pop psychology in the *Star* editorial.
That business about his trying to compensate in his designs for his
own physical deficiencies—he'd heard that before. People who
believed it had simply never looked at the record. If they did,
they'd find out that he had *never* compromised on safety for the
sake of economy, not even when he was young and his legs were as
strong as anyone's. The new attempts to save a few yards of concrete and a few tons of steel by endlessly "refining" the design with
the aid of computers, the pressure to lower long-established safety
factors, were not for him. Maybe his structures did cost more.
Maybe they were, strictly speaking, overdesigned in the sense that
they were built to standards higher than those in accepted industry
practice. Fine. If you wanted a cheap dam, a cheap tunnel, a cheap
airport, get somebody else. That's why he enjoyed doing business
with the Arabs—they had the money to do things right.

"Here we are, sir."

Roshek struggled to his feet and arranged himself solidly on his
crutches. The bell captain opened the door and handed him his
key.

"Thank you," Roshek said, fishing a ten-dollar bill out of his
pocket. "Here. Go buy yourself a new taxi whistle."

Roshek crossed to the far side of the room and sat down on the
bed facing the windows. If he had glanced into the adjoining room
of his suite, he would have seen a line of light under the bathroom
door. He had accompanied his wife to the airport earlier in the evening, and assumed she was well on her way to Los Angeles. She
had planned to stay with him in Washington until the end of the
week, but that morning, with uncharacteristic suddenness, decided
to return to California on the next available plane. She didn't explain why. Roshek noticed that she was unusually restless and with-
drawn, and suggested that she should consider doing what she had

often talked about, have a complete checkup at the Mayo Clinic. For some reason the remark had greatly irritated her, and had made her behave as if she could hardly wait to be out of his sight.

Roshek put the newspaper clippings on the bedside table and picked up the phone, shaking his head at the impossibility of understanding his wife. There were advantages in having her gone. One was the absence of tension in the air. Another was that he could call Eleanor from the comfort of his room instead of from a booth in the lobby. There were things he could discuss with his wife, however, that Eleanor seemed totally uninterested in. His work, for example. Were his structures more pleasing to the eye than those of his contemporaries? He hoped so, for graceful lines had been a goal all his working life. He was one of the first to take an architectural approach to bridge towers and overpass columns. He helped pioneer cable-supported roof design for large arenas, which brought elegance to what previously had been considered a problem in function and economics alone. He had striven many times in laying out such prosaic structures as chemical and manufacturing plants to lessen their effect on their surroundings, to keep them from assaulting the sensibilities of those who had to live with them. He had worried about visual pollution and environmental impact before the terms were coined. And he did these things before the scourge, the plague, the curse, had struck his legs, providing editorial writers with idiotic metaphors.

He placed the telephone beside him on the bed and dialed California. How happy she would be when she heard the news! He would try to tell her in a matter-of-fact way—too much excitement in his voice would be out of character. The initial euphoria, in fact, had passed, and he was beginning to consider it as a natural progression, as justice, that he should be chosen for a Cabinet post. He heard the phone ring at the other end, and he tried to imagine Eleanor walking across the room, tried to imagine the silken movements of her long legs, the carriage, the poise, the exquisite balance she brought to every gesture. He tried to summon up the image of her oval face, the black hair drawn tightly back, the alabaster skin, the subtle gray-green of her eyes, the smell of her, the *ambiance* of her. . . .

"Hello? Eleanor. It's Ted. How are you, my darling? Yes, I'm fine, and missing you terribly. I have some quite incredible news. To make sure you will be as happy as I am about it, I bought you something very nice I'll give you when I see you, which I hope will be next weekend. I want you to be in a proper mood for celebrating. . . ."

When she heard her husband's voice, Stella Roshek leaned toward the bathroom mirror and finished the job of redoing her makeup. Satisfied that no signs remained of the tears that had earlier reddened her eyes and streaked her cheeks, she took a deep breath and opened the door. She was going to have to confront him and she might as well do it now.

8

PHIL LIGHTLY TRACED THE OUTLINE OF JANET'S BODY, DRAWING HIS hands across her skin from head to toe and back again. He kissed her feet, knees, furry triangle, nipples, ears, eyes, and mouth. He pressed his face into the softness of her stomach and breasts and felt her body arch with pleasure.

"Well," she said, "you seem to have lost your reticence with me anyway. With more work you may become a tolerable lover." She smiled up at him, then laughed. "Even in the candlelight I can tell you're blushing."

"The girls back at St. Jude's High School didn't talk like you."

"How did they talk?"

"They said things like 'I can't let you put your hand there because it's too much of a commitment.'"

"Really? God! I can't imagine Kansas. Nothing happens when I try to think of it."

"It's a place with lawns to be mowed and garbage to be taken out. With mothers waiting for twenty-five-year-old sons to come home from movies. Where a woman as beautiful as you would set off riots in the streets."

He kissed her.

"I'm not beautiful," she whispered. "I'm cute. I'm a cute person who likes you very much."

Phil rolled onto his back and put his hand over his eyes. "Why can't I make love to you day and night? Why does life have to include lectures from Bolen and appointments to get my ass chewed out by Roshek?"

"How did Roshek get involved? You said Bolen wasn't going to tell him. When you barged in here tonight, you were so maddened by lust—saliva running down the front of your clothes and everything—you didn't give me the details."

"Was I an animal? Sorry."

"I loved it. Before, it was like deflowering a priest."

"I called a guy named Jeffers at the dam. He called Roshek and asked who the hell I was. Roshek was damned if he knew."

Janet was moving the tip of her tongue back and forth across her lips. Phil lowered his head to touch the tip of his tongue to hers. "Roshek called Bolen?" she said.

"And told him to have me in his office the minute he gets in from the airport. From your arms to his . . . what a shock to the system that's going to be."

"It was nice, though," she said, "seducing a priest. It made me feel deliciously evil."

"I'm far from a virgin, you know. I've screwed every Miss Kansas since 1948 and most of the runners-up, along with their sisters and mothers. You are in bed with a master. Bolen called me at home after work today and lectured me on how to act with the old man. I really would like to stay in bed with you for about two weeks straight. Let's plan to do it. We could use bedpans so we wouldn't even have to go to the bathroom."

"And blindfolded eunuchs to bring food. I'll see what I can find in the yellow pages." She thought for a moment, then said: "Roshek might want to compliment you for your concern about public safety."

"What he wants to do is jump up and down on my face. Apparently he's mad as hell. Even Bolen sounded scared. He told me not to defend myself if I valued my job. I guess I'll just have to let my natural cowardice shine through."

Janet moved her hand down Phil's chest and stomach and let it rest between his legs. "I think I know why I like you so much. Because you treat me like an intellectual equal, which I am. Because you are considerate and gentle and sensuous. Because you are hung like a stud horse." She broke into peals of laughter. "You always look so shocked when I say something raunchy. You must think I'm terrible! Just because I like to talk dirty doesn't mean I *am* dirty."

"Sorry to hear that."

"Because I love sex doesn't mean my life is filled with men. I'm very particular about who I let into my laundry. *Very* particular. You have no idea how many toads I've gone out with. Until you came along, I was beginning to worry that my playpen might atrophy. Don't laugh! In the last year or so you could count the lovers I've had on the finger of one hand. As a matter of fact, the finger of one hand was about all they—"

"I don't want to hear about it! I've got enough on my mind without your other lovers."

"That's just it. There aren't any."

"Good. Okay, now I want you to do something really perverted. Let's find out how liberated you really are. I want you to hug me and pat me on the head and tell me everything is going to be all right." He nestled his head on her shoulder and closed his eyes.

"Poor *baby*," she said, hugging him and patting his head. "Everything is going to be all *right*. That nasty old Mr. Roshek won't hurt you. If he says something that makes you cry, tell him to fuck off. You can always move in here and go on welfare."

"You are wonderful, Janet."

They made love again, then fell asleep in each other's arms.

Languorously, Eleanor James extended her arm to the bedside table and lowered the telephone receiver into its cradle. She laced her fingers across her stomach and raised her left leg in the air, foot extended, toes together, until it pointed straight at the ceiling. The skin was white and smooth. The leg was long and straight, thin but steely strong.

"It feels good to get out of my clothes and stretch after being cooped up in the car." Her voice was small, like a child's.

"I gather that was old hatchet face?"

"Yes. He thinks he's going to get some sort of government job. I wasn't really listening."

"Does he call every day?" The young man lying beside her raised his leg until it matched hers. By flexing his foot at the ankle he made the muscles ripple in his calf and thigh.

"Yes. He loves me. That's what you do when you love somebody."

Slowly she bent her left leg until the knee touched her chin while she lifted her right leg to full vertical extension. Her partner matched her movements. Their bodies were lithe and lean.

"How long are you going to string him along?"

"Until I get the money."

"Then what? Cut him off just like that?"

She watched her legs with satisfaction. "Oh, I don't know. There are advantages to being adored by a rich old man. He buys me jewelry. Did you know that he sits for hours and watches me move my legs like this? There should be more audiences like him. Change the record, would you, sweetheart? I get awfully tired of Ravel."

He strode evenly to the record player in the corner. She watched his young dancer's body through the V formed by her upraised legs. The shoulders tapered to a small waist and the buttocks were small and tight. When he returned to the bed, she noticed that he had a half erection. He lay on his side, supporting himself on one elbow. He touched her small, firm breasts. She gently closed her legs around his head.

"Why, Russell Stone," she said with a coy smile, "I do believe you want to make love again, and we've only been here an hour."

"You find that amusing?"

"Yes. Half of California thinks you're gay."

"Let them. It means that a lot of husbands trust me with their wives."

She lowered her legs and pushed herself into a sitting position. "Are you jealous of an old man?"

He shook his head. "I just don't see how you can do it. Go to bed with him, I mean. A cripple . . ."

"I want a studio of my own and he can give it to me. That's how I can do it. Besides, it's not so bad. I close my eyes and think of you. Or Baryshnikov."

"The whole thing is sick."

"I don't see him often. He can be very sweet. He's not as fierce as people think." She looked past him to the windows, to the trees, to the canyon walls on the other side of the river. "Often it's not intercourse he wants. He just wants to touch me. He treats me as if I were a fantastic work of art. He said that next to me the greatest structure he ever designed was like a mudpie."

"I give him credit for finding the key to your body: flattery."

She looked at him with round eyes. "Oh, Russell, I wouldn't talk about flattery if I were you. I've seen you burst into tears over a bad review in the *Examiner*. You shouldn't make fun of a man whose hospitality you are enjoying."

"Without his knowledge." He looked around. Through an open door he could see the enormous fireplace and the parquet floor of the living room. "It's weird, you've got to admit, making love in a room with a picture of a dam on one wall and Franklin Delano Roosevelt on the other. It's weird not hearing any traffic noises. I get the creeps when I'm not in the city."

"We're hardly roughing it. This is probably the most elaborate home in the whole valley. It even has a name, Creekwood, that's listed on county maps."

"Fancy place, all right. Still, I don't see how I'm going to stand it up here for two whole days."

Eleanor got up and slipped into a pair of jeans. "Let's take a walk by the river and fill our lungs with mountain air. You might like it."

She caught his hand and pulled him to his feet.

The river was well worth seeing. At the Sierra Canyon powerhouse ten miles upstream, the maximum amount of water was being released to generate electricity during the evening hours of peak demand. The tailrace water added to the flow pouring down the spillway sent the river close to overflowing its banks as it surged down the canyon.

It was an invigorating spectacle.

9

"WHAT HAPPENED, STELLA? DID YOU MISS THE PLANE?"

Roshek put the phone aside and watched his wife take a chair facing the bed. Her movements were controlled, as if rehearsed, and her eyes were full of quiet strength he had never seen before. Had she overheard the whole conversation with Eleanor? He tried to suppress signs of alarm as he recalled the terms of endearment he had used and the references to a meeting and a gift.

"I let the plane take off without me," she said evenly. "I've been waiting for you in the sitting room, watching it get dark."

Roshek made an effort to smile. "You scared the daylights out of me! I didn't see you when I came in." Then with concern: "Are you all right?"

"I'm fine. Wonderful, in fact, because I have finally made a decision about something that has made me miserable for years. I came back to tell you. Suddenly I couldn't stand the thought of putting it off a minute longer. Tomorrow I am going to file for divorce."

"Oh, now, Stella, for heaven's sakes! What brought this on? You're upset about something. I'm sure if we talk about it . . ."

She shook her head with quiet conviction. "You ask what brought it on. That you should have to ask . . . I suppose that's what brought it on. You've become so self-centered, Theodore, so sunk in yourself and your work that you are completely unaware of how profoundly you've insulted me."

"Eavesdropping on my phone calls, that's what brought it on. In your mind you've twisted something innocent into—"

"Nothing about Eleanor James is innocent," she cut in sharply. "Oh, yes, I've known about her from the beginning. I was at those cast parties in San Francisco, remember, when we first met her. I saw how she played up to you, how you fawned on her. For months you talked about her and found excuses to make trips to San Francisco. Then suddenly you stopped the talking, but not the trips. I can pinpoint almost to the day when your interest in her became more than . . . paternal. More than artistic." She turned away and fought to retain control.

Roshek tightened his lips, then said, "It's on an assumption like that that you want to end a marriage that has lasted—"

"You've been seen together!" she said, facing him and speaking with a harshness in her voice. "Friends have told me how a gray-haired old man is making a fool of himself over a gold digger half his age! No, no, don't tell me she's not a gold digger. You'd have to be blind not to see it. Don't tell me how innocent you are. I heard you on the phone. I'm not deaf. I'm not stupid."

It would be worse than futile, Roshek realized, to try to defend Eleanor or himself—the effort might send Stella into the lobby in hysterics. But he would have to do something to change her mind about a divorce, at least delay the filing until after the appointment and the Senate confirmation hearings. A divorce action would hardly make his candidacy more attractive. Clampett had specifically asked if his marriage was solid. Then there were the financial consequences should Stella claim as her share of community property half of his interest in the corporation.

"Maybe I have been making a fool of myself," he forced himself to say. "I suppose it is ridiculous of me to think that a young woman like Eleanor James could find anything attractive about . . . well, about a cripple. But even if she did, Stella, it wouldn't pose any threat to *us*. My feelings for her don't match my feelings for *you*."

She waved her hand and made a sound of contempt. "You have no feelings for me. Not as a person. Not as a wife. I'm somebody you practice speeches on at breakfast. I'm your social secretary. I cater your business dinners. You think of me as another one of your employees, that's all. Well, Theodore, employees can quit. They can quit and take their severance pay and try to build a life with less misery in it. That's exactly what I'm going to do."

"You are getting all worked up over nothing. . . ."

She laughed bitterly. "You know one of the things I'm looking forward to? Not having to listen to you say things like 'You are getting all worked up over nothing.'"

"But it's true in this case! Eleanor James means nothing to me compared to you! Absolutely nothing! I'm sorry I let myself slip into a childish infatuation. I'm sorry I've been so insensitive and thoughtless. I'll change. I'll never see her again if that's what you want. A divorce? Surely we haven't come to that. Not after all we've been through together."

Clampett had warned him that he was being indiscreet in his meetings with Eleanor, and he was obviously right. For the next few months he was going to have to be very careful. Restaurants and theaters in San Francisco were out. There were remote resorts where they could meet. There was Europe and South America. He looked at his wife, who sat facing him with unwavering composure. The possibility that she would yield to tears was plainly remote.

"Even if I believed you could change, it would make no difference. Eleanor James is only part of the problem. I want a divorce mainly because you . . . because you no longer want me as a woman."

"That's not true!"

"It is true. Look at me. Am I unattractive? I'm fifty-four years old. Everyone tells me, you have told me yourself, that I look ten years younger. I still get admiring glances from men."

"You are a very handsome woman, Stella." A very handsome woman who could get a court order freezing community property, thus destroying the corporation's financial flexibility. It could take years to assess the worth of a firm involved in dozens of joint ventures around the world. A team of lawyers could make a career of the case. "I haven't been paying as much attention to you as you deserve. I've been working too hard, trying to lift the firm into the greatness we seem close to achieving. The success we've been having, Stella, the fast growth, it's a kind of vindication of everything I believe in. Eleanor has distracted me, too, made me behave, I can see it now, like a fool. Have I made you feel as though I don't want you as a woman? Please, *please* forgive me. Come, sit beside me on the bed. . . ."

"No, Theodore, you can't manipulate me anymore. It's over. Nothing you say can make me forget the pain you've given me for four long years. Not once in four years have you touched me or shown me the slightest sign of tenderness. I can't forgive you. I can't forget it."

Roshek sighed. "A man can't be expected to sustain the same level of interest over three decades that he had during the honeymoon. Love might still be there, but it changes."

"Yes, it changes. It goes from something to nothing. Do you know why you lost interest in me? Don't deny that you did."

"I don't know," Roshek said, shaking his head and making a helpless gesture with his hands. "I'll make it up to you. I—"

"I know why. Because I had a hysterectomy. Yes, that is the reason."

"That's ridiculous!"

"From that moment I was incomplete in your eyes. Flawed. I have a scar . . . unobtrusive, but there it is, and when you saw it you turned away and never really looked at me again. You rejected me the way you would a structure that had been improperly designed."

"God, spare me the amateur psychology. I've had a dose of that already today."

"You began looking at other women differently—not as objects to impress and dominate and amuse, but as if you were appraising them. Like expensive cars. Oh, how your eyes lit up when Eleanor James smiled at you! No scars there, I could see you thinking. No missing parts—except perhaps for a brain and a conscience. You probably think of her the way you think of engineering designs you admire. I've heard you use the phrase a hundred times: a beautiful combination of form and function. You said that about Sacramento's new sewage treatment plant. Graceful lines, you said. Economical design. A beautiful combination of form and function. Do you tell Eleanor James she is more beautiful than any sewage plant? Is that what you whisper to her when she is caressing your wallet?" She rose and put her hand on the doorknob.

"Goddammit, Stella, sit down! We've got to talk this out."

"Don't raise your voice. It's a waste of energy. You don't frighten me anymore. You did once, did you know that? You are so decisive, so sure of yourself, so used to giving orders and holding hoops for people to jump through. I never knew quite where I was going or who I was, so I followed you and helped you pursue your goal, which, as I understand it, is to become the richest engineer who ever walked the earth. Well, I know who I am now. I am a piece of used, patched-up merchandise who feels that life isn't over yet. I know where I'm going, too: to the airport to catch a night flight. My luggage is waiting for me in Los Angeles. Goodbye."

"Close that door! A divorce is the last thing either one of us needs. Please, Stella . . ."

Roshek got to his feet and took several awkward steps toward her before his legs buckled. He went down on one knee and hung on to a chair to keep from falling to the floor. He grimaced. "I can't get up . . . help me. . . ."

She stood in the doorway looking at him sadly. "I never thought I'd see you resort to that," she said. "If you need help, I suggest you call the front desk."

When she was gone, Roshek cursed and pulled himself into the chair. He threw his head back and covered his face with his hands. She was going to ruin everything if she wasn't stopped. He needed a few months, then he didn't give a damn what she did. In his mind he ran through the names of attorneys she might turn to. In the morning he would call them and promise to make it worth their while if they stalled her. He would suggest going with her to a marriage counselor. He would offer to see a psychiatrist. He would send her flowers. She took a dozen pills a day . . . maybe she could be drugged in some way to keep her out of action long enough for him to . . .

He crawled onto the bed, his mind sifting through the alternatives. He needed time, and he vowed to get it one way or another. He pictured his wife, suddenly grown so hard and cold, totally unlike the woman he thought he knew. She had looked at him on the floor without a trace of sympathy. He rolled back and forth on the bed like a man in agony, eventually drifting into a sleep filled with terrible dreams.

10

A BATTERED GREEN VOLKSWAGEN BUG WITH A PLASTIC DAISY ATOP ITS aerial pulled into a parking space behind the Center for Holistic Fitness in Berkeley, California. A slightly built man with a thin beard got out and waved his arms several times in wide circles. His blue jeans were faded and tattered, and his T-shirt carried the message "DISTANCE RUNNERS DO IT LONGER." With a light step he walked around the one-story, cement-block building to the front door. He hesitated several times before going inside, once turning his back and taking several steps in the opposite direction.

The receptionist was impressed when he gave her his name.

"Dr. Dulotte is expecting you," she said with a smile. "I'll let him know you're here."

Scattered on a low table were sports, running, and health magazines. The man noticed that the cover of *Western Strider* was filled with a photograph of his face so twisted with pain that torturers might have been applying cattle prods to his genitals. "KENT SPAIN WINS AGAIN," the banner caption read. "See page 32 for his quick energy tips."

"Won't you have a seat?" the receptionist asked. "The doctor might be a few minutes."

"No, thanks. Sitting is bad for your lumbar."

He walked around the waiting room, studying framed testimonials from satisfied patients and photographs of smiling staff members. The Center for Holistic Fitness was a medical-mystical smorgasbord catering to a broad range of physical achievers and those wishing to be. Most of the customers were joggers and week-end tennis players, but there was a sprinkling of malfunctioning college and professional athletes as well. The building directory showed how far the services available spilled over the borders of the orthodox. Appointments could be made with a general practitioner, a podiatrist, an orthopedist, a nutritionist, a physical therapist, a behavioral psychologist, a life-style analyzer, a hypnotist, a naturopath, an acupuncturist, a foot reflexologist, a Buddhist priest (Mondays only), and a psychic schooled in astrology, meditation, and the reading of auras. The brainchild of David Dulotte, a doctor-businessman who was more businessman than doctor, the Center was under constant scrutiny by the appropriate divisions of the state government and the American Medical Association. Those on the staff with M.D. degrees didn't care what the A.M.A. thought, because they weren't members. They criticized it almost daily, in fact, for its lack of enthusiasm for wheat germ, biofeedback, and the vitamin B_{12} complex. B_{12} was one of the staples sold at the Center's adjoining store, which carried a bewildering array of health foods, sporting goods, and pharmaceuticals.

Dr. Dulotte was an enthusiastic, dapper, portly man with steel-rimmed glasses. He pumped Kent Spain's hand vigorously as he guided him into his office.

"Good to see you again, Kent, by golly! Have a chair!" He sat behind his cluttered desk and spread his arms. "What do you think of our little establishment?"

"It's not so little. You sure cover all the bases."

Dulotte chuckled appreciatively. "A guy walks in here with a complaint, or just some slob who wants to lose a belly, and he gets hit with everything under the sun. Something is bound to work, right? We give a patient a more complete workup than any hospital in the state, I shit you not. We do thermography, plethysmography, Doppler ultrasound, glucose tolerance, mineral analysis, every damned thing. We stare into their eyeballs—that's iridology—we slap 'em on a stress treadmill to see if they die of heart failure, and we make 'em swallow a Heidelberg capsule."

"Swallow a what?"

"A little gizmo that sends out radio signals as it travels through the gut. Don't look so amazed! Standard stuff you can get at a regular clinic if they have any imagination. But look how much farther we can go. We can calculate your biorhythms, ponder your alpha waves, teach you the lotus position, and flex your spine. We are the only place in the western states that does moxabustion. Sit down, will you? You make me nervous."

"I was sitting down in the car. Sitting down is terrible for you. Just what the hell is moxabustion?"

Dulotte clapped his hands with glee. "I love it! It's the very latest thing from ancient China. A jogger comes in with, say, a pain in the hip. Where it hurts, we put a little pile of wormwood leaves along with some secret herbs and spices—I don't know what exactly —and set it on fire! Honest to God! People say it helps! I think what happens is they get so distracted by the pain of the blister they forget about the original complaint. The research I've read on it suggests that it works best on old Chinese women who have never been exposed to anything but folk medicine. Unfortunately for us here at the Center, very few old Chinese women are into jogging."

"You're a quack, Doc. A regular Donald Duck."

"There are gray areas," Dulotte said with a shrug. "We use placebos just like establishment doctors, except ours aren't shaped like sugar pills. There was an article a while back in the *New England Journal of Medicine* that showed that the placebo is one of the most effective drugs on the market, with no side effects. Our policy here is to give the customer what he wants provided it can't be proven harmful in a court of law. What customers want these days is hooey from the Orient, so I'm importing everything I can lay my hands on. We're making so much money we are the envy of every clinic and medical corporation in the Bay Area. I'm thinking of selling franchises. I'll be the Colonel Sanders of holism."

From a cooler beside his desk Dulotte took a tall green bottle and poured two glasses of murky liquid. "Try this," he said. "Our newest item. Natural mineral water from Szechwan Province. Sold a ton of it already at ten bucks a quart. Can you imagine? Here's to your decision to turn pro! We'll make piles of money together. Bottoms up!"

Spain took a sip and made a face. "Tastes like dragon piss," he said, putting his glass down. "My decision to turn pro. That's a laugh, isn't it? A marathon runner turning pro? I'll be lucky if I make bus fare."

"You'll be surprised at how much you can make. Endorsements

are getting to be big business. Of course, it depends on what you are willing to endorse."

"On the phone you said if I gave your shoes credit for winning a race you'd give me twenty-five hundred bucks, is that right? I'll do it. I'm thirty-three years old and I'm not getting any faster. I'm not good enough to make the Olympics, so what the hell, I might as well make a few bucks while I can. God, when I think of the years I've spent trying to become a world-class runner! A lifetime. What have I got to show for it? Not a fucking thing. I can't even coach, because the colleges all want a high-school diploma at least. With twenty-five hundred I can get a better car and start looking for a job."

Dulotte smiled benignly. "Your problems are over if you do what I tell you. You are the biggest name I ever had a chance to work with. I made six grand for Frank Robutz last year and you've got twice the name he has."

"Six grand? Frank Robutz? Christ Almighty, he can't beat Orphan Annie."

"You are right. What kind of shape are you in?"

"Not the shape I was in a year ago. I'm only doing sixty miles a week. I used to do a minimum of a hundred. But I've been doing a lot of hill work. Every other day I do a double Dipsea. That's twelve miles, most of it either straight up or straight down."

"Can you win tomorrow?"

"I should be able to beat a bunch of housewives and businessmen. Hobbyists."

"Tommy Ryan is in the field."

"Yeah? He can be tough. My money is on him."

"And my money is on you. Tell me, what's your best time?"

"In the marathon, two twenty-one, but I haven't come within twelve minutes of that for almost two years. I tell you, Doc, I'm going down the tubes."

"You will still be the class of the field tomorrow. Fifteen hundred fanatics sweating and panting in their cute little outfits and you are the favorite."

"Big deal."

Dulotte glanced at his watch. "It's a little after nine. At about this time tomorrow morning, you'll be crossing the finish line in front of the Sutterton City Hall. The banks are closed on Saturday, but on Monday, if you will sign a personal services contract I have ready for you, you can be in the bank of your choice with a check for ten thousand dollars. What do you say? Eh?"

"Come on, cut it out. You can't make that kind of money off me, not even if I ran naked with Bobby Riggs tied to one leg."

"Oh, yes, I can. Look, your best days are behind you. Everybody knows that. Your times are getting steadily worse. What if you were to turn in your lifetime best mark tomorrow? On a course that is a lot harder than Boston? While wearing and eating and drinking and using products made by Jog-Tech, which happens to be my Hong Kong manufacturing subsidiary? I could run a series of ads in the running journals that would bring the Ponce de Leóns swarming out of the woodwork by the thousands."

"Ponce de who?"

"León. The first guy to spend a fortune and bust his ass trying to stay young."

Kent Spain began pacing back and forth in front of Dulotte's desk. "How the hell am I going to run my best time? By prayer? By magic?"

"No. By cheating." He let the words sink in. "A little cheating never hurt anybody. I dare say it got you through two years of high school."

Spain put his hands on the desk and stared at Dulotte. "What do you mean, *cheating?*"

"I mean cheating. Nobody will get hurt. You get ten thousand bucks for starters."

Spain collapsed in a chair and blew a stream of air through pursed lips.

"If you can learn to talk," the doctor added, "you can make twice that on the lecture circuit even after I take fifteen percent."

Spain suddenly straightened up and struck the desk top with his fist. "I'll *do* it! Ten thousand! For starters! Holy shit! What's the plan?"

Dulotte unfolded a map and traced a line. "The race starts here, follows a highway, then a fire road, then a trail through a national forest. What you have to do is run five-minute miles for the first fifteen miles. Ryan and a few others will be trying for five seven or five eight."

Spain looked worried. "I'll burn myself out. I'll have to crawl the last eleven miles."

"No, you won't. Look at the map." He tapped a spot with his

forefinger. "The trail comes out of the woods right here, goes across the top of Sierra Canyon Dam, and back into the woods on the other side. After that is a long stretch through heavy timber, downhill all the way. You'll be taking that on a bicycle, old buddy, catching your breath and whistling a merry tune, the breeze flowing through your kinky hair."

"A *bicycle!*"

"A bicycle. It's in the bushes waiting for you. Watch for a T-shirt tied to a limb. Make sure you are the first one to get there. There isn't another aid station until mile nineteen."

Spain was out of his chair again, pacing back and forth with lunging steps, wringing his hands as if he were trying to cleanse them of stubborn grease. "It won't work," he said. "It can't work. It'll never work. There's no *way* it can work."

"It'll work."

"If somebody clocks me at the dam, the monitor at mile nineteen will figure out later that something is haywire. You're nuts, Doc, totally out of your gourd."

"Which brings us to the real beauty of the concept. I am the monitor at mile nineteen."

Spain stopped and stared. "You?"

"Me." Dulotte resumed the tracing of a line on the map. "You'll be ten or fifteen minutes ahead of the field, and after dumping the bike you can sit down for five minutes and catch your breath."

"I hate sitting down."

"Walk, then. The course comes out of the woods here at the county fairgrounds. Trot the rest of the way as fast as you can. You'll be on a highway with people cheering you on. You will break the tape right here"—he tapped the map with triumphant finality—"in downtown Sutterton, the new champion of the Mother Lode Marathon, with a time just minutes off the world record. An amazing new lifetime best, achieved while festooned with Jog-Tech gimmicks."

Spain sank into a chair and watched the doctor empty the contents of a drawer onto the desk. There was a pair of ribbed rubber heel cups to guard against bruising and to provide "greater lift," a digital pedometer-watch, a Jog-Tech Living Jock Strap, a Micho-electronic Pulsometer that recorded pulse rate, blood pressure, temperature, and electrolytic balance. "This is the latest hardware,"

Dulotte said of the Pulsometer, "a hot item that goes for four hundred bucks."

Spain protested, "I can't wear all that crap! Must weigh ten pounds!"

"A little over a pound. You can manage. After the race you will say that your record-breaking performance was the result of being able to keep track of your body functions, scientifically adjusting your pace to your maximum feasible exertion rate. Of course, you will also say that you trained on our home treadmill—another four-hundred-dollar item—while drinking our vegetable-vitamin-almond consommé."

The runner lifted his upper lip in revulsion and turned away. "I feel sick," he said.

"We will make a killing. Sign here."

Thirty minutes later, the contract gone over and signed and the details of the race rehearsed, the two men shook hands, one beaming, one desolate. Dulotte raised a glass of Chinese mineral water to the marathoner, drained it, and smacked his lips. "You really ought to give this another taste, Kent," he said. "It's the best dragon piss in the world."

Just before lunch, Herman Bolen phoned Sierra Canyon and was told by an engineer in the powerhouse control room that Lawrence Jeffers had not yet made an appearance that day. He was expected at any time.

"He might have gone to Sacramento and forgot to tell us," the engineer said, trying to be helpful.

"You're probably right. Have him call me when he comes in."

"Sure will, Mr. Bolen. I'll put a note on his desk right now."

Odd, Bolen thought, walking slowly to the windows. Not like Jeffers to leave his whereabouts unknown. If he had found anything worth mentioning in the drainage galleries, surely he would have phoned late last night or early this morning before leaving for wherever he was. A trip to Sacramento—yes, that was probably it. Or a dental appointment. Still . . .

He returned to his desk and sat down, wondering if he should call the powerhouse again and order someone into the dam to look for Jeffers. He might have fallen down that accursedly long flight of concrete stairs and broken a leg or a hip so badly that he couldn't drag himself to one of the emergency phones. Or he might have had a heart attack despite his apparently robust health. In either case, Bolen would not appear in a very favorable light for having sent Jeffers into that dark hole at night.

Come, come, Bolen chided himself, you are overdramatizing the situation. If Jeffers was still inside the dam, someone at the site would have noticed his car. You would look pretty foolish if you launched a manhunt for a man who might come strolling into his office unconcernedly at any moment. Roshek would accuse you of overreacting to the fears of a young nincompoop by sending Jeffers on a wild-goose chase, then of overreacting again in mounting a search for him. "Jesus Christ, Herman," he could imagine Roshek saying, looking at him as if he were crazy, "haven't you got any sense at all?"

Best he wait a while longer and try to keep his imagination from soaring into fantasy. At the end of the afternoon, if Jeffers still hadn't reported in, he would make a few discreet inquiries.

He looked at his calendar. There was a meeting that afternoon at Southern California Edison's downtown headquarters about the plan to enlarge Sequoia Dam. If it dragged on, he would excuse himself at some point and make a phone call.

11

ALONE IN HIS OFFICE, THEODORE ROSHEK CLOSED HIS EYES AND TOUCHED his temples. For the first time in years he had a headache, a relentless headache that spread in waves from the center of his forehead. He hadn't slept well the night before in his Washington hotel room. The flight to Los Angeles had hit a stretch of rough air that made it impossible for nearly an hour to think about anything except the plane shaking itself apart. Even the limousine ride to the office was nerve-wracking, partly because of the congestion on the Harbor Freeway, partly because the driver seemed half drunk and nearly got them both killed with nonchalant lane changes.

At least he had had a small success with Stella. He phoned her from the airport and got her to agree not to see an attorney until they could discuss their problems further that night. The hardness in her voice, though, was unsettling. Further discussion was useless, she said, and he should make arrangements at once for moving out of the house. Surely he would have better luck with her face to face. He would play on her sympathies, and if that didn't work he would raise his voice, remind her of her own shortcomings, and exploit the guilt she must be feeling for walking out on a man who had given her a life of luxury. With luck he would break her down, make her fold up and cry the way he had on several previous occasions when they had argued. *He must not lose his temper.* If he shouted at her or threatened her, in view of the mood she was in now, he would lose all chance of keeping the marriage patched together.

He thought of the small gun he carried for protection in his attaché case. She knew it was there—it was at her insistence that he had started carrying it—and if their emotions boiled over one of them might make a grab for it. Unlikely, but nevertheless . . . He snapped the case open and removed the weapon from its velvet pocket, turning the cold steel over in his hand. The safety was on and it hadn't been fired since the day he bought it fifteen years earlier, but it still felt ominous and deadly. There might have been a reason for him to have such a thing at the beginning, before the days of airport security checks, when he was traveling alone to some of the most remote areas in the world, but hardly anymore. He hadn't even thought about the gun in a long time, and he half wondered if it still worked.

A red light flashed on his intercom. He depressed a small lever and heard his secretary's voice: "Mr. Bolen wants to know if you'll be going to the Southern Cal Edison conference. He's ready to leave."

Roshek put the gun in a drawer and felt glad to be rid of it. "Tell him I'll try to get there in an hour or so. After I talk to young Kramer, I want Jules Wertheimer on the phone. Set that up, please."

He broke the connection and jotted down a list of questions he wanted to ask Wertheimer, the only lawyer he knew that he trusted completely. He was a corporate rather than a divorce lawyer, but he would be able to provide some preliminary guidance. Could Stella freeze the community property, thus depriving the company of its freedom of action? Were there enough assets in the estate to satisfy her rights without giving her any part of the company? Could assets be concealed, perhaps by preparing a second set of books or by making transfers to overseas subsidiaries? Wertheimer would have some ideas.

Thinking about his wife claiming half his share of the corporation he had spent his life creating angered him, and the more he thought about it the angrier he got. He would hang on to full control no matter what California's ridiculous divorce laws said. She could have the Beverly Hills house, the Sierra Canyon house, the cars, the furniture, the art, the stocks, the insurance, everything, but not the business. If her attorneys didn't think that was a fair division, they could go *fuck* themselves. He tightened his hands into fists. He would try his best to keep the marriage intact long enough to secure the government appointment, but once he had that nailed down Stella could do whatever she wanted, except stick her fingers into the company. That he would never allow. Never!

His secretary came on the intercom again. "Mr. Kramer is here to see you."

Phil crossed the carpeting and sat down tentatively on a leather chair in front of Roshek's massive mahogany desk. Good God, Phil thought when he saw the expression on the old man's face, he looks as if he's going to spring at my throat! What's he so mad about— that I didn't bring a cap I could twist in my hands while he bawls me out? If he tries to slap me the way Sister Mary Carmelita did in grade school for shooting spitballs, he's going to have a fight on his hands.

"You're Kramer? You look intelligent. Why don't you act it?"

"I beg your pardon?"

"Tell me if I've got this straight. You have no practical experience except for a few summers' work with the highway department in Kansas or some goddam place. You've never been involved in the design or construction of a dam. You know nothing about the subject except what you've read in books, which is worse than nothing. You've come up with a cockamamie computer model that makes you think you can sit in an office five hundred miles from a dam you've never seen and understand it better than men with lifetimes of experience who are sitting right on top of it. Is that right?"

Phil stared, speechless. Was Roshek kidding? Was he trying to be funny? "No," he managed to say, "that's not right at all."

"It isn't? What's not right about it?"

Phil crossed and uncrossed his legs. "I don't know where to begin. You've put the worst possible interpretation—"

"Furthermore, you had the audacity to call the chief maintenance engineer on the site and lead him to believe that his headquarters people think something is wrong with his dam."

"I did not! I called him only to get some current meter readings. He may have thought I sounded excited on the phone, but he wasn't looking at what my computer program was telling me."

"He doesn't *need* to look at what your computer program is telling you, and neither do the managers of ten thousand other dams.

He doesn't *need* intimations from a greenhorn that he isn't doing his job properly. This company doesn't need and *I* don't need an employee casting doubts about one of our structures. We depend on two things for success: the ability to provide technical services of the highest professional quality, and the *reputation* for being able to provide them. Ruin our reputation and we are out of business, it's as simple as that. What you have been doing amounts to a whispering campaign against your own employer."

Phil waited until he was sure it was his turn to speak. Keeping his voice calm, he tried to make his point. "Mr. Roshek, I no doubt deserve some criticism for taking too much initiative. But the data clearly indicate, to me anyway, that some sort of investigation is called for."

"You're not an engineer. I hope you realize that. Not yet. Not by a long shot."

"I'm not a licensed engineer, that's true. In California you need five years' professional experience after graduation before you can apply. I have a doctorate in—"

"An engineer is more than a man with a diploma and five years' experience. True engineering can't even be taught in school, because it involves a man's personality, his willingness to consider every last detail, the way he respects the materials he works with, his sense of history and the future, and his integrity."

For Christ's sake, Phil thought, he's not listening to a word I say! He's using me to practice some sort of goddamned commencement address.

"Most important," Roshek went on, "is maturity. A sense of proportion. Judgment. A doctor wouldn't say to a patient, 'You probably don't have cancer. Then again, you might have. We'll know when we get the lab results. In the meantime, don't worry about it.' See how stupid that sounds? What you've been doing is along that line. Jeffers called me in Washington to find out what was going on."

"He did? I didn't mean to get everybody so upset. I didn't realize that a phone call would—"

"You didn't realize that you could have caused a panic? What if word leaked out that we were worried about the safety of the nation's highest dam? A secretary overhears part of your conversation, a switchboard operator listens in, rumors start flying, newspapers pick it up, politicians demand an investigation, environmentalists charge a cover-up . . . I've seen it happen. Over nothing. Because a prematurely smart college student gets excited over drivel in a computer."

Phil felt his cheeks turning red. He knew he should simply let Roshek's tirade run its course without risking disaster by fighting back, but he felt he should put up some sort of defense. Silence would imply that he agreed with Roshek's distortions. Besides, he was getting mad. There was nothing in life he hated more than to be accused of something he didn't do.

"Sir, I didn't say to Mr. Jeffers that I thought the dam was failing. I showed my surprise that so many of the meters were out of order and that the seepage was so high. I did tell Mr. Bolen, in private, that my program indicated something was wrong. Maybe I should have discussed it with him first before calling the dam, but I wanted to make sure I had the latest figures." Phil let his voice trail off because his words were being ignored. Roshek's eyes were wandering around the room resting on the photographs of his projects, and he was reciting their names like a litany.

"Sinai, Maracaibo, San Luis, Alyeska. These tremendous developments are as sound as the day they were built." He gestured toward a glass display in which was a realistic scale model of an earth and rock dam complete with tiny trees on the abutment slopes and a center stripe on the road across its crest. "Sierra Canyon Dam. Recognize it? Probably not, since your knowledge is confined to textbook abstractions. Not one of the structures this company has had a hand in designing has ever had the slightest question raised about its safety. Not one has suffered a failure of any kind. Engineered structures fail, yes, usually because foundation conditions aren't properly assessed. It was Karl Terzaghi, the father of modern soil mechanics, who said that when Mother Nature designed the crust of the earth, she didn't follow the specifications of the American Society of Testing and Materials."

I'm a dummy audience, that's all I am, Phil said to himself, wondering how much more he could take before boiling over.

"The structures I've designed will be in use two hundred years from now, if the civilizations of the future want them. Durability like that is a result of skill, hard work, intuition, and uncompromising insistence on top-quality work every step of the way. When a design philosophy like that is brought to bear, structures don't fail."

Did Roshek really believe that? Phil wondered. That if a skilled engineer did his best nothing could go wrong? The proposition was absurd on its face.

Roshek gazed with a kind of rapture at the display case. "Sierra Canyon Dam, about the supposed inadequacies of which you have developed such a lunatic obsession, has a design life of three hundred years. It is an engineering landmark, and not because of its height or its cost-benefit ratio."

"I don't have an obsession," Phil said quietly, "except possibly for a computer programmer I met recently."

"It represents an unprecedented effort to insure safety, from the thoroughness of the geophysical investigations right through to the ongoing system of inspection and maintenance. I insisted on the most extensive network of sensors ever implanted in a dam."

"Half of those sensors don't work anymore."

"There is a matter of justice involved, too. Of percentages. Of fairness." Roshek pushed his swivel chair away from his desk and looked at his legs. "I was struck by polio two years before the vaccine was developed that would have saved me. That's enough bad luck and injustice for one life." He looked up and seemed momentarily flustered by having become more personal than he had intended. Recovering, he glowered at Phil as if he were to blame for the indiscretion. "I've spent too much time on this already. I need to tell you just one thing. Stop concerning yourself with the dam. Is that clear? If you want to fool around with schoolboy computer models, use your own computers and your own time. That's all. You can go." He began assembling papers from his desk and placing them in his attaché case.

Phil had gradually slumped down in his chair while watching the older man's bizarre performance. If he understood the last remarks correctly, Roshek was saying that his structures could not fail because his legs already had, that there was a limit to the bad luck that could happen to any one man. This was the world-famous engineer, the paragon of logic and objectivity?

"Well?" Roshek said, eying him. "I said you can go."

Phil straightened up but did not rise. "Mr. Roshek," he said, "you've been very unfair. I thought you'd give me a minute at least to explain my actions. In my defense I could point out that—"

Roshek cut him off. "What do you mean, 'in your defense'? This is not a trial. I pay your salary and so I can tell you to do whatever

I want you to do. I'm telling you to drop Sierra Canyon Dam. Your ignorance of it would fill Chavez Ravine. You've caused enough trouble and I want an end to it. Yesterday, as you may or may not know, I was sworn in as president of the American Society of Civil Engineers. You should read the Code of Ethics. Point number two is that engineers should perform services only in their areas of competence."

"I was president of the student chapter in college," Phil said half to himself, "and I know the Code of Ethics, too. Point number one is that engineers should put the safety, health, and welfare of the public above everything else."

"What? What did you say?"

Phil stood up, his cheeks hot and his heart pumping. In a louder voice he said, "I don't deserve to be shouted at and treated like a child," amazed that he was saying anything at all. "In the past few weeks I've been closer to that dam than you. It's true that extensive foundation borings were made before construction, but the earthquake five years ago might have changed everything. It's not true that none of your structures has ever been questioned—the dam leaked so badly after the quake two million dollars had to be spent to plug up the cracks. The reservoir was filled this spring fifty percent faster than you yourself recommended five years ago that it should be."

Roshek was so astounded by the outburst that he couldn't find his voice. His mouth opened and closed and his eyebrows rose high on his forehead.

Phil tore a sheet of paper from a notebook and dropped it on the desk. "Here are the latest seepage figures from Gallery D. In every case they are higher than Theodore Roshek said they should be when he wrote the original specifications. Somebody should go down there right now and take a look, because next week may be too late."

Roshek crumpled the sheet into a ball and hurled it against the wall. He found his voice, and it was loud. "I don't need you to tell me how to look after a dam. I didn't order you in here to listen to your sophomoric opinions! Your opinions are more irrelevant now than they were before, because you are fired! Get out! If you are at your desk in the morning, I'll have you arrested for trespassing!"

Phil tried to slam the door on the way out but hydraulic hinges made it impossible.

12

JANET SANDIFER COULD HARDLY RECOGNIZE THE VOICE ON THE TELE-
phone. "Is that you, Phil?" she asked, smiling and frowning at the
same time. "You sound funny. Is that a jukebox I hear?"

"I've been waiting for you to get back from lunch. That's a jukebox, all right. I'm at a bar on Figueroa Street doing some research.
I'm trying to find out if it is possible to drink fifty bottles of beer
and still hold a pool cue. Fifty bottles of *cerveza*, I guess I should
say, this being a Mexican joint. Then I'm going roller skating on the
freeway."

"What are you talking about?"

"They got one of those little coin-operated pool tables here,
know what I mean? I'm locked into a big eight-ball shoot-out with
the meanest-looking illegal alien I ever saw in my life. I'm two dollars ahead. I haven't played a game of pool in years! I must be naturally gifted."

"What about Roshek? Did you talk to him?"

"If you were here, you could hold the stakes. Roshek? You mean
the distinguished engineer who has won any number of prestigious
awards? Yes, I talked to him. Did I *talk* to him! I practically told
him to go take a flying fuck for himself. I talked to him all right.
The man is a mental case, Janet. It was the weirdest thing I've ever
been through. I'm not kidding, somebody should rush him to a psychiatrist's emergency entrance. Christ, I knew he was ill-tempered,
but I didn't know he was a madman. He talked about my cockama-

mie computer program and called me a sophomoric greenhorn who was trying to wreck his company. He said if he saw me around there again he'd arrest me for trespassing. It was unbelievable! I'll do an impression of him when I see you and you'll think I'm exaggerating. That old fart needs help! I had the seepage figures neatly printed on a sheet of paper so he could understand the situation at a glance, and you know what he did? Threw it against the wall!"

"Phil, wait a minute. Are you trying to tell me that you got yourself fired?"

"What I'm trying to tell you is that I got myself fired. I went in there expecting a mild raking over the coals. I thought I'd leave thinking Roshek was a nice guy after all. Instead, my God, he went after me as if I were some kind of ax murderer. The most unbelievable part of all was that I talked back to him and tried to defend myself. That was stupid. I mean, that was stupid. I was dealing with a crazy person and I should have kept my big mouth shut. But there I was, good old painfully shy Phil Kramer, arguing with him like the sophomore he said I was. It really got vicious at the end—that's when we started throwing quotes at each other from the ASCE Code of Ethics."

"Oh, Phil, I'm so sorry. I know how much you liked your job."

"I'll find another. Now I can say I have three weeks' experience."

"If Roshek fired you in anger, maybe he'll take you back when he cools off."

"I'll refuse! I liked the job, sure, before I met him. You should have seen him hollering at me, running sores all over his face, giant warts on his nose and hands, broken yellow teeth, steam and stench rising around him, green wax leaking out of his ears. Work for him again? Not a chance. Not even if he gave me a cost-of-living increase."

"So you're going to get drunk, is that it?"

"I'm going to become a professional pool player. A hustler going from town to town. You can be my sidekick. You set the suckers up, I'll fleece 'em. It'll be a wonderful knockabout life, Janet! Just the two of us, alone together on the open road!"

"I have a better idea. Come over tonight with some grass. I'll thaw something for dinner and later I'll pat your head."

"It's a deal."

In the middle of the afternoon, Herman Bolen excused himself from the conference room and made a phone call. Again he was told that Jeffers had not been heard from.

"Is Chuck Duncan around, by any chance?" The young inspector could be sent into the lower gallery to see if anything was amiss.

"Chuck is gone for the day," the powerhouse engineer said. "I think he's going fishing on the lake for the weekend. Should I try to track him down?"

"No, that won't be necessary. Just make sure Mr. Jeffers gives me a jingle when he gets in."

Bolen returned to the conference room and resumed his seat between Roshek and Filippi. The table was covered with drawings, maps, and economic reports, but Bolen had a hard time keeping his mind on the subject under discussion: the cheapest way to raise Sequoia Dam. It was only three o'clock—if Larry had gone to Sacramento, forgetting his promise to call, he would hardly be back yet. In the meantime, there were more immediate problems to contend with, one of which was the lack of participation of Roshek, who after arriving an hour late had sat oddly subdued. At the moment, his eyes were closed and he was rubbing his forehead. Bolen himself had contributed little to the discussion beyond a few wise looks and noncommittal shrugs. Thank God Filippi had done his homework and was presenting alternatives well supported by facts. The complexity of his analysis had so far kept the Edison engineers from noticing that his two superiors at R. B. & B. were doing little more than filling two chairs. Roshek came to life long enough to point out that if the efficiency claims being made by Mitsubishi for its new turbine generators turned out to be realistic, it would be more than practical to add pumped-storage power generation at Sequoia, a good point that had, unfortunately, been gone over thoroughly before Roshek arrived. The Edison engineers heard him out respectfully, then went back to the problem of minimizing environmental impact during construction. There was no clay at the site, and unless a source could be found nearby, a long haul road would be necessary. In an effort to justify his hundred-dollar-an-hour consulting fee, Bolen suggested that it would be worth investigating a conveyor belt for the clay haul, especially if the borrow pit was at a higher elevation than the discharge point. He reminded the group that during the construction of the railroad fill across the Great Salt Lake a downhill conveyor equipped with generators had produced enough power to run the electric shovels doing the excavation.

* * *

At 2:00 P.M. Phil called Janet again.

"I've changed my mind," he said. "I'm not going to become a pool hustler. I'm three dollars behind and I think the dude I've been playing is a shark from Xochimilco. I'd break his thumbs if he weren't such a big bastard. Janet, I want a rain check on tonight. I'm going to drive to northern California. To the dam. On Interstate 5, I can make it in seven or eight hours. Don't try to talk me out of it. All I've got in life besides my health and your phone number is a computer program that the world's greatest engineers agree is a piece of shit. I want to see Sierra Canyon for myself. I'm going to try to get into the drainage galleries. If nothing is wrong, okay, a thousand pardons. What can they do to me for making one last effort to prove something is wrong? I'm already fired. If too much water is coming in, what will be the piece of shit then, the dam or the program? Me or Roshek?"

"I liked your first idea better."

By the time the meeting at Southern California Edison was over, traffic on the Hollywood Freeway had eased considerably. Herman Bolen had no trouble maneuvering his Mercedes 300SD into the fast lane. He would drop Roshek off at his home in Beverly Hills, then return to the office to clean up some paperwork before the weekend. One thing he would do was solve the Jeffers problem, even if it meant calling hospitals. Strapped securely into the seat beside him was Theodore Roshek. Roshek used the seat belt only when riding with Bolen, as a way of showing his disapproval of his partner's driving habits, which he thought were inappropriately flashy. "Your image usually suggests prudence and propriety," he had told Bolen on one occasion, "as it should, but when you are behind the wheel of a car you become as idiotic as the average teenager. I think you'd be happier as a test pilot than an engineer."

Bolen could have retaliated by pointing out that Roshek's image could stand a bit of improving as well. The gray felt hat he always wore made him look like something out of an old Humphrey Bogart movie. Without criticizing the hat directly, Bolen had once offered to buy him a new one. Roshek declined by saying that the hat he already had was fine. "It's an old friend as well as my good luck charm." "Don't mention good luck charms to our clients," Bolen had replied, and quite humorously, too, he thought, "because they might wish us to use devices and methods of a more rational nature."

"How did your chat with Kramer go?" Bolen asked by way of making conversation and to satisfy his curiosity. "Impressive young man, don't you think? Still a little wet behind the ears."

Roshek, preoccupied, turned his gaze back to Bolen. "The chat with Kramer? That went very well. I fired him." Noticing the dismay that came over Bolen's face, he added: "I know he was a favorite of yours, but he gave me no choice. He had the nerve to come into my office, look me straight in the eye, and tell me how to run my business. Never saw such impertinence in my life. He must have missed a spanking somewhere along the line."

Bolen looked straight ahead for a full minute before speaking. "He wasn't a favorite of mine, particularly," he said, using a casual tone. "It's just that I felt he was intelligent and serious-minded. I thought he might develop into a valuable employee. It surprises me that he said anything to anger you." He wondered if he should try to get Roshek to rescind his action, at least until the situation at the dam could be evaluated. It wasn't likely that emergency measures would have to be taken, but if they were it would be disastrous if the press learned that the one man who tried to sound an alarm was fired for his trouble. "Was it really necessary to let him go?" he ventured. "Seems a bit extreme." Bolen tensed himself for a possible outburst. In the last few years, the merest hint that he felt one of Roshek's decisions was less than perfect sometimes provoked a volcanic reaction.

"It was either that," Roshek replied calmly, "or turning the company over to him to run his way while I went back to a drafting board. Maybe I was a little hard on him. He started in on his ridiculous computer model and it was more than I could stomach. I told him to keep his nose out of what he didn't understand and what didn't concern him, and before I knew it he was raising his voice to me, which wasn't too smart in his position. He should have known I wouldn't tolerate that. I had to shout at him to make myself heard. I haven't shouted at anybody in years—I mean really shouted. I almost enjoyed it."

Roshek squirmed in discomfort as Bolen, with a burst of acceleration, knifed into a gap that had formed in an adjacent lane. "Herman, would you mind cutting our speed forty or fifty percent? You aren't Paul Newman. A glance in the mirror will convince you of that."

Bolen lifted his foot from the accelerator, worked his way over to the right lane, and took the Santa Monica Boulevard exit westbound. Both men lowered visors to block the rays of a setting sun.

"I rather liked Kramer's enthusiasm," Bolen said. "Dismissing him could backfire. What I'm thinking of is—"

"We have more important matters to discuss. You and Calvin might have to run the business for the next few years."

With that abrupt announcement, Roshek began a summary of his meeting with the President's aide. He brushed aside Bolen's attempts at congratulations by pointing out that the appointment was yet to be made. "Other people are being considered. I do believe I have the inside track. There must not be any negative publicity about the firm. There must not be a juicy divorce between Stella and me, which is my main problem at the moment."

"Good heavens, Theodore! Stella wants a divorce?"

"Keep your eyes on the road. Yes, she dumped that on me last night in Washington. Her mind seems made up. I won't bore you with the reasons except to say that she has some. Tonight I get one last chance to talk her out of it."

"No wonder you were so quiet this afternoon! I thought you weren't feeling well."

"I'm not. I'm sick at the prospect of that ungrateful bitch—I'm sorry, but that's how I now think of her—pulling this on me. If she makes allegations and demands that I have to answer in court, then I think my chances of getting the appointment will be zero. I got the clear impression that what Washington wants is a wife who is a party-giver, not a mudslinger. I can't let her ruin me and the company. I *won't* let her."

The Mercedes made several turns along streets lined with forty-foot-high palm trees. Roshek's home was in the Spanish style, with thick walls, a red tile roof, and a broad lawn outlined with succulents and cactus. The car glided up the curved driveway and stopped at the front entryway. Behind a double wrought-iron gate was a carved wooden door.

"Wait until you see I'm inside," Roshek said, trying to figure out how to unbuckle his seat belt. "She might have changed the locks."

"Do you want me to push your chair?"

"No, let me struggle with it myself. If she's watching from a window, she might feel a twinge of pity. Just get the chair out of the car and hand me my crutches. How the Sam Hill do you unhook these belts?"

Bolen reached over and depressed the release catch. Silently the lap and shoulder straps were drawn into their receptacles. "You never were very good with small mechanical devices, were you, Theodore? Unless a thing has at least five hundred moving parts or is worth ten million dollars, it doesn't engage your attention."

"Then why haven't I paid more attention to my wife? She might cost me ten million dollars. Of course, she has only one moving part. Her mouth."

Bolen walked to the passenger side, removed the collapsible wheelchair from the back seat, and expanded it into position. Roshek managed to get out of the car and into the chair without assistance. As Bolen handed him his crutches, he decided to risk bringing up the subject of Kramer and the dam one last time.

"Did you by any chance take a look at the seepage figures Kramer compiled? He told me he was going to ask your opinion of them."

"He handed me a sheet of paper," Roshek said, turning his chair away from the car. "I crumpled it up."

Bolen shook his head gravely. "Seepage is high. More grouting may have to be done. I called Jeffers last night and asked him to take a look around in the lower galleries."

Roshek looked up at Bolen with mild exasperation. "What did he find?"

"I expect him to call in a report any minute."

"Let me know what he says. Now, if you'll excuse me, I have an appointment with my loving wife."

Bolen touched Roshek's arm to detain him. "We should face the possibility that Kramer has blundered onto something serious."

"Goddammit, Herman, whose side are you on, mine or that fucking kid's?"

"I'm on your side and the firm's side," Bolen said, keeping his voice low. "But it may be that new leaks have sprung up that call for grouting, overhauling the drainage system, lowering the reservoir, or whatever. We can take such corrective action quietly, without the public hearing about it, provided we don't have a disgruntled ex-employee running around shooting his mouth off.

Kramer could go to a newspaper and make himself look like a hero at our expense. As you said, we don't need any bad publicity."

Roshek sagged. "Christ," he said through clenched teeth, "as if I didn't have enough on my mind."

"Suppose I tell him you are willing to give him another chance."

"You mean hire him back? Apologize to him? I'm not that desperate."

"You don't have to even see him. I'll tell him that I have your okay to assign him to the London office. I haven't met a man yet who hasn't jumped at London. That will get his mind off Sierra Canyon. Six months or a year from now we'll terminate him when it won't seem connected with trouble at the dam . . . if there is any trouble."

"Good. I like it. Just don't mention his name around me again."

Bolen returned to the driver's seat. He watched Roshek push the gates open, wheel himself to the door, and try his key. When the door swung open, he turned and mouthed the words: "Wish me luck." Bolen waved reassuringly, then released the brake and coasted down the driveway to the street.

Driving east on Santa Monica toward the freeway, he planned the actions he would take when he reached the office. Time, he learned long ago, could be spent most efficiently when priorities were set in advance. Identify the tasks that had to be done at once, those that wouldn't suffer too much from delays, and those with "float time," to use the technical scheduling term, and attack them in that order. In the present case he would phone Kramer and tell him "the good news"; he would track down Jeffers wherever he might be; and, finally, he would permit himself thirty minutes—not a minute more!—to daydream about what it would be like to control the company in Roshek's absence.

II

The Race

13

SEVENTY MILES AN HOUR WAS THE MOST PHIL'S AGING MUSTANG WOULD
do without shuddering uncontrollably, so he held it at that speed
while keeping one eye on the rearview mirror for signs of the Highway Patrol. In a racing car he could have gone twice as fast in perfect safety, for Interstate 5 through California's Central Valley was
broader, straighter, and smoother than any speedway. Too broad
and straight, in fact. Drivers tended to fall into a kind of follow-
the-leader trance brought on by the monotony. Cars innocently
parked on the shoulder were sometimes the cause of multiple rear-
end collisions.

There was little chance that Phil would doze off and try to drive
over the top of a parked car. He was too keyed up by what he per-
ceived as the urgency of his mission and too aware of the
significance of the region he was passing through, which he had
heard his father talk about so often. He drove with both hands
clamped on the wheel, leaning forward in an unconscious effort to
urge the car beyond its natural limits. He read every road sign and
studied every feature of the landscape, surprised at how much
seemed vaguely familiar. According to his father, the Central Valley was a cradle of technological innovation and one of the world's
greatest displays of engineering achievement.

Phil's father, Carl Kramer, had been Road Superintendent of
Sedgwick County, a job that carried considerable prestige around

Wichita, but that, Phil had discovered upon joining R. B. & B., sounded comically provincial to California ears. Phil had both loved and admired his father, and missed him now just as much as he ever had. He was a thoughtful, studious man whose honesty and warmth and intelligence had seemed as innate as the quality of his voice and the color of his eyes. His interests ranged far beyond the duties of a husband, father, and county engineer. He was a serious student of the history of engineering. If, as he had maintained, a man cannot consider himself educated unless he knows the history of his own profession, then he must have been one of the most educated men in the world. Hardly a year had gone by that both Kansas and Kansas State did not ask him to join their engineering faculties and develop a history course. Always he turned them down, although he did give several lectures a year on both campuses. He liked his low-pressure county job. He liked driving over the network of farm-to-market roads that was largely his creation and stopping to talk to farmers, ranchers, policemen, and merchants. His professional ambitions had been confined to his son. When he died, Phil was in his first year of graduate school. "Keep up the good work," he had written in his last letter. "You've got something extra and there's no telling how far you can go." He said things like that so often and with such conviction that Phil sometimes almost believed him.

Phil looked toward the east, where a thin haze obscured the horizon. Behind that haze were the Sierra Nevadas, where, his father had told him, more major dams had been built than anywhere else on earth. A dozen powerful rivers surged out of the high country and through the foothills to join the north-flowing San Joaquin, rivers like the Kings, the Merced, the Tuolumne, the Stanislaus, and the American, some of which contained so many dams that the water was almost "staircased" from one end to the other, the water behind one dam lapping at the toe of the dam upstream. Mammoth Pool Dam, Pine Flat Dam, Wishon, Courtright, Don Pedro, Pardee, and Camanche—Carl Kramer could have named them all—dams that in exchange for wild rivers generated power, controlled floods, created recreational lakes, slaked the thirst of San Francisco and Los Angeles, and supplied the irrigation water that had transformed a desert into a fantastic engine of agricultural production. Ten percent of everything grown in the United States came from the four-hundred-mile-long Central Valley, thanks to water from the mountain reservoirs, distributed by means of a vast network of canals and pipelines.

East of San Francisco, I-5 passed Stockton, an apparently unexceptional city of 115,000 that most non-Californians had never heard of. In the early decades of the twentieth century, a series of earthmoving machines were developed in Stockton that revolutionized the way land was leveled for irrigation, the way dams and roads were built, the way canals were dug, even the way wars were fought. A small Stockton manufacturing firm named Holt & Best, which later moved to Peoria, Illinois, as the Caterpillar Tractor Company, came up with the continuous steel tread that enabled farm and construction machines to work on soft and marshy ground and that led to the ubiquitous crawler tractor as well as the military tank. Several Stockton mechanics experimented with mounting steel blades on tractors so that dirt could be carved out of the ground and pushed from place to place without the need for loading it into trucks—and both the bulldozer and the motor grader were born. In the 1930s, an affable welder named Bob LeTourneau, a giant of a man, God-fearing and Bible-quoting, combined the bulldozer, tractor, loader, and truck into one machine that could dig, carry, and spread dirt without assistance from other machines. The scraper, as the hybrid was called, characterized by huge tires and an engine that overhangs the front axle, is now common everywhere in the world that earth is moved. LeTourneau later moved his Stockton fabricating shop to Longview, Texas, where in his spare time he founded a college that combined technical courses with Holy Scripture.

Phil noticed that several times in the two-hundred-mile stretch between Bakersfield and Stockton the freeway crossed or paralleled the California Aqueduct, which he had learned from his father was part of the most ambitious water redistribution system ever built. After World War II, to get water from the northern part of the state, where it wasted to the sea, to the Central Valley and the Los Angeles Basin, where it was needed, California spent two billion dollars on eighteen dams, five power plants, fifteen pumping stations, and five hundred and eighty miles of canals. The hundred-yard-wide California Aqueduct, the north-south backbone of the system, rivaled the world's greatest rivers in its capacity to carry water.

Even the freeway Phil was on belonged on a list of outstanding civil engineering achievements. Interstate 5 between Bakersfield and Modesto was the longest major highway ever built on new right-of-way—twin ribbons of concrete two hundred miles long stretched across the empty lower slopes of the Coast Range, bypassing every town and village. When it first opened, it lacked even a single rest room or gas station.

Surrounded by so many superlatives and so much engineering history, Phil wondered if maybe he qualified for some sort of list or record book himself. He was possibly the most presumptuous, reckless, megalomaniacal, and plainly ridiculous young engineer in the world. Here he was driving through a wonderland with famous projects right, left, and underfoot, headed for one of the most famous of all, to prove if he could that it was a grave threat to public safety. Phil Kramer, a sophomoric greenhorn from Wichita, Kansas. What a joke! He should have stayed home where he knew how people thought and where the things that people had built were still on a scale that could be grasped. Maybe designing curbs and gutters and living with Mom was the best kind of life for him, despite his father's dreams. A man could make mistakes in Kansas, and make a fool of himself, too, but not on the fantastic scale that was possible in California.

Once he got to the dam, what then? He still hadn't made up his mind what he would do if the people in charge laughed at him and slammed doors in his face. Maybe the whole trip was a mistake he would regret forever. He was acting emotionally, out of anger at getting fired unfairly, in the hope of finding something that would embarrass Theodore Roshek, the only person in the world he had ever hated. Hardly healthy motives for embarking on an engineering investigation. He should have stayed calm and thought things over.

How are you going to explain this to your mother, he asked himself, easing up on the accelerator, especially if you wind up in jail? How are you going to tell her that her pride and joy blew a perfectly good job by mouthing off to the company president? She's going to want you to fly home so she can press cold towels to your forehead. You must be crazy as well as stupid. And what about Janet? She should have seen you were goofy from too much Mexican beer and talked you out of leaving town. Your father would have if he were still alive. Or would he? He believed in digging for facts, and he believed in acting on them once they were in hand.

He was passing Sacramento. Through the right-hand window of the car he could see rays of a setting sun glinting off the dome of the Capitol Building. If he was going to turn back or spend a night in a motel, this would be a good place to stop. There was an off-ramp coming up on the right. He let it go by, stepping on the gas and swinging over to the fast lane. "I *am* calm," he said aloud. "I *have* thought things over." Turning back now after coming so far would prove he was crazy. By pushing on to Sutterton, now only an hour and a half away, the worst that could happen was that he would be proved wrong. Better to be proved wrong than crazy. "When you feel you are right about something," his father had told him more than once, "stick to your guns come hell or high water."

Hell and high water. If his theory was right and he had acted too late, there was liable to be plenty of both.

The air conditioner in the window above the sink hummed valiantly, but the late afternoon heat in Stockton was too much for it. Emil Hasset sat across the kitchen table from his son, sweat rolling from his face into the creases of his neck. He had removed his holster and the jacket of his guard's uniform and rolled his sleeves above his elbows. When he lifted his forearms off the oilcloth, there was a sound like paper tearing. By leaning back in his chair he could reach into the refrigerator for two more cans of Coors. He slid one across the table.

"You're not gonna chicken out on me, are you, Freddy?"

"If you get caught, the cops will come straight to me. I'm still on probation."

"What can they prove? If you don't see the armored truck coming down the road, take the plane back to the airport and you're in the clear. Christ, look at it from my point of view. I've never bailed out of a plane before and you do it every weekend."

Freddy Hasset, a small man with thin brown hair, looked uncomfortable. He hadn't looked fully at ease since returning from San Quentin, where he had spent three traumatic years for knifing a man in a barroom brawl. "You could join the club and take a few practice jumps. If you don't, you're a cinch to break your neck."

"Not a chance. I'm going to jump out of a plane just once in my life, and that's tomorrow. With you right behind me. With two hundred thousand bucks at least."

"And with Lloyd shooting at us all the way down."

"Goddammit, let me worry about Lloyd. He'll be back at the supermarket trying to figure out how to dial the cops. He's used his gun once in fifteen years and that was to crack some walnuts with the handle. When I drive off and leave him at the dock, he'll be so surprised it'll take him an hour to find his holster. Do you want to spend the rest of your life in Stockton tapping the till at the pool hall and chasing cheap pussy and getting in knife fights? Living in this dump with your old man, who ain't going nowhere either? Mary Lou was right what she said the other night. We're losers. Now we've come up with a way to be winners . . . big winners."

"You got a steady job, at least."

"Sure I do. Twelve years, never missed a day, and they still pay me four-fifty an hour. No raises, they said. Valley Financial Transfer is a little on the shorts at the moment, they said. They'll be on the shorts at the moment, all right, when I get through with them. Oh, how they've been screwing me! Now I need you, Freddy. You're the only one I can trust. You got to do your part. If you don't land on the road to pick me up, I've had it. I've *had* it."

"I don't know, there's something funny about the deal."

"What's funny about it? When we took the other car up to the canyon, you thought it was great. Now you think it's funny? You liked the little cabin I rented and you said the clearing was perfect. A couple of months up there while things cool off and we're home free. All you gotta do is get the plane."

"I got a Cessna reserved. A two-seater."

"Is it easy to jump out of?"

"A snap. Only problem is it's a little tough to open the door against a hundred-mile-an-hour wind. So I'm going to take the door off at the airport. It's a ten-minute job with a Phillips screwdriver. You won't mind a little breeze in the cockpit, will you? You'll be strapped in with a seat belt."

Emil Hasset beamed paternally at his son, then laughed. "Oh, you gotta admit this is sweet, Freddy. The plane will crash *way* the fuck and gone and nobody will know *where* the fuck we are."

"You're sure we can find the cabin from the air?"

"Easy. Look at the maps. It's four miles downstream from a dam. Promise me you'll pick me up after I hijack the truck. Look me in the eye and promise."

"I promise. I'll be there. We got to be due for some good luck."

Freddy Hasset seldom smiled because his teeth were bad, but he smiled now. "You know what, Pop? You're gonna look awful funny floating out of the sky in your guard's uniform."

"I sure as hell will, and I'll be laughing the hardest."

14.

WILSON HARTLEY, SUTTERTON CHIEF OF POLICE, WIPED THE MELTED butter from his chin and took the phone from his wife. Corn on the cob was impossible to eat neatly, and the same could be said for many of his favorite foods: spaghetti, artichokes, spareribs, cracked crab, roast turkey. Whenever his wife served any of those, the dining-room table quickly took on the look of a municipal dump.

It was Karsh, the night sergeant. "Sorry to bother you at home, Chief, but I got a guy on hold who alleges that he wants to talk to you personally if at all possible. He further alleges that his name is Herman Bolen and that he is calling from Roshek, Bolen & Benedetz in Los Angeles."

"For Christ sakes, Karsh, put him through." Hartley recognized the name of the engineering firm that was in charge of the dam and assumed that some sort of security problem had arisen. He left the table and carried the phone to his desk in the next room, wire trailing behind him and a napkin dangling from his belt.

"I don't know if you remember me," Bolen said when he was on the line. "We met during the dedication ceremony ten years ago or so."

Hartley didn't remember. "Yes, of course I remember. How are you, Herman?" People tended to become tense when talking to the Chief of Police, so Hartley had gotten into the habit of using first names and a friendly manner in an effort to relax them.

"I'm fine, thank you. Mr. Hartley, a matter has come up that has to be handled with some discretion. I'm sure you know Lawrence Jeffers, our maintenance chief at the dam."

"Larry? Sure I know him. Go deer hunting with him every year. We've never come close to shooting anything, because when he starts whistling and singing all the animals run for their lives. Are you going to tell me Larry is in some kind of trouble? That would be hard to believe."

"I'll come right to the point. He's been missing all day. To put it as precisely as possible, I talked to him twenty-four hours ago and haven't been able to locate him since. He didn't show up for work and he doesn't answer his home phone. What worries me is that he promised to call me first thing this morning. Now, it may be that I'm worried over nothing. He may be missing only as far as *I* am concerned. For all I know, he's having dinner with you right now or visiting a sick friend and simply forgot to call me or tell his co-workers where he would be."

The Chief assured Bolen that Jeffers was not immediately at hand, and agreed that it was odd for a man so trustworthy to drop out of sight. "You want me to take a look around, is that it? Make a few inquiries?"

"Exactly. But I don't want to get anybody alarmed unnecessarily. I was about to start calling hospitals in the area, then I realized that you probably have a system for doing that. What I am really trying to find out is if there is any *reason* for me to be worried. I don't know his personal habits, whether he has a woman, where he goes after work. To be quite frank, I don't want to embarrass myself or him by starting a search for a man who may not be lost."

"I get the picture. Tell you what. I'll swing by his house and see if his car is in the garage and I'll call on a few of his friends around town. If I don't find him, I'll call the Highway Patrol and the hospitals to see if he's been in an accident. Any idea at all where he might have gone?"

"Maybe to Sacramento. You might also check for his car at the powerhouse parking lot."

"Right. Give me a phone number and I'll call you back in a couple of hours."

"Thanks very much, Mr. Hartley. I had a hunch you would know how to handle this."

Next, Bolen tried to reach Phil Kramer by phone. Failing, he stared absently at a pile of papers on his desk, wondering what he would do if Hartley failed to find a trace of Jeffers. If that happened, he would simply have to send somebody into the drainage gallery to look for him, even if it meant admitting that he had ordered Jeffers to make a night inspection. Would he have to admit that? He could say that he had been talking to Jeffers on another matter and heard him say he was going into the dam. . . .

Bolen frowned and picked up a sheet of paper. It was a note from his secretary:

After you left for SoCalEd a call came in from a Mr. Terry of the California Division of Dam Safety. He said he's seen the latest figures from Sierra Canyon and feels that a field investigation is called for, which he is going to conduct himself tomorrow (Saturday). He was unable to reach Mr. Jeffers at the dam and wonders if you would like to accompany him. He will arrive there about noon.

Charlene

"God*dammit!*" Bolen said. Why does the *state* have to get involved? It wasn't more than a month ago that Dam Safety had made one of its regular inspections, and the new seepage figures weren't *that* bad. Now he might have to get up at dawn in order to get to Sutterton by noon, unless he wanted to fly his own plane, which gave him a backache on long flights. *Damn* that Jeffers! He picked a hell of a time to go fishing or get drunk or whatever it was he was doing. He deserved a chewing out and would get it, make no mistake about that. Jeffers was a nice man, yes, but sometimes he carried that everything-is-wonderful, whistle-while-you-work act a little too far. There's a two-hundred-million-dollar dam to be looked after, Larry, let's not forget that. Oh, I hope Hartley finds you. What an earful you're going to get! I'll show you a side of Herman Bolen you never dreamed existed.

When Phil saw the dam, he felt his sense of purpose weaken again. He drove slowly, part of the Friday-night stop-and-go traffic on Sutterton's Main Street, unable to take his eyes off the dark, looming wall that filled half the night sky. He hardly noticed the floodlit City Hall, the bandstand in the square, the Wagon Wheel Saloon, the banner stretched across the street announcing the Third Annual Mother Lode Marathon. The road across the dam's crest was marked by lights, and to take in the entire glowing line Phil had to put his face close to the windshield. The dam was so over-poweringly high and huge it was hard to accept it as man made, and it was hard to imagine the lake behind it. "Jesus," he said softly. The dam was a mountain. It would stand as long as there were mountains anywhere.

And yet, towering over a town it miniaturized, it was obviously not a mountain. The great hills and cliffs on either side were higher and more massive, but it was to the dam the eyes were drawn. It was a *presence*, intense and sullen, that was threatening in a way the mountains were not. It was alien and the mountains were not.

A few blocks from the downtown district, Main Street reverted to a country road, passed through a grove of tall pines, and climbed to the top of the canyon along a shelf cut in a rocky slope. Phil drove carefully past a line of parked construction machines and warning flares. On a promontory above the dam was an overlook where the teenage occupants of a half-dozen cars were listening to music, drinking beer, and ignoring the view. Phil parked and walked to the railing, stretching his arms and legs. It was 10:30—he had made it from Los Angeles in just over eight hours, with only a single brief break in Marysville. The cool breeze off the lake carried the scent of evergreens and fresh water and was sweet relief after the heat of the Central Valley. The only sounds were the strains of rock music from the cars parked nearby and the distant roar of the spillway water plunging into the river a thousand feet below. To Phil's right was the shining black expanse of the lake, its surface divided by a yellow trail of reflected light from a three-quarter moon, its shore-line defined by low, furrowed hills with higher hills behind them. The snowy ridges and peaks of the High Sierras were outlined against an enormous bank of dark clouds in the far distance. Breaking through the surface of the lake directly below the overlook was a doughnut-like circle of concrete that Phil knew was the top of the intake tower. Slightly to the left and only barely higher than the water was the crest of the dam and the two rows of highway lights that merged at a point on the other side of the canyon. On the valley floor below the dam was a brightly lit rectangle that was the electrical switchyard. Between that and the downstream toe of the dam, out of sight beneath a shoulder of the hillside, was the entrance to the underground powerhouse. Farther to the left, in the distance, Sutterton was a sprinkle of pinpoint lights.

Gazing at the dam, Phil began to appreciate how foolish he must

have looked to Roshek and Bolen. Studying a mathematical model
and drawings of a dam was one thing, confronting the reality of it
was another. It was so enormous and so magnificent, so *permanent*.
It spanned the canyon gracefully and seemed to resist the weight of
the lake with ease, anchored so solidly in the abutments and the
foundation bedrock that no force on earth could dislodge it. The
computer images and columns of figures that had struck Phil as so
significant suddenly seemed irrelevant, random patterns of light
without substance, meaningless marks on paper. Roshek was right,
it was ridiculous to think that he could gain any real understanding
of a structure from a distance of five hundred miles with nothing
but abstract symbols to go on. Once again he had half a notion to
drive back to Los Angeles before making a bigger fool of himself
than he already had. Maybe he owed an apology to Roshek.

On the other hand . . . there was always that other hand. If he
had learned anything in engineering school, it was always to give
proper consideration to the goddam other hand. The seepage figures were not irrelevant and abstract. The dam looked sleek and
powerful and permanent on the outside, but what about on the inside? Deep within its bowels, if the meter readings were correct,
were possibly fatal flaws. The dam was colossal and enormously
strong, but so was the lake.

He climbed into his car and headed down the hill. He reminded
himself that in recent years he had overcome most of his childhood
shyness. He had found the nerve to make himself heard in groups,
to introduce himself to a beautiful woman, and to talk back to his
elders. He would not allow himself now to be driven back into his
shell by a mere *dam*.

Herman Bolen was in the study of his home in Westwood, a
phone pressed to his ear. "Yes, Mr. Hartley. I appreciate very much
the trouble you've taken. Please call me at this number at any time
of night should something turn up later."

He replaced the receiver on its hook. So, Jeffers's car was nowhere to be found and neither was Jeffers. He was not with friends,
his ex-wife, his daughter, or his neighbors. He was not in a Sutterton bar. His car had not been in an accident of which the police or
the Highway Patrol were aware. He was not in a hospital or a jail.
Where was he, then? Bolen didn't like the most likely answers to
that question. Either he had driven off any one of a hundred preci-

pices that lined the mountain roads around Sutterton or he was still inside the dam. Maybe on his way from the Administration Building to the powerhouse a wasp had flown through a window, causing him to lose control and go off the road above the portal of the tailrace tunnel. He was not dead inside the dam at all, but rather dead inside his car at the bottom of the discharge channel. Dead, unfortunately, in both cases.

Before he could decide on the next step, the phone rang again. It was another policeman, this one identifying himself as Officer Baker of the Beverly Hills police.

"I'm calling from the home of Mr. and Mrs. Theodore Roshek," the voice said. "The Rosheks have been involved in a family dispute. A fight, I guess you could say. Could we put Mr. Roshek in your custody for the night? Tomorrow we will know how serious the injury to Mrs. Roshek is and whether she wants to press charges."

"Jesus, Mary, and Joseph . . . I'll be there in fifteen minutes."

15

PHIL DECIDED TO PRESENT HIS CASE TO LAWRENCE JEFFERS. LAY OUT ALL the evidence and let the veteran maintenance engineer decide whether or not there was anything to get excited about. But Jeffers wasn't answering his phone. He wasn't answering his doorbell, either. The house, which Phil found without much trouble, was dark and apparently occupied only by a continuously barking dog. The garage was empty, and on the path from the porch to the street was the morning paper.

Plan B was set in motion from a phone booth next to a gas station. With a stack of dimes and the county phone book, Phil started in on the eleven listed Duncans.

"I'm trying to reach Chuck Duncan," he explained to the woman who answered his fifth call, "the inspector who works at the dam. Have I reached the right place?"

"Sure have. I'm his mother. Chuck went to the drive-in movie with Burt and Carla and the Peterson girl. This wouldn't be Mr. Richardson, would it?"

"Sorry. Do you expect him home soon?"

"Not hardly on Friday night. He might not come home at all, which is another story." She laughed with a twang in her voice that reminded Phil of his Aunt Lorene in Topeka. "The movie's probably out by now, seeing as how it's after ten. You could try the Wagon Wheel. They oftentimes go down there and stay till all hours."

"The Wagon Wheel?"

"On Main Street. I knew you were from out of town, which is why I thought you might be Mr. Richardson."

"Main Street. Thank you, Mrs. Duncan."

The Wagon Wheel was a kind of museum of the Old West, or at least of old Western movies. In front was a hitching post and a plank walkway covered by a low roof. Along one side was a fence made of overlapping wagon wheels. In back was a rusted tramcar, part of a display of early mining methods that had sunk into disrepair. The nature of the clientele was suggested by the vehicles that were nosed into the walkway like horses at a trough. One of the vehicles was, in fact, a horse, a handsome, well-curried beast that, judging from its twitching ears, didn't care for the music drifting through the swinging doors. Not a bad form of transportation, Phil thought as he parked and locked his car, for a person who planned on getting drunk. A horse could take you home even if you were unconscious. Most of the customers had arrived in pickup trucks with snow tires, roof racks for skis and rifles, bobbing heads in the rear windows, and plastic statuettes on the dashboards. For the first time since leaving Kansas, Phil saw a pair of fuzzy dice. He memorized a bumper sticker for use in the travelogue he would sooner or later present to Janet:

GOD, GUNS, AND GUTS
That's what made America great

It was country-Western disco night and the Wagon Wheel was packed. Phil stood inside the doors accustoming his eyes to the dim light and his ears to a noise level that was close to the limits of the endurable. Music for the evening was being provided and electrically amplified by a shaggy octet called Coley Hollenback and His Shi—— Kickers. There were plaid shirts, jeans, cowboy hats, tooled leather boots, and beards. The women as well as the men were dressed as if they were on their way to a rodeo, and not as spectators. There was singing, dancing, and shouting. Nobody fell silent and stared at the newcomer the way they did in television commercials; Phil could have secretly emptied a six-gun into the ceiling. Hanging resignedly on the walls were the stuffed and moth-eaten heads of a moose, an elk, and a buffalo.

Phil wedged his way to the bar and managed to attract the attention of a bartender, a large, unpleasant-looking man with a sun-burned nose and forehead.

"Do you know Chuck Duncan?" Phil shouted over the din.

"Old Chuck or young Chuck?"

"Young, I guess. The inspector at the dam."

"Yeah. It's the old man I never met."

"Is he here?"

"Who wants to know?"

"We work for the same company. His mother sent me."

The bartender shrugged, stepped onto a case of beer, and peered through the haze over the heads of the dancers. "He's in the corner booth. The blond kid with the stupid expression. Tell him I said that."

Phil skirted the dance floor to avoid getting injured and picked his way between crowded tables to the booths that lined the wall. In the corner was a passive party of four, Duncan and, if Phil remembered correctly the words of Mrs. Duncan, Burt, Carla, and the Peterson girl.

"Are you Chuck Duncan?"

The young man Phil addressed turned and tried to focus his eyes. His expression wasn't stupid, exactly, but was an argument against combining alcohol and marijuana. "What?" he said.

Phil repeated the question in a louder voice.

The man smiled. "Speaking," he said.

Aside from the effect chemicals were having on his mind, Duncan appeared to be no more than nineteen years old. Hardly a person you would entrust with your fears about the structural integrity of the world's highest embankment. "My name is Kramer. I'm with Roshek, Bolen & Benedetz in the Los Angeles office."

"Yeah? Well, I'll be fucked."

"Could I talk to you for a minute?"

"What?"

"I said could I talk to you for a minute? The music is so loud I can't hear myself think."

"Great, isn't it?"

"Let's go outside."

"I've been outside."

"Come on. Your friends don't want to listen to us talk about piezometers and pore pressures. It'll just take a minute." The girl next to Duncan was only partly contained by her red flannel shirt, which was unbuttoned to her waist. Phil nodded and smiled at her on general principles and to apologize for the interruption. He took Duncan by the arm and gently urged him to his feet. The young inspector yielded, mumbling, and let himself be guided through a side door.

"Let's make this fast," Duncan said when they were outside. "That goddam Burt is going to move in on Carla, I know he will." The cool night air, the streetlights, and the effort of walking had seemed to bring him out of his trance.

"Don't worry," Phil said reassuringly. "He's on the wrong side of the table. She can't hear a word he says, anyway."

"The son of a bitch will find a way. He's done it to me before."

"Look, I don't want to take up any more of your time than I have to. Where can I find Lawrence Jeffers?"

Duncan sat on the fender of a car and crossed his arms. "Beats the shit out of me," he said. "He didn't show up for work today. Nobody knows where he is. The big bosses in L.A. are looking for him, too, I hear. His ass is going to be in a sling. Did they send you up here looking for him? God, this air feels good. It's too hot in that fucking place."

"Nobody sent me here. I . . . I'm on vacation. I'm one of the guys that looks over those sheets of readings you compile every month. I'm on my way to Reno and thought I'd stop here and see if I could get a look at the drainage galleries."

Duncan grimaced and shook his head. "You don't want to see the drainage galleries."

"I don't?"

"No."

"Why not? It would give me a feel for what those numbers mean."

"You don't want to see the drainage galleries because it is a pain in the ass. An extreme pain in the ass. You climb down two hundred steps. Then you climb back up two hundred steps. It's dark. It's wet. It's the total shits. You want to get a feel for it? Stand under a cold shower in the dark with your clothes on. Then climb up and down the stairs of a fifteen-story building with a Water Pik stuck up your rear end. That'll give you a feel for it." Duncan chuckled, pleased with the image.

"It's that bad, is it?"

"I deserve a raise for taking readings down there. Go back to Los

Angeles and tell the big bosses Charles O. Duncan deserves a raise
for risking his life every month. And for being a beautiful human
being. Last time I went down there, I thought I was going to
drown. Do I complain? Noooo . . ."

"A lot of water comes in?"

"A lot of water. You know what I call this dam? Leaking Lena.
This year is the worst. I bet we pump more water out of Gallery D
alone than goes through the turbines."

Phil took a notebook from his shirt pocket, flipped it open, and
scribbled a few words. "I had no idea it was so bad. I definitely
will recommend you for a raise. On your last monthly report there
was a whole bank of meters you didn't include. Why was that?"

"I took the readings, but Jeffers told me to leave them out. They
were too goofy, he said. Some were zero, some were off the high
end. Every year more and more of those meters go out of whack
and we quit reading them. I'm hoping they'll all conk out so I can
quit going down there. Those meters are all a bunch of bullshit,
anyway. Ask Jeffers, he'll tell you. I know guys who work on other
dams around here and they don't have to climb down holes and
read meters. Listen, I better get back inside. Burt's probably got
both arms inside Carla's shirt by now."

"Wait a minute," Phil said, putting a hand on Duncan's shoulder.
"Those readings from the broken meters, have you still got them?"

"Sure I got them."

"Can I see them?"

"Why not?"

"Where are they?"

"In the trunk of my car."

"Where's your car?"

"I'm sitting on it. You think I'd sit on a car that wasn't mine?
Some of those guys in the saloon are *mean* bastards."

Phil followed Duncan to the back of the car, and noticed for the
first time the R. B. & B. logo on the door. While Phil looked on,
Duncan opened the trunk and sorted through a box full of manila
envelopes, occasionally holding one up to the light and squinting at
it.

"I still want to go into the dam and see the meters for myself,"
Phil said. "If Jeffers isn't back tomorrow, will you take me? First
thing in the morning?"

"No way. Saturday's my day off. First thing in the morning I'm going to the middle of the lake with my fishing gear. Maybe on Monday."

"Monday's too late. How about right now?"

Duncan straightened up and looked at Phil in amazement. "Man, you got to be crazy," he said, slamming the trunk and handing over an envelope. "I wouldn't go into that hole in the middle of the night for a million bucks. Well, maybe for a million. You say you're on vacation? How come you look sober and talk drunk?"

"Is there anybody else who would take me in?"

"Not at eleven-thirty at night. People around here got more sense than that. I'm going back into the bar and peel Burt's hands off Carla. Nice to meet you."

Phil followed him along the wooden walkway trying to squeeze out a few more scraps of information.

"Could I go into the galleries alone?"

"Sure, if you could get past Withers."

"Who's Withers?"

"Newt Withers, the night engineer at the powerhouse. He'll look you over on closed-circuit TV, and if he doesn't like what he sees he won't raise the door. You're with the company, so he might let you in. What's the big hurry, anyway? Do the big bosses think something's wrong?"

"No, the big bosses think everything is fine. I'm just curious, that's all. I guess you're right—it's crazy to think of taking a tour tonight. If Jeffers isn't around in the morning, I'll just forget the whole idea."

"That's what I'd do. Mail the envelope to me when you're through with it, okay? And say hello to old man Roshek when you get back to L.A. I've never met him, but I hear he's a real sweetheart."

"Sure will, Chuck, and thanks for the information. Good luck with Carla."

The long-distance operator's voice was reedy: "I have a collect call for Janet Sandifer from Philip Kramer. Will you accept the charges?"

"Yes, Operator, but he's got a lot of guts."

"Janet! It's Phil! I'm calling from my phone-booth command post in the heart of downtown Sutterton. Am I interrupting anything?"

"Only a shower. I'm dripping wet."

"Don't say things like that. I'll drool into the mouthpiece and electrocute myself."

"How are things going? Found out anything?"

"I struck pay dirt, as they used to say around here in 1849, in the form of the meter-reader whose figures we've been using. From what he told me, I'm surer than ever that all hell's about to break loose. The trouble is, he was both stoned and crocked and may have been exaggerating. You should have heard him spill his guts when I told him I would recommend him for a raise."

Janet laughed. "You told him that? I'm sure your recommendation will carry a lot of weight."

"He gave me a list of readings that weren't in the last report. I know you have a terminal in your office with dial-up ports. Have you got keys to get in? . . . Okay, here's what I want you to do—feed the new figures into the program. I'll give you the phone number of the R. B. & B. computer and the password that will give you access. I doubt if they changed it just because I got fired."

"For God sakes, Phil, it's after midnight! I'm stark naked and ready for bed."

"No time for sex now. Put on one of your no-nonsense business suits and get your ass down to the office. I'll call you when you get back to find out what the new readings mean."

"I could get arrested."

"So could I. If the computer shows what I think it will, I'm going to try to break into the dam. There must be some way to break the security system and get past the control-room operator. I'm going to get a motel room now and study the plans while you do your job."

"Are you all right? You sound as if you're hyperventilating. Are you stoned and crocked?"

"I see everything with an almost mystical clarity."

"Don't give me that bullshit."

"Right. I'll give you the figures. Got a pencil ready?"

Janet sighed. "Okay," she said, "fire away."

16

THEY DROVE FOR SEVERAL MINUTES WITHOUT SPEAKING. ROSHEK WAS in the passenger's seat staring straight ahead, his eyebrows drawn together and his deep-set eyes narrow. Twice he lifted his hands as if about to make an explanation, then let them drop. Both men were uncomfortable, and neither seemed to know how to begin a conversation. Bolen glanced at his partner and was struck by the uncharacteristic aura of confusion and defeat that surrounded him.

"Do you want to tell me what happened?" Bolen asked gently. "The police were rather vague."

Roshek wet his lips and swallowed before replying. "I can't recall everything," he said in a distant voice. "That is very . . . unsettling. I've been drunk a time or two in my life with hangovers that lasted for days, but always I could remember what I did or said down to the smallest details. Not now. There are several minutes missing." He raised a hand to his forehead. "My God, maybe I should see a doctor."

After a pause, Bolen ventured to ask another question. "The police implied that you struck her and that she ran from the house. Is that true, Theodore? There was physical violence?"

Roshek took a deep, ragged breath. "We were sitting in the living room. We talked about our life together. The pros and the cons. It was like compiling a feasibility study. We both tried to be calm and not to say anything that would irritate the other. It was a terrible strain. After an hour or two of pressure we both more or less cracked at once."

Bolen turned into his driveway. The garage door opened automatically and closed when the car was inside. He turned off the engine and looked at Roshek, who was still staring straight ahead.

"I didn't know either of us was capable of such hostility," Roshek said, speaking in a monotone, "such hatred." He bent his head forward and rubbed his temples. "I don't know what made it surface. I remember feeling outraged at the way she rejected my offer to meet her more than halfway. I took the blame for her unhappiness. I offered to spend more time with her, not as a tactic but because I genuinely felt sympathy. When I saw that she was not going to yield on the divorce, I made a generous settlement offer if she would delay filing. Nothing got through to her. I suppose she thought I was trying to manipulate her, buy her off with money. I don't know. I could feel anger rising inside of me like hot water in a boiler. We raised our voices. Insults came, and curses. In a matter of seconds we were screaming at each other. At one point she said, 'Don't threaten me,' but I don't remember threatening her. I do remember calling her an ungrateful bitch and throwing a wineglass against the wall. I didn't throw it at her. I definitely did not throw it at her." He lifted his head and looked at Bolen, astonished at his own words, apparently finding it hard to believe that the story he was telling involved himself. "She ordered me out of the house, Herman. I refused to go. I told her I would not be forced out of a house I bought and paid for myself. I told her the only way I would leave was feet first in a pine box or at the point of a gun. She ran to a phone and asked the operator for the police. I lost control of myself when I heard that. I lunged across the room, leaning on furniture to keep my balance, shouting at her to hang up. A lamp got knocked over." He turned away and sighed again, deeply. "I lifted a crutch and brought it down, trying to knock the receiver from her hand. I believe I hit her wrist. Yes, that must be it. She screamed. The sound will stick in my mind forever."

Bolen studied him. Roshek's face was twisted as if he were in pain. His hands, pale and thin with prominent veins, were clamped on his knees like the talons of a bird.

"Let's go inside," Bolen said. "We'll have a brandy and talk some more if you want to."

"It's at that point," Roshek went on, "that my memory lets me down. I can see Stella on her knees clutching her arm like a wounded animal. She was looking up at me with terror in her face as if she were afraid I was going to kill her. I don't remember her running out of the house, but I see the French doors to the patio standing open. I hear her wailing in the distance and pounding on the neighbor's door. I fell into a chair and sat there like a zombie. An hour must have gone by before the police came. I agreed with them that Stella and I couldn't stay in the same house. I gave them your name." He opened the car door and swung his feet to the floor. "I can't believe any of it happened. We were both like crazy people."

Bolen got the wheelchair out of the back seat and helped Roshek into it. "The police were very understanding, I'll say that," Bolen said, pushing Roshek along an enclosed walkway to the house. "They saw the importance of trying to keep the matter private. I'll talk to Stella myself in the morning. There's to be a hearing of some kind. If she doesn't press charges, the whole thing will be quietly dropped. Naturally you can stay with me and my wife as long as necessary."

"Forgive me for causing you so much trouble. I'll be forever in your debt."

"Nonsense. It's I who am indebted to you."

In the foyer, Bolen's wife told him that two phone calls had come in for him while he was gone. One gentleman didn't leave his name; the other, a Mr. Withers at the Sierra Canyon powerhouse, wanted a return call.

Janet Sandifer, alone in a shadowy sea of deserted desks, chairs, and typewriters, opened her notebook and dialed the number Phil had given her. There was a ringing signal followed by two sharp clicks. A steady tone indicated that she had reached the Roshek computer and that it was "up." She pressed the telephone into a recessed cradle on top of a terminal housing. A row of letters and numbers silently appeared in green on the cathode ray tube, followed by

Roshek, Bolen & Benedetz
HQ   Technical bank
Los Angeles
Please identify

"At this point," Janet said to herself, "I cross the line into law-breaking. Amazing what a basically decent woman will do for a good lay."

Her fingers moved deftly over the keyboard. One by one, letters appeared on the screen:

> **Philip Kramer   RB&B**
> **Hydro Design Section**
> **HQ   Los Angeles**

When she pressed the Enter Key, the words vanished and were replaced with:

> **PASSWORD**

Carefully, Janet typed

> **Grand Coulee**

> **INCORRECT**
> **Try again**

"Whoops," Janet said after looking more closely at her notes. She had capitalized the wrong letters.

> **gRand cOulee**

The machine responded immediately with the words

> **ACCEPTED**
> **On line**
> **Line clear**
> **Instruct**

> **List Column 7**
> **Enter**

Within three seconds the screen was filled with program titles. She moved the Cursor line to the seventh item on the list, the Kramer Dam Failure Model. At the touch of the Enter key the screen went blank, then displayed a message at the top:

> **CONGRATULATIONS!**
> **You have reached the amazing**
> **Kramer Dam Model**
> **Use it in good health**

Authorized personnel only
Violators will be towed away

Janet worked as fast as she could. She was breaking the law, and she didn't want to spend all night doing it. Which laws applied to what she was doing she wasn't sure. Grand theft, probably. Or, if Phil's program turned out to be worthless after all, petty theft. Unlawful entry, maybe. If impersonating an engineer was a crime, then she was probably guilty of that. Since she was female and the engineer she was impersonating was male, there was an element of transvestism involved as well. Fortunately, she thought, trying to comfort herself, that wasn't illegal in California.

Recall values of
5-22-81

5-22-81
Values recalled

Add new values
Meter bank 9
Gallery D
Sierra Canyon Dam

Ready

Piezometers
A 17
B 35
C 0
D 0
E 35
F 29
H 21
I 35

Strain gauges

Ready

A 0.2
B 0.2
C 0.5
D 0.7

```
E 2.5
F 4.1
H 9.1
I 0.0
J 0.0
```

Observation wells

Ready

```
A Overflow
B Overflow
C Overflow
```

Mode Four
Best Case
Evaluate
Instruct

One moment, please
I'm thinking

Janet leaned back and waited. It took the computer three minutes to evaluate the condition of the dam under the most optimistic assumptions.

BEST CASE
Begin lowering reservoir
Make visual inspection
Galleries C & D

She jotted down the response, then bent over the keyboard and made another request:

Mode Five
Worst Case
Evaluate
Instruct

When the response came on the screen five minutes later, she couldn't help smiling. Phil had told her what he had put in the program to indicate a failing dam that was beyond salvation:

RUN FOR YOUR LIVES!

When she got back to her apartment, it was after 1:00 A.M. and her phone was ringing. It was Phil.

"I'm calling from the beautiful Damview Motel in Sutterton, California, Gateway to a Mountain Wonderland," he said cheerfully. "If you project the plane of the surface of Earl Warren Lake in a southwesterly direction, I am under seven hundred feet of water."

"Sounds like a good spot to be. If your theory is right, you are doomed."

"Janet, remember when I told you not to remind me of your body because I might drool into the telephone and electrocute myself? I want to take that back. I've been thinking it over. The wattage used in telephones is so small you wouldn't even get a shock, much less a fatal incident."

"I wasn't worried. From what I've noticed, you don't drool with enough accuracy to hit something as small as a telephone mouthpiece. Is that why you called?"

"You know why I called, sweetheart. I've been calling every ten minutes. Were you able to rape the Roshek computer?"

"Sure was."

"And?"

"And I got a hell of a scare. It was creepy being in an empty office building. That is, I *thought* it was empty. I was glued to the terminal when I heard a noise. I looked up and here were these three black dudes advancing on me with clubs and rocks! Actually, they were janitors and they were carrying mops and buckets. They apologized for scaring me. They turned out to be really nice. When I left, the oldest one, a dignified man with white hair, walked me to my car to make sure I'd be safe."

"That was nice of him."

"I thought so, too. So I invited him home. He's here with me now. One thing is leading to another, and in a few more minutes I'll be pregnant."

"I hope he won't mind if we talk business for a second. What did the computer say?"

"What I'm sure you knew it would. It suggests that you run for your life."

"Did you ask it for the most likely points of failure?"

"Yes. It said there weren't enough data to be precise, but that it would courageously make a guess. Got a pencil? Upstream, between stations fifty plus seventy-five and fifty plus ninety-five, elevation five six five. Downstream, between stations fifty plus forty-three and fifty plus nineteen, elevation three seven five."

Phil read the numbers back to make sure he had them right. "Sounds like the contact between the fill and bedrock. Water must have found a way through the grout curtain under the core block at Gallery D. I've been studying the plans, and if I can get into the dam I'm sure I can find the place."

"What's next?"

"I'm going to call Bolen at home. He's a reasonable man and he thinks I'm only half crazy. He should be interested in finding out that nobody knows where his chief maintenance engineer is, that three observation wells are overflowing, and that the inspector who reads the meters says it's so wet in the lower galleries he needs scuba gear. Maybe Bolen will authorize me to make an inspection. He knows I know more about the dam now than anybody other than Roshek. I'm not going to call Roshek because he is a paranoid schizophrenic as well as a turd."

"What if Bolen tells you to mind your own business?"

"I'll make an inspection anyway. If I can't bluff my way in, I might go down the intake tower. There's a little elevator, a man-cage, inside. The problem would be getting to the top—it sticks up twenty feet above the water. I was thinking of stealing a yacht and climbing the mast."

Janet groaned. "This is sounding worse and worse. You'll get caught and thrown in jail if you don't kill yourself first. Either way there is nobody to take me out to dinner."

"Why not look on the bright side? You are a very attractive woman and you will have no trouble finding yourself another engineer."

"Don't make me laugh. I learn from my mistakes."

17

PHIL TURNED ONTO THE POWERHOUSE ACCESS ROAD AND IMMEDIATELY had to hit the brakes: both lanes were blocked by a double chain-link gate. "Shit," he muttered. "Duncan didn't mention this."

He left the car with the headlights on and the engine running to examine the obstacle. The hinge posts were four-inch steel pipes set in concrete. The padlock in the middle weighed at least three pounds and looked smugly impregnable, and the length of chain it joined in a loop would withstand a week of hacksawing. The good news was that there were no electrical connections anywhere on the gate or adjoining fence, which meant that if he could somehow force it open, alarms wouldn't go off up and down the Pacific Coast.

He returned to the car and sat behind the wheel pondering the alternatives. Climbing over the fence and walking the half mile to the tunnel portal would be no problem, but that is hardly the way an inspector from the Occupational Safety and Health Administration would arrive, and it was a federal OSHA representative he had decided to impersonate. The United States government didn't send its agents slinking along lonely roads in the middle of the night like escaped felons. He could try picking the lock with a piece of wire. No, that would take all night. If the local police had a key to the gate, maybe he could bluff them into opening it. No, too risky. He had to act fast if he was going to exploit Bolen's absence—his wife had told him on the phone that he would return home within the hour.

With his arms folded on the wheel, Phil lifted his eyes from the gate to the massive bulk of the dam looming in the background. The great structure seemed to be asleep, bathed in faint light from a moon that now was high in the sky. Dams for Phil had always been the most inspiring and admirable symbols of the engineer's art —stunning, audacious, thrilling. Sierra Canyon was different. There was something sinister about it and dangerous. The longer he gazed at it, the more uncomfortable he felt. Calm down, he cautioned himself, there is no immediate threat. The uneasiness you feel is an emotional response to the knowledge you have of the dam's inner workings. The dam was so goddam big! An enormous jungle cat, sleek and muscular, crouched in the canyon, its back arched against the force of the lake. Phil felt like a gnat in comparison. If he advanced any closer, that big cat might choose to obliterate him with a flick of a paw.

But dams and jungle cats, Phil told himself in an effort to keep his determination from eroding, can have physical problems that don't show on the surface. The most powerful and ferocious beast can be hobbled by a thorn and killed by a ruptured artery. He put the car in reverse and slowly backed away from the gate. "What I need," he said aloud, "is a way to get this car past that gate. Something simple and elegant that would honor the holder of a doctorate from one of the Midwest's finest institutions of learning."

When the car was a hundred and fifty feet from the gate, Phil stopped, checked his seat belt, shifted into low, and raced the engine. Grabbing the wheel tightly and bracing himself, he let out the clutch. Tires squealed. "Something subtle and sophisticated," he said as the car shot forward.

A speed of forty miles an hour proved sufficient to break the gate apart, cave in the grill, flatten the front tires, rip off the front bumper, and smash one headlight. The nice thing about driving an old car, Phil thought, shaking off the effects of the impact, is that a few more scratches don't make any difference.

Set into the base of a vertical wall of rock was a steel hangar door that marked the mouth of the powerhouse access tunnel. Next to it was a concrete panel into which were countersunk a microphone and a loudspeaker. Phil, a roll of plans under his arm and a clipboard in his hand, pushed a large black button. A red light went on and a hiss came over the loudspeaker followed by a voice.

"Control room."

"Is this Mr. Newt Withers?" Phil asked crisply.

"This is Withers."

"I'm Charles Robinson of the Occupational Safety and Health Administration." It was the biggest lie Phil Kramer had told in his entire life. When the state of Kansas was admitted to the union in 1861, Charles Robinson was elected Governor.

"Come again?" Withers asked.

Phil repeated his *ad hoc* name and affiliation. "I trust you've been expecting me," he added.

There was a pause. "What did you say your name was? Robinson?"

"Mr. Withers," Phil said with mock impatience, "didn't Mr. Jeffers or Mr. Bolen tell you that there might be an OSHA night inspection this weekend?"

"I'm sorry, nobody said anything to me. I'm not supposed to raise the door without authorization."

"What time did you go on duty?"

"Ten o'clock, sir."

"Nobody left a message for you?"

"Not that I noticed. May I ask how you got through the upper gate?"

Phil raised his voice slightly. "With a key that Herman Bolen gave me earlier today in Los Angeles. Your communications seem to be less than adequate. It makes me wonder what else might be. I told Larry Jeffers yesterday and Herman Bolen this morning to be sure that all powerhouse personnel were notified of the new OSHA program. They assured me there would be no problem and that I would be admitted at any time of the day or night."

"I don't know what to say," Withers said defensively. "My standing orders are—"

"If I'm not let in after clearing the visit with the officers who are in charge of the structure, I'll have to assume there's something you're trying to hide."

"It's not that. We had an OSHA inspection a few months ago. We got high marks."

"The marks were not as high as you apparently think. There were questions raised about air quality—the air you have to breathe, Mr. Withers. There were lights burnt out in the inspection galleries. The subcontractor replacing the rotor of the Unit Three generator was not conforming to standard safety procedures. Excuse me, I don't mean to blame you for the failure of others to keep you informed. Here's what I want you to do—call Lawrence Jeffers and Herman Bolen at their homes right now. I'll wait here. Don't worry about waking them up; tell them I ordered you to call. They will confirm our recent discussions and give you the okay to let me in. If they don't, I'll have to file a report with my superiors in Washington as well as with the State Division of Dam Safety."

"Yes, sir. I'll do that right away."

The red light went out and the loudspeaker fell silent. With luck, Phil thought, Bolen won't be home yet and nobody will answer Jeffers's phone. Withers will be on the spot then and will probably yield. Phil turned away and looked up at the dam. "No need to look so surly," he said, addressing it as if it were alive. "I'm only trying to help. If you have a thorn in your paw, it should be taken out—don't you agree? Then we can be pals."

After several minutes two floodlights went on above the panel, illuminating Phil like a singer on a stage. He turned and squinted.

"Would you stand on the center of the platform, please," Withers asked over the loudspeaker, "and look at the camera?"

For the first time, Phil noticed a camera housing on the rock wall five feet above his head. He saw the lens retract to put him in focus.

"May I ask what the cylinder is you are carrying?"

"This? A set of plans of the dam's instrumentation and inspection tunnels."

"Would you unroll them, please?"

Phil did so, realizing that Withers wanted to make sure he wasn't concealing a rifle or a bomb. He held the sheets toward the camera. "You can see the Roshek company seal in the lower corner," he said.

"Yes, I see it. Are you carrying any metal?"

"Just a belt buckle."

"What about the clipboard?"

"Plastic." It was in fact a children's item Phil had bought in the School Daze section of an all-night grocery store.

"If you are carrying any other metal, an alarm will sound in the Sutterton police station when you go through the detector. I'm going to raise the door high enough for you, Mr. Robinson, but not for your car. You'll have to walk down the tunnel. If you have instruments that are too heavy to carry, you'll have to come back in the morning when my boss is on duty."

"Fair enough."

There was a rumble as the ponderous door rolled upward. It stopped with the lower edge five feet above the pavement. Phil ducked inside and heard it thunder shut behind him with reverberating finality.

"This is Herman Bolen speaking."

"Oh, yes, Mr. Bolen. Newt Withers here. Thanks for returning my call. Excuse me for calling so late, but I had a question to ask and I couldn't locate Mr. Jeffers."

"Is everything all right up there? No sudden leaks or anything, I hope." Bolen laughed briefly.

"Everything is fine, as far as I know. Nothing shows on the board."

"Good. I must say I was surprised to get the message that you called, because I was about to phone the powerhouse myself. Something came up and I had to leave the house for a time. I'm trying to find out what happened to our Mr. Jeffers. He's been missing for over twenty-four hours."

"I know he didn't come in today. The local Chief of Police called earlier to ask if I knew where he was."

"Withers, I have to tell you that I'm a little worried about what might have happened to him. It may be that his car has gone off the road somewhere . . . that's what I'm most afraid of. Another possibility is that he's had some sort of accident in the lower drainage tunnels. When I talked to him on Thursday night, he said he was thinking of checking a few meters before going to bed. No reason to get excited," Bolen added quickly when he heard Withers's low whistle. "All of this is just supposition on my part."

"If he was in the dam, wouldn't his car still be here? I didn't see it in the lot when I came in."

"Good point. Still, I'd like to have somebody take a look around down below. What I want to avoid is a general alarm, missing-person bulletins on television, and that sort of thing. That would be embarrassing to the firm and to Larry, too, if it turns out that he has simply wandered off somewhere without telling anybody. Can you take a break and go down to the lower galleries?"

"Well, I'm not supposed to leave the control room for longer than ten minutes. Going down to the bottom and back would take a half hour. The OSHA inspector said he was going to check Gallery D. That was twenty minutes ago. . . . When he gets back, I'll ask if he—"

"What OSHA inspector?"

"The one you talked to this morning. The one you gave the key to the upper gate to. The reason I called you a few minutes ago was to make sure he had proper authorization. You and Jeffers were out, and he seemed to be getting hot, so I decided to let him in."

"I don't know any OSHA inspector. My key to the upper gate is locked in my desk."

Withers moaned. "Oh, God, no. He said his name was Charles Robinson. He said he was here to make a night inspection and that you knew all about it."

"I don't know anybody by that name. He must be the fellow who tried to reach me when I was out. He knew I was gone, that's why he told you to call me. The man is a phony."

"If he's a phony, he sure knows his business. He knows this dam inside and out. He even had a set of R. B. & B. plans of the tunnels. Should I call the cops?"

"He had a set of plans? What did he look like?"

"Tall guy, maybe six foot two. About twenty-five years old. Reddish hair."

"Does he take big steps when he walks, like a farmer stepping over two furrows at once?"

"Yeah, I guess you could say that."

Bolen cursed quietly. "It sounds like Kramer. Can you turn on the parking-lot lights from where you are? See if you can find his car with your camera."

"Just a second. Let's see . . . yep, that must be his car, right next to mine. Wait till I focus. Got it. Looks like a Mustang, six or seven years old, pretty banged up."

"Call the police. Your OSHA inspector is Phil Kramer, an engineer Roshek fired about twelve hours ago. He is convinced that the dam is going to fail any second. He's absolutely possessed by the idea, which is why we had to let him go."

"Is he violent? Jesus, I'm in here alone."

"I don't think there is any chance of violence. As far as I know, he is perfectly rational except when it comes to the dam. Unless I miss my guess, when he comes up from below he's going to want

you to declare an emergency. He's never been inside a dam and has
no idea of how much leakage there is. When he sees the way water
comes in, he'll think it's about to bust."

"I hope the cops can get here before he gets back."

"Withers, if it can be arranged, I don't want him charged with
anything. Best for us is if the police restrain him and keep him from
going to the newspapers until I get there. I'm coming up to meet a
Dam Safety inspector from Sacramento at noon. We don't want rumors getting started about the dam. See the point? I'll take charge
of Kramer when I get there. I'm sure I can talk some sense into his
head. Let's keep this quiet if we can."

Bolen had been talking on the wall phone in the kitchen of his
home. When he hung up, he turned to his wife and Roshek, who
were having coffee at the kitchen table. Roshek had obviously
grasped the entire picture from hearing only one side of the conversation. There was color in his cheeks and the fire had returned to
his eyes. He looked almost normal.

"We should throw the book at that kid and try to keep him
behind bars for life. He's a menace to the company."

Bolen nodded tiredly. "We'll talk about it in the morning. Let's
all try to get some sleep. I'll wake you, Theodore, if Withers calls
with any unusual news."

18

PHIL SQUEEZED PAST THE CAR THAT WAS PARKED BEHIND THE SIXTH turbine. Was there a workman of some kind in the tunnels, he wondered, despite the hour? If there was, he would bluff him the same way he bluffed Withers. He sprinted up the flight of steel stairs and pulled open the door marked "DANGER, NO ADMITTANCE." He grabbed a flashlight from the rack and headed down the tunnel at a half trot. He couldn't help smiling at the success of his acting début. His officious and faintly irritated manner had completely fooled Withers. The poor guy was kept on the defensive by a barrage of questions about working conditions, handrails, fire extinguishers, first-aid kits, and anything else that had popped into Phil's mind. Withers never had a chance to demand identification or to ask questions of his own.

The tunnel was better suited to screams of fear than to smiles of satisfaction. It was no bigger than the culverts under his father's county roads, so poorly lit by the widely spaced overhead bulbs that he had to turn his flashlight on, and so wet he had already ruined his shoes. God, he wondered, casting his light onto the mineral-stained walls and the swiftly flowing rivulet in the gutter along the walkway, if there is this much water coming in at the elevation of the river what's it going to be like a hundred and fifty feet lower?

The air was stale, and the tunnel seemed to get smaller the deeper into it he advanced, although he knew that was just his imagination. For the first time since childhood, he felt a touch of claustrophobia, not enough to make him turn back, but enough to make him remember with unsettling clarity being held in a closet at the age of five or six. His tormentors were a group of laughing playmates who were unmoved by his terror—they were moved, finally, by his mother, who heard his muffled screams from the backyard. Now Phil had the feeling that the fear that overcame him then was lurking deep within him still, and would surface again if he let it. He pushed on, each footstep making a splashing sound that reminded him of the way he used to stomp around in the puddles that formed after summer rains in Wichita. He wished he could be transported suddenly to Kansas and out of the dreary tunnel whose walls seemed to be pressing in upon him—Kansas, where the horizons were always miles away.

At an intersection with a cross tunnel, Phil unrolled the plans and rested them on his upraised knee. He hardly needed to refer to them again, but the sight of the detailed technical drawings, complete with dimensions, cross-sections, and explanatory notes, helped him keep his intellect in control rather than his emotions. There was no mystery about the tunnels, the drawings seemed to say, and nothing to be afraid of. You aren't lost in Hell or the sewers of Paris.

To the right was the inspection tunnel that penetrated the rock of the north abutment. Straight ahead was the way to the base of the intake shaft. To the left, that's where he wanted to go.

The side tunnel was definitely smaller, Phil thought, proceeding with more caution—no more than seven feet in diameter. Jesus, I can see why Duncan hates to come in here. A man could shout his lungs out and shoot off a cannon and not a living thing would hear him. At least in the sewers of Paris there would be rats to take notice, or maybe gendarmes. If I really was an OSHA inspector, I'd raise hell about these tunnels—not enough light, terrible air, treacherous footing—and maybe I will anyway. Something should be done to make seepage water come in through the underdrains and the radial collector pipes, where it's supposed to, instead of through cracks and joints in the tunnel walls. This is a hell of a mess. . . .

Phil stopped at the top of the main stairwell, which descended at a steep angle. The beam of his flashlight had little effect on the gloom below him. There was a faint sound of rushing water that he felt sure could not be normal. He stood very still and listened.

Water was dripping and trickling around him and flowing in the gutter alongside the walkway, but the sound that held his attention was deeper and stronger, like that of a waterfall plunging into a pool.

He started down, taking the steps as quickly as he could. According to Duncan, there were two hundred of them. If he tripped, he would never stop rolling.

Two hours after midnight on Saturday morning, the bars of Sutterton were closing. Two police cars were on duty, one stationed across from Randy's Roadhouse south of town, the other across from the Wagon Wheel Saloon. Experience had shown that as the patrons of the town's two largest establishments debouched onto the streets, the sight of police cars hastened the onset of sobriety.

Car Two was at the Wagon Wheel. Officers John Colla and Lee Simon were relieved at the display of temperance and good behavior. Nobody seemed interested in disturbing the peace or anyone else. Nobody needed police assistance to stand or walk.

There was a rush of static on the two-way radio as the dispatcher asked for their location. Colla, behind the wheel, picked up the microphone. "Car Two at the Wagon Wheel. Quiet as a church picnic."

"We've got a two two three at the powerhouse. Engineer on duty is Withers. Proceed NFS."

The policemen glanced at each other. Two two three was the code for a trespass under way. NFS meant no flashing lights or siren.

"Which Withers is that, Chet?" Colla asked. "Newt?"

"Yes. The intruder is thought to be one Phil Kramer, who used a false name and story to get in. Purpose unknown. Suspect is somewhere inside the dam and doesn't know we've been called. Newt has locked himself in the control room and will raise the door when you ring the buzzer."

Colla started the engine and pulled away from the curb. A U-turn put him on the way to the dam. "Weapons?"

"Nothing showed on the metal detector. Suspect has no known record. May be unstable. Known to be a fanatic about the dam and thinks it's going to fail."

"What about the upper gate?"

"Your key number fifteen should open it. If not, Newt has some of his people on the way who can let you in."

"Sounds tricky. Are we getting any other help?"

"Highway Patrol is sending a car."

"Roger. Out."

Officer Simon unlocked the glove compartment and removed a ring of keys. "We might have a psycho on our hands," he said.

"Sounds like it. I hope he's one we can sweet-talk."

His hope for using psychology rather than force was undermined by the sight of the demolished upper gate.

After saying good night to Roshek, Herman Bolen waited in the hallway outside the guest bedroom to see if he would go to sleep or sit up working himself into a temper. When the slit of light under the door turned black, Bolen sighed in relief. "At least I've got *him* out of my hair for a while," he breathed, going down the stairs to his den. He sat at his desk and dialed the powerhouse.

It was amazing how complicated life had suddenly become. Questions about the safety of Sierra Canyon Dam were raised by the latest inspection reports; one of the company's most reliable employees was inexplicably missing and guilty at the very least of gross thoughtlessness; Roshek announced that he might abdicate his throne for a few years, then proceeded to terrorize his wife and get evicted from his own house by the police. Now this thing with Kramer. It was surprising enough that Kramer had talked back to Roshek and gotten himself fired, but going to Sutterton and lying his way into the dam was almost unbelievable. That kid will wind up in jail if Roshek has his way. Bolen was disgusted with himself for making such a terrible character judgment, and wondered if there was mental illness in the young engineer's background. A call to the boy's family or the Menninger Clinic might turn up something.

"This is Herman again," he said when Withers answered. "Any developments?"

"The cops are on their way but not here yet."

"Good. Kramer hasn't showed up again?"

"Still down in the hole, I guess."

"Don't let him in the control room. If he throws a fit in there, he could really do a lot of damage."

"You think he'll throw a fit? Christ, I'm glad these big windows are bulletproof."

"I don't know what he might do. I completely misjudged the man. I don't think we have to worry about bullets, though . . . unless the police get excited and start shooting. I hope they'll use minimum force. I've been thinking about my last conversation with Kramer. He was particularly upset about what he regarded as excessively high seepage in Gallery D. Can you tell me anything about conditions there from where you sit?"

"Gallery D? There are a few remote-reading pore-pressure sensors, I think. I'm strictly electrical, you know, not trained in hydraulics. Hang on while I take this on another phone—the lower gallery panels are on the other side of the room. . . . Mr. Bolen? There are three dials here for Gallery D. Two show zero, and the third is stuck on the high end. I think they're out of order. I've worked here six months and the readings never change. I can check the current drain for that reach of the electrical network . . . one second. Let's see, looks like about a third of normal. I would guess two of the three pumps aren't working."

"Two pumps out? That means there might be a few inches of water standing on the tunnel floor. If there is a break in the high-pressure line from the third pump, Kramer will think the lake is coming in. Don't let him scare you."

"I understand."

"One more thing. If those pumps are out, get somebody to put them back on line immediately. We don't want the inspector from the state to find a pile of broken-down machinery."

At the bottom of the steps, Phil found himself in darkness standing in water that came to his thighs. Don't get excited, he told himself, just because the overhead lights are out and the pumps aren't working. The situation was hardly normal, but there was no proof that a catastrophe was pending. What he wanted was proof. Leaving the roll of plans on a dry step, he waded forward toward the sound of surging water, the beam of the flashlight penetrating only as far as the next veil of water dripping from the tunnel crown. Fifty feet from the foot of the steps, he found what he assumed was the main source of the flood—a vigorous upwelling of water from beneath the surface. He groped with one foot to try to determine if it was erupting from a boil-out on the floor or from a broken pressure pipe, but the force of the jet was too great. His foot was knocked aside and into a submerged object that seemed roughly cylindrical and covered with canvas or cloth that was snagged on the tunnel wall. It yielded and rolled away as he pushed past it.

Deeper in the tunnel, Phil's flashlight illuminated a rectangular chamber. On the left wall was a half-open steel door marked Gallery D. There, he knew, he would find the proof he needed.

He kept fear in check by concentrating on the technicalities of the job to be done. He already felt vindicated for breaking in. The fantastic amount of water demonstrated beyond argument that the drainage, pumping, inspection, and monitoring procedures that Roshek was so proud of were inadequate. Further, his computer program, while perhaps far from foolproof, had at least revealed that *something* was haywire. Even if the submerged jet was the result of a ruptured discharge pipe, he was justified in sounding some sort of alarm. For one thing, if emergency pumping was not begun at once, the water level would rise so high that all the pumps and monitoring devices in this section of the structure would be put out of action. He had evidence enough now to wipe the look of contempt off Roshek's face and to dissolve Bolen's attitude of condescension. But Phil wanted to check his larger theory as well, that the dam as a whole contained fundamental weaknesses. For proof of that, he wanted a look at the meters in Gallery D that were still above water and functioning.

The passageway behind the door descended gradually and after only eighty feet Phil was in water up to his chest. He stopped and shined his light ahead, wondering how much farther he had to go to reach the meter bank. Twenty feet away he saw a shimmering horizontal band that made his mouth open and his flesh crawl: a sheet of water under extreme pressure was jetting from one wall of the tunnel to the other from a jagged crack. The volume of water grew as he watched it, and he saw several small pieces of concrete at the base of the stream scoured loose and shot across the tunnel with the force of rifle bullets.

"That's not seepage," he said, taking several backward steps and trying to swallow, "and that's not a broken pipe. That's a fucking *breach. . . .*"

He turned and waded toward the main tunnel as fast as he could, wondering if he could make faster progress by swimming, aware for the first time how slippery the footing was. Slippery? Holding the flashlight aloft in one hand, he lowered the other to the walkway, having to submerge his head and shoulders to do it. He scraped the side of his palm along the concrete and brought it to the surface. The flashlight confirmed his suspicion: his cupped hand was filled with clay. The incoming water was carrying with it part of the embankment. He poured the clay into the pocket of his shirt and fastened the button. Ten feet away, sudden waves of water in the main tunnel began closing the door to Gallery D. With a desperate lunge he was able to jam his arms through the narrowing gap and force the door back far enough to pull himself through. He no longer was worried about verifying a theory, or saving his career, or getting the last word with Bolen and Roshek. All that mattered now was escaping with his life. Gasping, he pushed his way toward the steps. Blocking his way was the submerged fountain, which was gushing upward now with ten times its earlier force and sending a boiling mass of water against the tunnel crown. Phil plunged wildly forward and into the cold, stiffened arms of Lawrence Jeffers.

In the powerhouse, needles on two dials assumed to be inoperative rose from zero to the high ends of the scales.

Theodore Roshek couldn't sleep. He fumbled in the darkness for the lamp on the bedside table. When the light was on, he lowered his feet to the floor and put the telephone in his lap. He would call Eleanor. She had never been particularly sympathetic when he wanted to discuss matters she considered "heavy," but maybe when she heard what he had gone through she would forgive him for waking her and say something to cheer him up. Just hearing her voice would make him feel better. Unfortunately, there was a busy signal when he dialed Creekwood, the house on the Sierra Canyon River. She had probably turned in for the night and, as usual, had taken the phone off the hook.

He put his head on the pillow and lay staring at the ceiling.

In the kitchen downstairs, Herman Bolen was at the stove making another pot of coffee and waiting for the phone to ring.

19

WHEN THE SMALL JET OF WATER IN THE TUNNEL FLOOR ERUPTED INTO a full-fledged geyser, the increased force dislodged the snagged body of Jeffers and rotated it upward in a sudden cartwheel, the arms projecting grotesquely. Before the body landed on him, Phil caught a flash of glassy eyes protruding from a death mask that was frozen in an expression of terror even greater than his own. Phil hurled himself backward in fright, dropping the flashlight and losing his balance. His hoarse shout was stopped by the water that closed over his head as he fell. When he regained his footing, he was in total darkness. He waded toward the sound of the upsurging water, again encountering the body, which was floating face up and blocking his way. Phil filled his fists with the cloth of the dead man's shirt and pushed the body ahead of him. Taking a deep breath and ducking his head beneath the surface, he drove forward using the body as a shield and as a way of keeping his balance. Once past the jet, which was shooting upward like the stream from a broken hydrant, the water level came to his waist—a foot higher than it was on his way in ten minutes before. Phil struggled forward, pushing the body, orienting himself by keeping one foot on the edge of the walkway. At the base of the steps he looked up and saw faint lights far above him. Thank God, he thought, the lights are out only at the bottom. He began the upward climb one step at a time, pulling the ungainly body behind him. After advancing twenty feet he released his grip and sat down gasping for breath.

The body slipped down several steps and became wedged in the gutter between the walkway and the curving wall of the tunnel. Phil tried to clear his thoughts. Was there time to drag the body out and save himself as well? What was the point of risking his life to retrieve a corpse? He felt a coldness growing on his legs and wondered if it was a sign that he was going into shock. Peering down through the semi-darkness, he saw that the stairwell below him was completely flooded. Silently rising water was creeping over his feet, calves, and knees. He rolled away from it and clambered up the steps on all fours toward the distant lights.

Withers cursed his own stupidity. Why did I let that guy in? Raise the door only for people you know or who have authorization arranged in advance—that's what the orders are. Oh, Jesus, it's going to be my ass when Jeffers gets here, or Bolen, or any of a half a dozen other people. But I thought it would be my ass if I *didn't* let him in! How was I supposed to know he was a phony? He knew all the right things to say. Anybody would have done what I did.

There were four closed-circuit television screens mounted on the wall. One displayed the access tunnel entrance and parking area, one the electrical switchyard, one the generator deck, and one the turbine deck. The last two were usually focused on dials, but they could be panned remotely to take in any part of the chambers. By manipulating two small levers, Withers trained Camera 4 on the door leading to the inspection galleries. He moved his eyes back and forth from 1 to 4, hoping that the police would appear before the intruder.

A buzzer sounded and a light flashed on the hot-line phone to Pacific Gas & Electric's Power Control Center in Oakland, from which the power grid in northern California was monitored.

"Sierra Canyon."

"Power Central. Rancho Seco may have to cut back in a few hours. We'll need an extra twenty megawatts from you during the morning peak. I guess you can handle that? We show you at eighty-six percent of capacity, not counting Unit Three. Are you spilling? What's your afterbay elevation?"

"We're spilling two feet, but the afterbay is drawn down. An extra twenty will be no problem."

On the fourth television screen, Withers saw Kramer burst through the door at the end of the turbine and drape himself over a steel railing, apparently trying to catch his breath. He was gulping air, his shoulders and chest heaving. Or was he vomiting? Squinting, Withers couldn't tell. Where were the goddam cops? "Can I get back to you?" he asked the dispatcher.

The voice from Power Control Central went on in a monotone: "Checking our printouts on Sierra Canyon, there seems to be a frequency fluctuation during the last thirty minutes or so. Nothing serious, just a hair. What do you indicate at your end?"

"Look, I'm awful busy right now. I'll call you back in about thirty minutes. . . ."

"At three in the morning you're busy?"

"I got a slight problem here. I'll explain later."

Withers hung up and rose out of his chair staring at the monitor. Kramer's clothing and hair looked wet. His eyes were wide and his mouth was hanging open. "Holy Christ," Withers whispered, "a pipe must have burst and hit him with spray. He looks like he's flipped his lid completely." As he watched, Kramer closed his mouth and swallowed with difficulty, glancing behind him as if he were being pursued. He lunged down the short flight of steps to the floor of the turbine deck, out of the camera's view.

Withers lowered himself into his chair and swiveled toward the windows that lined one wall of the control room. He would have to stall Kramer until the cops arrived. Remain calm and reason with him. Hope that he wouldn't go berserk. Withers ground his teeth at the thought of how much damage a madman could do. Unit 3 was off line and the generator deck was strewn with tools and equipment that could as easily be used to destroy as repair. A sledgehammer or a bucket of bolts thrown into one of the spinning rotors would cause a terrible amount of damage. If something like that happened, Withers realized, because he had admitted a man without clearance, he would be out of a job and could forget about ever getting hired again as a powerhouse operator.

The apparition that appeared on the other side of the windows was like something out of a bad dream. Kramer's clothes were soaked and torn and his face was streaked with blood from a cut on his scalp. The expression on his face was that of a man who was in a desperate battle with private demons, a man who had only a tenuous connection with reality. He ran drunkenly across the tile floor, skidded to a stop, and pressed his hands against the glass. The voice Withers heard over the intercom was high-pitched and breath-less.

"The dam is failing! We've got to sound the alarm! The dam is failing!"

Withers nodded sympathetically but did not move.

"Can you hear me? The dam is failing!"

Withers leaned forward to bring his lips close to a microphone on the counter top. "Yes, I can hear you."

"The lake is breaking into the tunnels. . . . One man is dead already. . . . We've got to warn the town. . . ." Kramer looked wildly around, then hurled himself to the end of the windows and tried to open the control-room door. "Unlock the door! What's the matter with you? The dam is failing!"

Withers concentrated on presenting an unruffled appearance even though his pulse was racing and beads of sweat were forming on his forehead. He was gripping the edge of the counter so tightly the tips of his fingers were white. Did Kramer say a man was dead? "I can't open the door," he said. "It's against regulations. Clearance would have to be obtained from—"

"Fuck regulations!" Kramer shouted. "This is an emergency! We've got to do something right away, warn people, get our asses out of here. . . . Are you crazy? Isn't one corpse enough? Maybe the dam can be saved . . . we've got to get on the phone. . . ."

"Calm down, Mr. Kramer. You are all excited."

"Sure I'm excited! Jesus Christ!" He frowned. "You called me Kramer. How did you know my name was Kramer?"

Withers hesitated, hoping he hadn't made another terrible error. "I talked with Herman Bolen a few minutes ago. He was able to identify you. When you say 'corpse,' do you mean—"

"Get him on the phone! Let me talk to him. When I tell him what I've seen . . . Call him! Call anybody! You goddam dummy! Do something!"

"Mr. Bolen will be here at noon. You can talk to him then."

Kramer shook his fists. "By noon the dam may not be here! Sutterton may not be here! Unless you get in gear, you'll be floating around in that chair in the middle of San Francisco Bay. *The . . . dam . . . is . . . failing.*" He rolled his eyes in disbelief at the lack of effect the words had on Withers. "The dam is failing and I have to deal with a robot." He whirled around and saw the row of offices that lined the opposite wall of the lobby. He ran from one to another trying the telephones, throwing them aside when he couldn't get a dial tone.

"The phones are dead," Withers said. "The switchboard is turned off when the staff leaves at five. Mr. Kramer, you've got to get hold of yourself. Why don't you sit down at one of those desks and take a nap? We'll talk things over later." Where the hell were the cops?

Kramer tightened his fists and walked back to the control-room windows. "You think I'm a raving fucking lunatic, don't you?" he said. "Bolen told you I had a fixation about the dam failing and that I wasn't to be taken seriously, is that it? Protect the company's reputation."

"You *think* the dam is failing. You don't *know* the dam is failing. If the dam was failing, the instruments would—"

"The instruments are out of order! Ask Duncan, he'll tell you. This whole joint is out of order. I *know* the dam is failing. With my own eyes I have . . ."

Kramer slapped both hands over his face, digging his fingernails into his forehead in frustration and apparently not feeling the blood on his cheek. His shoulders were trembling. Withers stood up, studying him, hoping he was about to succumb to some sort of seizure.

Kramer lowered his hands. He had managed to erase the tension from his face. The men stared at each other through double panes of bulletproof glass. When Kramer spoke again, it seemed to Withers that he was making a great effort to keep his voice from cracking and to keep from talking too fast.

"I am not a crackpot," Kramer said, making precise gestures. "Until yesterday I worked in the hydro design section of Roshek, Bolen & Benedetz in the Los Angeles office. I have been worried about the structural integrity of this dam for three weeks. I got fired because I explained my suspicions to Roshek and lost my temper when he wouldn't take them seriously." He stopped for a deep breath. "I came here to see if I was right or wrong. I lied to you to get in because it seemed like the only way. A thousand pardons, Mr. Withers, for the trick I played on you." His voice and face had become calm. As he continued, he gave a convincing impression of being utterly relaxed. "I was just down in the lower drainage galleries and I found that my worst fears were true. The lake is breaking in under pressure even as we stand here having this friendly discussion. I saw two breaches. Each one is bringing water in at about five or ten thousand gallons a minute, I would guess."

Withers gradually realized that Kramer's voice and expression had taken on a patronizing quality, as if it were he, Withers, who had to be humored.

"I'm sure you realize, Mr. Withers, as an engineer, that water coming in under pressure is— how shall I put it?—bad news."

"I . . . I'm not an engineer."

"I am. I have a Ph.D. in civil engineering. My area of special interest, as luck would have it, is the prediction of dam failures. Some people immerse themselves in hydrangeas or collect miniature whiskey bottles. I study dam failures. One thing you learn when you pursue such an interest is that it is a poor sign when leakage is under pressure. Another poor sign is the presence of clay, which shows that the impervious core is not as impervious as might be wished, and is being scoured away by the water under pressure, to which I have just alluded." He dipped a finger into his shirt pocket and extended it toward Withers. "See? I scooped this up from the invert in the lower gallery. From under four feet of water." He drew a gray line on the glass between them. "That's clay from the core." He laced his fingers together. "What this all means—the pressure, the clay, the rapid increase in flow—is that the dam is failing. That's it in a nutshell!" He smiled as if pleased at himself for finding words that even the dumbest child in kindergarten could comprehend. "As simple as that. The dam is failing! Now, Mr. Withers, what should two intelligent adults do when confronted with a failing dam?" His face clouded over and his voice began to rise. "Should they alert the authorities or should they converse like two fucking idiots? *Get on the phone!*"

"I'm not an expert or a specialist on hydraulics . . ."

"*I* am an expert and specialist on hydraulics!" Phil shouted. "I am a foremost goddam authority!"

". . . and I'm not going to cause a furor just because you are telling me things you may be making up or imagining, or that are based on misinterpreted data. In the morning the appropriate people can check out what you say."

"Fuck the appropriate people! There may not be any morning! We don't have time to go through channels, you dumb son of a bitch! You know how much time was lost at Baldwin Hills because the first people on the scene went through channels? We may have hours and we may have minutes. This dam may be ready to split open like a watermelon dropped from a truck." Phil pounded his fists against the windows. "One man is dead already and we may be next! You want to stay here? Fine. Then open the outside door so I can get the hell out. Otherwise I'm going to grab a crowbar from downstairs and tear this place apart. I'll smash these windows and knock your teeth out!"

Withers was sweating profusely. "What man is dead? Who is dead?" Could it be that Jeffers had had an accident in the inspection gallery? Kramer might have blundered into a broken pressure main and found Jeffers unconscious while snooping around in Gallery D. That would scare anybody half to death; no wonder he was so agitated.

"How should I know? The guy whose car is parked behind the turbines, I guess."

"Did you see him?"

"He landed right on my head! Did I see him? My God, I *danced* with him."

"What did he look like? A high forehead?"

"He looked terrible! He looked dead!" Phil lifted his eyes to the television screens behind Withers. His eyebrows rose. "Hey, did you call the cops?"

Withers turned to the monitors and saw a police car in the parking lot. A touch of a button switched the camera to close focus. The face of a policeman appeared on the screen. "Newt? This is Lee Simon. You okay? What's going on?"

Withers picked up a second microphone. "I'm okay, Lee. I'll raise the door. Drive to the end of the tunnel and come up the steps to the control room."

"You got a trespasser?"

Phil pounded on the glass again. "Don't let them in! Tell them to wake up the town!"

"Yes, but no trouble so far. He's on the control-room deck."

"Is he armed?"

Withers looked at Kramer, who was holding the sides of his head as if to contain an explosion. "I don't think so." He pushed the button that raised the roller door at the mouth of the access tunnel.

"You've got to be out of your mind," Phil said, edging away. "We'll all drown. . . ."

"Look, Kramer, the police aren't going to charge you with anything. Bolen just wants you held until he gets here. Stay cool and everything will be fine, okay? Do us both a favor. . . . Where do you think you're going?" He cursed when he saw Kramer run for the stairs to the lower decks. He picked up a microphone and shouted into it: "Touch those generators and you'll spend the rest of your life in jail! That's a promise!"

20

A CAR FROM THE COUNTY SHERIFF'S DEPARTMENT ARRIVED WITHIN minutes of the police. Withers told the deputies to post themselves at the portal of the access tunnel in case Kramer tried to escape in that direction, then turned his attention to officers Colla and Simon, who were standing in the control-room lobby awaiting further instructions.

"He's back in the inspection galleries," Withers said. "See those stairs? Two flights down is the turbine deck. Go to the far end of the chamber and you'll see a steel door. I saw him go through there on the monitor."

"You're sure he's not armed?"

"Almost positive."

"Can he cause any damage?"

"Not if you keep him away from the generators. He could break some instruments and pull out some wiring, but nothing too bad."

"We'll stand guard downstairs until some of your people get here who know the tunnels."

"Right." Withers's attention was caught by a red light flashing on an instrument panel to his left. "Wait a minute. . . . Christ, he's in the elevator."

Although Withers had never been in it, he knew there was a man-cage inside the walls of the intake tower. He should have realized that Kramer would be aware of it. The red light showed that it was in use, and a dial showed that the cage was at the seven-hundred-foot level and was rising steadily toward the top landing at eight hundred and thirty feet. With a slight smile, Withers reversed the position of a toggle switch labeled "Override." The arrow stopped and began to swing slowly to the left. It would take the cage about five minutes to return to the bottom of the shaft, and when it got there the intruder would be met by Withers and the two policemen. He unlocked the control-room door and ran toward the stairs. "Come on!" he shouted, waving for the policemen to follow him. "He's trapped in an elevator. We've got him now!"

The footsteps of the three men as they ran down the steps masked a faint, throbbing vibration in the hum made by the generators. In the control room, a series of lights went on indicating a drop in frequency, then went out as circuits were shorted out by water. Two phones began to ring.

The elevator was little more than an open framework built over a three-foot-square platform. A waist-high grillwork fence shielded the passenger from the concrete walls of the shaft. One wall of the shaft was covered with water pipes, ventilation ducts, and bundled electrical conduits; another, in a two-foot-wide, two-foot-deep vertical inset, carried the steel rungs of a ladder that ran the full height of the tower.

Phil reviewed in his mind the drawings of the tower he had studied at the motel. At the highest landing was a flight of stairs leading to a hatch cover. Once he got past that, he would be outside, twenty feet above the surface of the lake and about two hundred feet from shore.

As the cage rose, it rattled disconcertingly against its steel guide channels. Phil steadied himself against the railing and looked upward. The steel doors through which the reservoir intake gates could be reached were eighty feet apart, each one marked by a light. He kept one hand on the control handle, pressing it hard against its upper stop in an effort to force the cage beyond its fixed and agonizingly slow speed. With enough of a head start, he felt sure, he could swim to shore, find a phone, and sound an alarm before Withers and the police figured out where he had gone.

He kept his eyes on the last light, now about a hundred and fifty feet above him, and watched it slowly approach. With a lurch, the cage stopped moving. "Now what?" he said aloud, rattling the control handle. His first thought was that water had risen high enough to short out the generators . . . but no, the lights in the shaft were still on. Maybe power was only temporarily interrupted. "Come on, you bastard!" he shouted, kicking the grillwork fence and slamming the handle back and forth.

When the cage began to descend, Phil guessed that Withers had discovered where he was, and was using some sort of emergency hookup to bring the elevator to the bottom. He climbed to the top of the railing, caught hold of one of the ladder rungs as it went by, and stepped out of the cage. He flattened his body against the ladder until the upper framework had passed on its way down, then began climbing. The rungs were so wet from water trickling down the wall that he had trouble keeping his footing, and the steel was so cold he was afraid his hands would stick to it if he stopped moving. He kept his eyes fixed on the light above him and tried not to think about what would happen if he lost his grip.

After several minutes of steady hand-over-hand progress he reached the top landing. He stepped off the ladder and through a rectangular opening in the concrete wall. The clanking and creaking pulleys and cables stopped—the cage had reached the bottom. The faint sound of excited voices, confined in the narrow shaft, drifted up to him. The committee that had been waiting to welcome him was disappointed.

Phil ran up the stairs, pushed open the hatch cover, and climbed outside. With a profound feeling of relief in escaping from what could have been a death trap, he sank to his knees to catch his breath and look around. He was on the outer rim of the tower, the structure that had looked like a concrete doughnut floating on the lake when he first saw it from the overlook. The moon was in the western sky and would soon be out of sight, but it was still bathing the valley in light and casting a trail across the water. The sky was full of stars and there wasn't a trace of movement or sound in the air. The dam, visible as a low wall that stretched away as far as the eye could follow, seemed to be a natural part of the landscape.

It was a scene of such tranquility that Phil began to wonder if his brain was playing tricks on him. Had he simply imagined what he had just been through? For more than an hour, he had been trying to escape from a surrealistic nightmare, his bloodstream laced with adrenalin and screams never far from his lips. But under the starred canopy of the night sky and in the silence of the surrounding forests there was nothing but perfect peace. His feelings of terror, panic, and impending disaster seemed almost absurd. Perhaps a flawed and failing dam existed only in his mind. Perhaps Withers, the bloodless robot-clone, was right to ignore the ravings of a hysteric.

If I'm nuts, he thought, getting to his feet, they can lock me up. If I'm not, I'd better get a move on. The water I saw jetting into the lower galleries was no illusion. I didn't imagine that dead body—I can still feel the clammy arms around my neck. I've got to get to a phone. . . . The cops are probably already on their way to head me off.

Phil placed his car ignition key in the right side of his mouth between his cheek and his gum. In the left side he put two dimes he had in his pocket—they would be handy if the only phone he could find was in a public booth. He removed his shoes, socks, shirt, and slacks, and folded them in a neat pile. "If things work out right," he said to his clothes, "I'll come back for you."

He turned and leaped off the edge of the concrete, cupping his testicles in one hand and pinching his nose shut with the other. The shock of the cold water gave him new energy, and he pulled for shore with clean, strong strokes.

21

HERMAN BOLEN LAY ON HIS SIDE IN BED SCOWLING INTO THE TELEPHONE. The connection was poor and he had to strain to hear the words. "He said he saw a dead body?"

"Yes, sir," he heard Withers say. "It must be Jeffers. When I went with the police to the elevator, I saw his car behind the last turbine."

Bolen collapsed onto his back and stared at the ceiling. Jeffers! Dead! Dead because I sent him into the hole in the middle of the night . . . or was he? "Is it Jeffers or not?" he said in sudden exasperation, throwing the covers aside and sitting on the edge of the bed. "Is there a body or isn't there? Didn't you go down to make sure?"

"Things have been so hectic around here I haven't had a chance."

"Send somebody else, then! Have you called Cooper and Riggs?"

"They got here a little while ago. They're outside helping the police—"

"Goddammit, Withers! I want somebody to go down below *right now!*" Bolen covered the mouthpiece with his hand and turned to his wife, who was standing on the other side of the bed pulling on a robe. "The *stupidity* of this guy," he said in a strained whisper, shaking his head in amazement, "is absolutely incredible." He turned back to the phone and asked Withers what else Kramer had said.

"He said water was jetting in all over the place and bringing the dam in with it. He dug some dirt out of his shirt pocket with his finger and streaked it across the glass, as if that was supposed to prove something."

"Good Lord!"

"I didn't let that bother me because you already told me he was going to say the dam was failing. My dials showed two pumps were out, so I knew water was accumulating. When he saw a dead body, or thought he saw one, I figure he got hysterical. You should have seen him screaming and waving his arms. He's definitely psycho. I don't think his version is going to have much relation to the way things really are."

"For everybody's sake, Withers, I hope he was hallucinating. What's your version of the way things really are?"

"Looks like all three pumps are out in the lower gallery. I'm getting no current drop on the sump circuit. The remote sensors in Gallery D have shorted out, too. My guess is that Gallery D is flooded."

"Wonderful," Bolen said with heavy sarcasm. "Just wonderful. And Kramer? You say the police have him cornered?"

"They saw him run across the road by the left overlook wearing nothing but his shorts. He's hiding in one of the buildings in the construction yard. They think they'll have him in a few minutes."

"What construction yard?"

"Mitchell Brothers has a contract with the county to widen the road."

"Get hold of Leonard Mitchell and give him the job of pumping out the lower tunnels. We've got to get those three sump pumps back in action, and I mean immediately. My God, we've got a guy from Dam Safety coming in at noon! Tell Cooper and Riggs to leave Kramer to the cops. I want a report from them on what's going on down below. I'm going to leave Beverly Hills right now." He looked at his bedside clock—it was 5:30 A.M. "I think I can be there in three hours. There's no commercial flight until eight o'clock and there's no airport at Sutterton for the company Lear, so I'll take my own plane. I'll land on top of the dam."

Bolen hung up and began dressing hurriedly. "I'll try to be back by late this afternoon," he said to his wife. "When Theodore wakes up, tell him I had to go to Sierra Canyon because of the Kramer situation and that I'll call him as soon as I can. Would you mind calling Stella? See if you can get her not to press charges."

In the guest bedroom downstairs, Roshek carefully replaced the receiver of the extension phone. He pulled himself out of bed into a chair and stared into the darkness, his jaw muscles tense and his lips pressed into a thin line.

After scaling the rocky slope from the lake to the road, Phil stood shivering, wondering which way to turn. Sutterton was at least a mile downhill to the right. The overlook was closer, up the road to the left, but he didn't recall seeing a pay phone there. Across the road were fuel and water tanks, what appeared to be an asphalt plant, and several corrugated-metal buildings. Against the sky he could see wires fanning out to the buildings from a nearby pole. One could be a telephone line. He trotted across the road, cursing under his breath whenever his bare feet landed on a pebble.

Just before he reached the shadows on the other side of the road, a car rounded a curve. For an instant, Phil was caught in the beam of the headlights. He sprinted between two parked crawler tractors, hoping he hadn't been spotted, and tried the door of the largest building. It was solidly locked. He ran to the rear of the building, which was set close to the steeply rising mountainside, and saw a row of horizontal windows hinged at the top. He broke one out with a rock and climbed carefully inside, and as he did so he heard the car slide to a stop in the gravel. The crackle of a two-way radio and fragments of a conversation confirmed his fears—it was the police.

"Suspect in construction yard on Sterling Road. Negative, cliff is too steep to climb. May be inside one of the buildings. Look, just send everybody up here, all right? We'll keep him from getting out."

Phil hugged himself in the cold, his eyes gradually becoming accustomed to the darkness. Looming over him were the shapes of two off-highway earthmoving trucks with tires eight feet high and cabs that could only be reached by ladders. One was on blocks with its rear wheels removed. On a workbench beneath the windows was a pile of oily rags. He grabbed a handful and dried himself, smoothing down the goose bumps on his forearms. What appeared at first glance to be a man standing against the wall staring at him turned out to be a pair of white coveralls on a hanger. He put them on, knocking over a rack of tools in the process. Outside, a second car arrived, and a third. In a momentary flash of headlights, Phil got a look at his surroundings—in the far corner was an office partitioned from the main area by walls of glass and plywood. He picked his way toward it, feeling the floor with a toe before each step.

"No shooting," he heard an authoritative voice say. "There's fuel tanks all over the place and maybe dynamite, too."

"Yes," Phil whispered, groping forward, "let's have no shooting. The suspect hates shooting."

In the office was a desk and on the desk was a phone. He raised the receiver to his ear and closed his eyes in relief when he heard a dial tone. Sixty seconds later Janet Sandifer was on the line.

"Phil, my God it's five in the morning! Where are you? Did you get in the dam?"

"Getting in was easy, getting out was the bitch. The cops are after me and they've got me cornered in a garage. The dam is failing, I'm sure of that now. Water is pouring into the tunnels under pressure. You've got to sound the alarm. . . ."

"What?"

". . . and raise all the hell you can. The dam is failing and I can't get anybody to believe it. I'm about to be arrested for trespassing or some goddam thing. Tell everybody the dam is failing. Call the towns downstream, call the Sheriff, call your mother. The state has some sort of disaster office . . . call that."

"The dam is failing? You mean right now?"

"Right now. What I am faced with here is a dam in the failure mode."

"You're putting me on. You sound funny. Your voice—"

"I'm not putting you on! If my voice sounds funny, it might be because I'm scared shitless! I'm surrounded by cops with guns! There are thousands of people asleep below the dam and I'm the only one who knows it's failing. . . ."

"Can't the cops see it failing?"

"There's nothing to see unless you know exactly where to look. Water is probably oozing out of the downstream face right where the computer said it would, but it's still dark and I can't get anybody to listen to me. You're my only hope. . . . This is the only phone call I'm going to be able to make. I may sound funny but I sure as hell don't feel funny. I feel like crying, if you want to know the truth. Janet, there's still time to evacuate the town. You've got to believe me! I know I'm right! I'm not joking! You've got to do what you can . . . please, please, please!"

"I believe you. I'll do what I can. How much I can accomplish from Santa Monica I don't know, but I'll do my best. Phil? I'm worried. About you. Don't take any more chances. You've done enough. Okay?"

Phil closed his eyes in relief. "Whew! I knew I could count on you. I've got to hang up. Good luck!"

"Don't take any more chances! Promise?"

"Just one more. Then I'm through. Then it's up to you. There's one more stunt I can try. . . . Read about it in the papers tomorrow."

When Chief Hartley arrived at the construction yard, a patrolman apprised him of the situation. Prints of bare feet had been found leading to the rear of the main building, where a pane of glass had been broken. A sheriff's deputy trying to look inside with a flashlight had nearly been hit by a wrench thrown by the suspect.

"Give me the bullhorn," Hartley said, "and I'll see if I can talk him out." He crouched behind his car with several aides and raised the bullhorn to his mouth. "This is Wilson Hartley," he said, his voice booming through the still night air and echoing off the cliff behind the building. "Sutterton Chief of Police. You might as well give yourself up, Mr. Kramer. Just stroll through the door with your hands up and you won't be hurt. Don't make us throw in a cannister of tear gas. You won't like it at all."

He lowered the horn and listened for a response. Surprisingly, he got one. Six times in his thirty-year career as a peace officer he had been involved in capturing runaway teenagers, escapees, and burglars who had hidden themselves in buildings of one kind or another. Never had one replied to his initial appeal for surrender.

"Do you promise not to shoot?" came a call from within the building.

Hartley widened his eyes at the deputy next to him. "We don't shoot trespassers in Caspar County," he said into the bullhorn. "My men won't shoot unless I give them a direct order."

"Good," was the muffled reply, "because I don't have a gun. You have a big edge on me there. I hate guns and shooting. Guns and shooting are inimical to life."

"What did he say?" Hartley whispered to the deputy.

"I didn't catch it. Something about life."

"If you can get them talking," the Chief went on in a whisper, "they usually won't do anything crazy. Setting up lines of communication is the key."

"I heard that," said the voice from inside the building. "Communication works both ways. Get a policeman talking and he usually won't do anything crazy, either. How do you like police work? Does your wife worry?"

Hartley frowned at the bullhorn and flicked the switch on the handle back and forth several times. "We can talk about that later," he said, once he was satisfied that he understood the mechanism. "Right now we want you to come out before somebody gets hurt. There are a lot of men out here who would like to go back to their regular duties."

"So would I," said the voice. "I know we can talk later, but we should talk now. The dam is failing, did anybody tell you? I know because I am a civil engineer. Kansas State. You and your men should be waking up the town instead of terrorizing a civil engineer who is trying to do everybody a favor and who is sure he is right and whom you can't help liking once you get past his shyness that is a carryover from God knows what in his childhood."

"Jesus," Hartley whispered, "this guy is a real fruitcake."

"I heard that," said the voice. "I am not a fruitcake. I resent that."

Hartley shook the bullhorn angrily. "How the fuck does this thing work, anyway? How do you turn the goddam thing off?"

"Must be stuck," said the deputy.

"The reason I am talking so much," said the voice, "is that I'm stalling for time. I'm checking a few things out in here. I'm not quite ready to come out, but almost. There, I think I'm ready. Are you ready, Sheriff?"

"I'm not the Sheriff, I'm the Chief of Police. We're ready. Take it nice and slow. Keep your hands over your head."

"I will not keep my hands over my head. That is a self-incriminating posture that would prejudice my chances for a fair trial. I intend to appeal this case all the way up to the Board of Direction of the American Society of Civil Engineers. See the garage door, Sheriff? I'm going to push a button that opens it. Then I'm coming out. I mean, I'm coming *out*."

Before Hartley could respond to what he sensed was in some way a rejection of his ultimatum, the door, suspended from a track at the roofline, rolled to one side with a rumble, revealing an opening large enough to pass the largest construction machines. Hartley peered into the shadows inside the building and was startled by the sight of two headlights winking on. There was the roar of a diesel engine and a fifteen-ton dump truck leaped into view. One of the huge tires caressed the Chief's car and knocked it aside as if it were made mostly of fiberglass rather than steel, which was in fact the case. Before anyone could react, the truck was out of the yard and turning left on the highway.

A deputy raised a rifle. "Say the word," he murmured, aiming.

"No shooting," Hartley commanded, jumping into his car. "He might lose control and crash into a house. Try to pass him and stop your car across the lanes. I'll radio ahead for a roadblock. He won't get far in that thing."

Hartley stepped hard on the gas and took off in a cloud of flying gravel. He turned on his roof lights and his electronic siren and overtook the truck in less than a minute. As he tried to pass on the left, the truck swerved right onto the narrow road that crossed the dam. "Where the hell does he think he's going?" Hartley said, braking and cramping the wheel hard right into the turn. "He'll never make the hairpin curves on the other side."

The deputy beside him had rolled down his window and was aiming his rifle again. "Let me take his tires out, boss."

Hartley pursed his lips in indecision. "Jesus, I'll bet those big fuckers cost five thousand bucks apiece. Well, okay, go ahead. . . . Wait, he's stopping! He's raising the dump. . . ."

He slammed on the brakes and hung tight to the wheel as the car skidded to a stop with its nose under the tail of the truck.

"Come on," Hartley said, "let's get him."

But before they could open their doors the car was jolted violently as ten tons of crushed rock slid out of the upraised dump and landed on the hood and engulfed the sides. By the time the two men had crawled out of the rear windows, a line of seven police and sheriff's cars had formed behind them and the truck was lumbering away, its upraised dump outlined against a graying sky.

22

PHIL STOPPED THE TRUCK WHEN HE SAW THE NUMBERS 50+00 STENCILED
on the concrete shoulder of the crest road. According to the figures
Janet had relayed to him when he called her from the motel, the
most likely point of failure on the downstream face was between
nineteen and forty-three feet past this point. He climbed down the
ladder from the cab to the ground. He was dressed in the white
coveralls he had found in the garage and a pair of ill-fitting rubber
knee boots. A quarter of a mile away approaching headlights and a
siren told him that one of the police cars had gotten around the pile
of rock.

He climbed over the guardrail and looked down at the face of
the dam, which angled downward at a two-to-one slope into the
shadows and mists far below. The only sound was the thunder from
the bottom of the spillway. In the left distance at the base of the
dam on the other side of the river was the parking lot for the
switchyard and the powerhouse. There were half a dozen cars there
now, including his own. Despite its two flat front tires and its
crumpled front end, the sight of his beloved jalopy was comforting,
a link with his carefree past. His tongue touched the ignition key—
still wedged between his cheek and gum.

The crest of the dam was a thousand and fifty feet above sea
level, the predicted failure point at three seventy-five. He had a
long climb ahead of him. From a distance the face of the dam
looked as smooth as a tabletop—in fact it was composed of rough

chunks of quarried rock measuring several feet on a side that protected the underlying layer of compacted earth from erosion. Phil swung himself over the guardrail, hung for a moment from the edge of the concrete road platform, and dropped five feet to the top of the slope. Above him he heard a car stop and doors open. He clambered downward as quickly as he could without losing his balance.

"Get back up here," a voice shouted, "or you're going to be in a whole shitpot full of trouble!"

"I'm already in a whole shitpot full of trouble," Phil replied, scampering downward across the rocks.

"Stop or I'll shoot!"

Phil stopped. Two policemen were looking down at him from twenty feet above. "You wouldn't shoot a harmless, unarmed engineer. The Chief told you not to shoot without a specific order from him. Aren't you going to follow me? I want you to. I want to show you where the dam is leaking. Then you'll know I'm not the nut you imagine. Well?"

"Son of a bitch. John, radio that he's going down the dam about two hundred yards from the spillway. Send some men to the bottom. I'll chase him down. You stay here in case he doubles back."

The policeman vaulted the rail and dropped to the top of the slope. He cupped his hands to his mouth and shouted at the figure scuttling down the rocks below him. "I'll give you one last chance to stop. If you make me climb all the way down this fucking dam, I'll wring your neck when I catch you."

There was no answer.

Power Control Central was on the line again. "Rancho Seco has to cut back more than we thought," the dispatcher said. "We need forty extra megawatts from Sierra Canyon, not the twenty we asked for earlier."

"No problem," Withers said, filling his voice with confidence, "We got plenty of water here."

Riggs and Cooper had arrived and let themselves into the control room. "Hang on a second," Withers said to the dispatcher. He covered the mouthpiece with his hand and told Riggs and Cooper that Bolen was on his way. "He's really pissed. He wants you to make a visual inspection of the galleries and have a report ready when he gets here."

Riggs, the older and heavier of the two, groaned. "The *lower* galleries?"

Withers nodded. "Gallery D. Look for a dead body. The kid said he saw one. Could be Jeffers. Get going, I've got Power Central on the line."

The mention of Jeffers galvanized Riggs and Cooper. They looked at each other and left for the tunnels on the run.

"Okay," Withers said into the phone, "so you need some extra juice. Forty megawatts? No sweat. Want it in a lump?"

"Feed half onto the line in thirty minutes and the rest thirty minutes later."

"Right. Gotcha."

"Are you having some kind of trouble up there? You said you were going to call me back and you never did."

"Trouble? No trouble. Well, we had a little trouble with one of our employees. Ex-employee, actually. He was sick and I told him to go home but he wouldn't go and started throwing up all over the place and it was a mess around here, I want to tell you! He's gone now and everything is quiet." Withers looked at one of the television screens and narrowed his eyes. A thin line was coming from the half-open door at the end of the turbine deck, a sparkling line like a piece of tinsel. Was that water?

"Good," said the dispatcher. "Glad to hear it. One other thing. We definitely have a frequency problem in the foothills sector of the grid. Could be Sierra Canyon, could be one of the automatic plants downstream. What do you show? Give me the readings for each of your units."

Withers swiveled his chair to the right and glanced at the bank of frequency meters. All arrows were on zero.

"What the goddam hell—?"

"Beg pardon?"

Withers was half out of his chair, leaning toward the dials. "I can't quite see them from here. I'll call you back in a minute. I'll check the graph traces, too, for the last couple of hours."

"Do that."

He hung up and ran to the generator meter bank. He tapped his finger on the glass dial coverings and gave the panel housing a rap with the heel of his hand. Nothing flickered. Every dial within his field of vision indicated zero. "That goddam son of a bitch," he said, running back to his chair. "He must have tripped all the circuit breakers or some damned thing." Cursing, he made a series of connections to try to find out how much of the system was affected. The overhead lights dimmed, then came on more brightly than before as a backup diesel-electric generator in the next room coughed into life. On the television monitor behind him, the silver strand he had seen emerging from the turbine deck doorway grew into a small waterfall that bubbled down the short flight of concrete steps. Through the windows he saw Riggs running toward him shouting and waving his arms.

Phil stood on a flat rock and slowly turned in a small circle. As closely as he could estimate, he was standing on the coordinates that the computer program indicated was the likeliest point of failure. But there was no failure. There was no leak. The sky was light enough now to enable him to examine the face of the dam for a hundred feet in every direction. There wasn't the slightest trace of moisture anywhere. It was as dry as Death Valley.

"Well, shit," Phil said, glancing at the policemen who were working their way toward him from both above and below. "So much for mathematical models." He sank to a sitting position, hit his arms wearily on his knees, and hung his head. He noticed soreness in his legs. Two hours of climbing up and down stairs and ladders, running through tunnels, swimming across lakes, and climbing down dams was having its inevitable effect. He should never have given up jogging.

The policeman who had been chasing him from above arrived first. He stood beside him for a moment catching his breath and looking at him with an expression of revulsion that turned down the corners of his mouth. He said: "I'm Officer Lee Simon, badge one four six three, and I place you under arrest in the name of the Sutterton Police Department. I'm forced by law to caution you that any statement you make can be used against you, and sure as hell will if I have anything to say about it. Couldn't you give yourself up at the top instead of making me climb all the way down here and rip my pants, you goddam cocksucker?"

Phil sighed profoundly. He looked up with misery on his face. "I made you climb down here to show you the leak in the dam. As you can see, there is no leak, which puts me in . . . an unfortunate light. There is an old proverb in the computer industry: 'Garbage in, garbage out.' What that means is—"

Hands landed on each of his shoulders. There were three police-men around him now, the two new arrivals breathing hard and not looking friendly.

"See these?" the first policeman said. "Handcuffs. See this? A nightstick. Put out your hands so I can snap on the cuffs or I will introduce the stick to your head."

"Well put," Phil said, "but handcuffs won't be needed. I give up. I'm sorry I put you to so much trouble."

"I'll bet you are," the policeman said, locking Phil's wrists to-gether. "I'm going to be so sore I won't be able to walk for a week. Let's go."

Phil was pulled to his feet. He winced at the pain he felt in his calves and thighs. "Suppose I go limp," he said. "Would you carry me to the car?"

"Go limp and we'll kick you along the ground like a soccer ball."

At the bottom of the dam they walked in single file along a path formed by the juncture between the embankment and the natural hillside.

"Looking at the dam bathed in the dawn light," Phil said, "you'd never guess it was about to burst apart, would you? It looks im-pregnable."

"Jesus, what a job," one policeman said, ignoring Phil's remarks. "I was going fishing today. Now I'll have to spend hours writing a report on our apprehension of this fucking asshole."

"Appearances can be deceiving," Phil went on. "Fact is, the dam is hemorrhaging. Whether it can be saved by fast action, I don't know, but if the success I'm having in warning people is any indi-cation, I'll lay you eight to five it won't even be here at noon."

"Would you knock it off, kid? Explain yourself in court on Mon-day. We're going to put you in a nice jail. The nicest jail we've got. You can talk about the dam to all the new friends you'll meet there."

"You don't have to put me in jail. It would be a waste of the tax-payers' money. Just drop me off at the bus depot."

"The jail's already there, so we might as well use it."

"You look like intelligent men. All hell is breaking loose inside the dam. The lake is pouring into the inspection galleries right now. Sooner or later it's going to find its way to the downstream face. Start counting minutes then. Instead of hauling me to jail we should all be sounding an alarm."

"Tell it to the judge."

The policeman leading the way warned the others of a muddy patch ahead.

"You can't put me in jail," Phil said in a voice edged with alarm. "I'll be drowned. I haven't done anything. I'm a first offender. I'll never break into a dam again, I promise. I didn't steal anything or cause any damage."

"No damage, eh?" said the policeman behind him, poking him in the shoulder. "You totaled the Chief's cruiser by burying it in rocks, that's all."

"I did? It was an accident. I pushed the wrong button. I was trying to turn on the radio. My God, don't put me in jail now!"

"There's more than when we came up," said the policeman in the lead, jumping over a rivulet. "Shit, my shoes are soaked."

Phil stopped walking. "What's the elevation of the jail? Is it below the inundation line for a catastrophic failure of the dam?" He looked down at the feet of his rubber boots, which had sunk partly out of sight in mud. Crossing the path ahead of him was a stream of brown water several feet wide and an inch or two deep. He traced its course with his eyes to the point where it emerged from the lower edge of the rock blanket on the dam's face. He was poked on the shoulder again by the policeman behind him, who told him to keep moving. Phil stood rooted, looking back and forth from his boots to the dam. His expression changed from desolation to triumph. "Wait a minute! This is it! This is the leak! The dam is failing!" He jumped in the air. "Hallelujah, the dam is failing! I *told* you I wasn't nuts, but you wouldn't listen!" The smile left his face and he slowly covered his mouth with his manacled hands. "Holy God," he said in an awed whisper, "the dam *is* failing!"

He was grabbed by both arms and pushed roughly forward. "Spring water," one of the policemen said. "Lots of springs in the hills this time of year."

"This is no hill, this is a dam," Phil said, trying to twist free. "Spring water is clear, this is muddy." He was being hustled along the path so quickly his feet were barely touching the ground. "You know what's going to happen? The leak is going to get bigger and bigger until there'll be no stopping it. . . . We've got to tell the authorities. . . . Let me go—"

"We are the authorities."

They had arrived at a group of waiting police cars. Phil was thrown into a back seat. He lunged to the far door and tried to open it, but there was no handle. He rolled onto his back and saw Officer Simon pointing his nightstick at him.

"You are going someplace where you can calm down," the policeman said. "If we run into an engineer, we'll tell him we saw a trickle."

"I am an engineer," Phil yelled, "and I'm telling you that that trickle won't be a trickle for long! The town has got to be evacuated! Can't you see that? Are you completely stupid?" He instantly regretted using the word "stupid."

Simon shouldered his way into the car and pushed the end of his nightstick against Phil's upper lip until his head was bent back against the seat. "You run your business and we'll run ours, okay? Yours is trespassing and destroying city property. You're not an engineer as far as I'm concerned. To me you're just one more piece of shit." He twisted the end of the stick slightly and Phil's lip along with it. "Now, either you apologize for what you just said or I'll give you some purple knobs."

"I am sincerely sorry for what I just said."

Simon glowered, then backed out of the car and slammed the door. Phil rolled his face into the upholstery and made no sound during the ten-minute drive to the Sutterton city jail. His feeling of misery derived not only from his failure to convince anyone that a disaster was impending and from his aching legs and smarting lip. When Officer Simon's nightstick was telescoping his nose, he had swallowed his car key and twenty cents.

Janet Sandifer poured herself a glass of orange juice and carried it along with her phone to the dining-room table. She sat down and positioned two sharpened pencils alongside a sheet of paper on which she had made a list of the agencies she would call. First was the State of California. If the highest dam in the country was folding up, the state would surely want to be among the first to know.

Dialing 411 brought the patronizing recorded voice that always infuriated her: "You really can help reduce phone costs by using your directory. If the number you need is not listed, an operator will give it to you. Please make a note of it."

"Why should I make a note of it, you jerk," Janet said, "so I can report dam disasters every day?"

A female voice came on the line. "Directory assistance for what city?"

"Probably Sacramento, but maybe Los Angeles."

"For Sacramento Directory Assistance, dial 916-555-1212."

"I know that. Maybe the state department I want has a branch down here."

"What department is it?"

"I'm not exactly sure. I want to report an imminent dam disaster. An impending dam disaster."

"How do you spell that?"

"Either way it starts with 'I.' Who should get such a report?"

"For state offices beginning with 'I,' I have Immunization and Inheritance Tax."

"How about 'D' for disaster? Doesn't the state have something called a disaster office?"

"'D' as in Donald? I have the Diagnostic School for Neurologically Handicapped Children and the State Board of Dental Examiners."

"I guess I better try Sacramento."

"Is the dam in Sacramento?"

"No. Sacramento is flat. Thanks for your help. I don't know how the phone company gets such good people to work so early in the morning."

"If you are unable to find the state office that you need, dial 916-322-9900."

"That's the state's information number?"

"It's just listed as 'If you are unable to find the state office that you need.'"

"Thanks very much. Jesus Christ."

An operator in Sacramento reminded Janet that most state offices were closed weekends and would not even be open weekdays at five-thirty in the morning.

"There must be somebody open in state government besides yourself."

"A very few."

"Name one."

"Janitorial."

"No good. What else?"

"Emergency."

"That's it! That's it exactly. I've got an emergency to report. A big dam is failing and I thought somebody around there might want to do something about it. Like get out of the way."

"You don't sound serious."

"I'm deadly serious! I'm also exasperated. I've been on the phone for five minutes and still haven't been able to get through to anybody. The biggest dam in the country is in terrible trouble and I can't find out who should be told."

"Well, all right, I'll put you through to the Office of Emergency Services."

"Marvelous."

"There are numbers for radiation hazards, earthquakes, war, and so on."

"Anything! Hurry!"

There was a buzz followed by a deep voice that was clipped and all business. "Emergency Services. Hawkins."

"I'm calling to report a failing dam. Have I reached the right office?"

"Sure have. You're on the oil-spill hot line."

"I can't help that. Sierra Canyon Dam has been breached. Sutterton should be evacuated at once."

"Are you calling from the dam?"

"No, Santa Monica."

"Is this the Southern California Disaster Center?"

"Oh, God. I sometimes think of myself in those terms, yes, but at the moment I'm a private citizen trying to warn you about a leaking dam."

"All dams leak, lady. How did you get on the oil-spill hot line?"

"Would you forget that, for Christ sakes?"

"You're a long way from Sierra Canyon. You had a vivid dream, is that it?"

Janet inhaled and exhaled between clenched teeth before replying. "An engineer at the dam called me and asked me to alert the state. He told me water was breaking into the drainage galleries and that it was only a matter of time before it found its way through the whole embankment."

"It was nice of him to call you. Funny he didn't call us. Or the police."

"He didn't call the police because . . . because the police were calling *him*. Everybody up there has his hands full, don't you see?

The engineer had only time for one call, so he asked me to sound the alarm."

"Sorry, that's not how it's done. I'm not going to order an evacuation and mobilize disaster relief at the suggestion of a housewife in Santa Monica who didn't sleep well. I think you're a practical joker and I ask you nicely to get off the oil-spill hot line."

"I'm not a housewife and I don't give a shit about the oil-spill hot line! You mean you're not going to do anything? What the hell is the Office of Emergency Services for? Wait till the newspapers hear about this!"

"Tell your engineer to notify the local jurisdiction, which in this case would be the Sutterton Police Department or the Caspar County Sheriff's Department. The local jurisdiction will appraise the problem and take the necessary steps, which might include contacting this office to activate the state's warning and coordination functions."

"My engineer didn't notify the local jurisdiction," Janet shouted angrily, "because the local jurisdiction has its head up its ass! As far as *your* ass is concerned, it will be in a sling if you don't do something!"

"I don't appreciate that kind of language from a lady."

"Then you are a sexist pig as well as a schmuck klutz and you can fuck off!"

Janet slammed the receiver down and stormed around her apartment cursing the State of California, the Office of Emergency Services, and the cruel gods that brought Phil Kramer into her life. After several minutes of raging she sat down and dialed the next number on the list, vowing never again to get involved with a man who felt strongly about anything. While listening to the ringing signal, she decided to try a slightly different tack; the plain truth was apparently not persuasive enough.

23

WITHERS WATCHED RIGGS RUN PAST THE CONTROL-ROOM WINDOWS AND stop at the door, fumbling with his keys. The phone rang and he answered it automatically. It was Leonard Mitchell, the contractor.

"Yes, Mr. Mitchell, thanks for returning my call. Would you hang on a second?"

Riggs burst into the room, gasping. "Water . . . water is pouring from the gallery entrance . . . got to shut down. . . . Water is running into the turbine wells. Shut everything down. . . ." He ran to the master panel and started throwing switches. Withers leaped after him and grabbed his arm.

"What are you doing? We can't shut down. . . . I've got to start feeding in an extra forty megawatts—"

"Water . . ."

"What water? What water are you talking about?"

Riggs pointed at the television monitors. "That water. I hope we can save the generators. . . ."

When Withers looked at the screens, it was his turn to gasp. Water a foot deep was surging through the doorway and splashing on the floor of the turbine deck. As he watched, stunned, a horn began to sound rhythmically.

"There goes the warning horn," Riggs said, manipulating the controls that would bring the massive generator rotors to a halt. "Give me a hand, will you?"

"Where's Cooper?"

"In the tunnels to see if he can find where the water's coming from."

Withers swallowed hard. "The dam is failing. That's what Kramer said."

"Look," Riggs said sharply. "Water is coming into the turbine deck, that's all we know. Could be a ruptured discharge line. Could be a crack on the upstream side of the core block, like the one we had five years ago, or in the abutment granite. Could be a dozen things that don't mean the dam is failing. We've got to shut the place down and find out what the problem is. Come on, we've got work to do."

Withers nodded and picked up the phone. "Mr. Mitchell? We need a dozen of your men and some pumps. Got any pumps at your yard across from the south side overlook?"

"A few small ones. How much water have you got? Did I hear something about the dam failing?"

"No, no, nothing is wrong with the dam. Water is coming into the powerhouse, and we've got to get it under control before it damages any equipment. We think what happened is three of our own pumps stopped at the same time. The horn? A warning that something is wrong in the drainage system. We've got water at the rate of—oh, ten cubic feet a second. Can you handle that?"

"I'll round up some men and equipment and be right over. How are you going to pay for this—cost plus fifteen percent, or what? I'll have to bill this out at weekend labor rates, you know."

"Just keep records on everything. Mr. Mitchell, keep this under your hat till we know what we're up against. We don't want a panic."

"I understand. I'm on my way."

Withers showed Riggs the banks of inoperative gauges. Everything relating to sections of the embankment lower in elevation than the generator deck was dead.

"Christ," Riggs said, grimacing, "that really puts us in the dark. No way of telling what's going on. Water must have gotten into the utility conduits and shorted everything out."

They were interrupted by Cooper, who was red-faced and puffing and whose clothes were drenched. "I got as far as the centerline intersection," he said, collapsing into a chair. "Lights went out, so I came back. Couldn't tell if the water was coming from the intake tower or the lower gallery stairwell. Could the lower tunnels be flooded and the stairwell, too? Doesn't seem possible."

Riggs pulled a set of engineering drawings from a rack and spread them on a table. He turned the sheets until he came to a cross-section of the embankment that included the intake tower. "I'll bet the kid did something when he was running around loose. Maybe when he was in the tower he managed to open one of the bulkhead doors and let the lake in."

"That might be it," Cooper said, nodding, then shaking his head in dismay. "If it is, we'll have to lower the reservoir to the level of the bulkhead to get it closed. That'll take a week. The water districts and the P. G. & E. will love it."

"We'll look like a bunch of fucking clowns." Withers groaned. "Especially me."

"Can you stop the goddam horn?" Cooper asked. "It's driving me nuts."

Withers cut the horn circuit. A heavy silence settled over the control room. With power production stopped and the generators stilled, there was not even the customary electrical hum. "Well," he said, looking at the other two men, "do you think we should tell the Sheriff and the Chief of Police we've got a crisis on our hands?"

"Not yet," Riggs said. "Maybe with Mitchell's pumps we can dry everything up and keep the whole thing quiet."

"How are we going to keep it quiet," Cooper said, "when we've shut the plant down? I think we should assume the worst."

"Call Roshek," Riggs suggested, "and ask him what he wants us to do."

"Not me," Withers said. "I'm not going to let him chew my ass out."

"Call Bolen, then."

"He's in his plane on his way here to take charge of Kramer."

Riggs walked to the door. "Turn on the phones in the offices. I'll call the air communications center in Oakland and see if they can reach Bolen by radio."

"Let's call the police, too, just in case," Cooper said.

Riggs disagreed, insisting that it should be Bolen's decision.

When Riggs was out of the room, Cooper again urged Withers to alert the police. "We should start lowering the reservoir, too," he said.

"You want me to drop the spillway gates? Not unless somebody tells me to with more authority than you. There's two feet of water going over the top now. If I drop the gates, there will be twenty-two feet. That would cause a good-sized flood all by itself. It would take out Sutterton's Main Street Bridge, for starters. Let's see what Bolen says. If we can't get through to him, then we'll decide."

Cooper jumped to his feet and strode to the door. "I'm not going to sit here twiddling my thumbs. I'm going to drive around outside and look things over. If I see anything that isn't a hundred percent normal, Newt, I'm sounding an alarm whether you guys want me to or not. Piss on the company's reputation."

The phone rang. Withers answered it while waving goodbye to Cooper. On the line was Bill Hawkins of the Office of Emergency Services in Sacramento.

Hawkins said with a trace of amusement in his voice, "We just had a call from a woman in Santa Monica who said that the dam you have there is busting up. Now where do you suppose she got an idea like that? Hello? Are you there?"

"A woman from where said what?"

"A woman from Santa Monica said poor old Sierra Canyon Dam is on its last legs. A friend of hers, she said, called her from there and told her that water was coming in on all sides. Just a crackpot, eh? Thought I'd give you a jingle anyway. Amazing, the rumors that get started."

Withers whistled. "Kramer must have gotten to a phone. . . ."

"Come again?"

"We had a nut up here a while ago and we had to call the cops on him. He must have a girl friend who's trying to make us look bad."

"So everything's okay? Water is not coming in on all sides?"

"No, just into the powerhouse."

"Just into the powerhouse. Water is coming into the power-house." Hawkins repeated the words slowly, as if he were laying them on a table for examination.

"We've got a flow that may not be normal. A crew is on its way to check it out. We've shut the plant down."

"If enough water is coming in so that you've had to shut the plant down, it sure as hell is not normal. Say, I'm glad I called! This is only the Office of Emergency Services. I suppose if your dam is dissolving we'll hear about it on the eleven o'clock news."

"We are having a problem, that I grant you, but we don't think it is serious. We'll know in a few minutes. I'll call you. I know the emergency procedures. Your number is on a list we have posted on the wall, just after the local jurisdictions."

"Yes, leave us not forget the local jurisdictions."

"Excuse me, I've got a call on the other line. Be talking to you."

On the other line was an irate dispatcher from Power Control Central.

"What's wrong up there? We just got a big drop in frequency. Are you ready to start feeding in the extra power? Why didn't you call back with those readings?"

"I was just going to. Say, about that extra power. We've got some percolation—well, it's more than percolation; it's an actual flow—coming into the turbine bays and we've had to shut down the plant. That explains the drop in frequency."

"You've *what*? My God, for how long?"

"Don't know. We've got to pump out the drainage galleries before we can find out what the problem is."

"Is the dam in danger?"

"Oh, hell, no. Oh, shit, no. Listen, soon as I get a report I'll get right back to you."

"If you aren't back on stream in thirty minutes, we're going to have one hell of a brownout."

"Thirty days is more like it."

"You're kidding! Tell me you're kidding!"

Withers hung up and took the next call. The monitor showed that the flow into the turbine deck had slacked off. Maybe the leak or rupture was self-clogging.

"Newt? This is Luby Pelletier over at the Butte County Disaster Office in Oroville. Remember me? We met last year at the Public Safety Conference."

"Yes, Luby, I remember."

"How is everything up your way this fine day?"

"Wonderful, terrific. Say, would you mind—"

"The dam isn't falling apart or anything, is it?"

"Well . . ."

"We just got a weird call from a woman in Santa Monica—"

"Jesus! She must be calling everybody in the whole goddam state!"

"You know her? She said she was a psychic who just had a vision of Sierra Canyon disappearing and swarms of people running naked into the woods. Who is she?"

"We don't know, exactly. A friend of hers used to work here."

"I guess that's how she knew so much about the dam. She mentioned the intake shaft, the drainage tunnels, stuff like that. Came to her in a flash of light, she said. I could hardly keep from laughing."

"Look, Luby . . ."

"She said predicting the future was her main gift and that she had a special fondness for disasters. The big stuff. I told her I didn't put much stock in that bullshit, but that I'd check out what she said."

"As it turns out, we do have a small problem. At least, we hope it's small." Withers kept his eyes on the television screen. The flow seemed to be increasing again.

"Of course, I didn't actually say 'bullshit.' People who claim they can see the future have terrible batting averages. One lucky guess for every five hundred misses. Nobody remembers the misses."

"Luby, I'm awful busy and I'm going to hang up. We may have to evacuate the town." From the other side of the lobby, Riggs was nodding to him and holding up a phone. Apparently he was getting through to Bolen.

"Look at the philosophical pickle it puts you in," Luby Pelletier rattled on, chuckling. "If you foresee something, you can make sure it doesn't happen. So what was it you foresaw? See what I mean?" He paused, then added, "What did you say about evacuating the town?"

"I'll call you later. Don't make any plans for today."

As Withers took the next call—the phone rang the instant he hung up—Riggs shouted to him over the intercom that air traffic controllers had located Bolen in his plane over Fresno. Withers acknowledged the news with a wave. Lee Simon was on the phone.

"Your friend Kramer led us on a merry chase," the policeman said, "but we've got him under lock and key now."

"Great. Keep him out of everybody's hair till my boss gets here."

"Did he wreck anything inside the dam?"

"We don't know yet. He may have opened some valves. We've had to shut the plant down while we check things out."

"Yeah? That skinny son of a bitch is a good argument for police brutality. Say, Newt, we saw a wet spot at the bottom of the dam a while ago. Thought I better mention it to you. A spring, probably. Been raining a lot lately."

"A wet spot? Where?" Like the caress of a feather, goose bumps advanced across Withers's shoulders.

"About a hundred yards from the riverbank on the north side. Your friend Kramer got all excited when he saw it, but he gets excited about everything."

"Is it just a wet spot or is there a flow of water?"

"Sort of a trickle. About as much as you see in the gutter when somebody up the block is washing a car. Think it means anything?"

"Cooper is in his car right now. I'll call him on the radio and have him take a look. Lee, are you at home? I know you worked all night, but don't go to bed yet. I got a horrible feeling we've got big trouble. Stay by the phone and I'll call you back."

Withers got on the radio, reached Cooper, who was on his way to check the gauges in the tailrace valve house, and directed him to a vantage point next to the switchyard parking lot. Withers's phone was ringing again, but before answering it he jotted down the names of people he had promised to call back.

"Powerhouse, Withers speaking."

"This is the news desk of the Sacramento *Bee*. We're tracking down a rumor that Sierra Canyon Dam has been mined by former members of the Iranian Secret Police. According to our source, the blasts are set to go off in thirty minutes and Sutterton should be evacuated."

"Is your source a woman in Santa Monica?"

"You know her? Anything to what she says?"

"I'll call you back."

Cooper's voice came over the radio loudspeaker announcing that he had arrived at the overlook.

Withers leaned into his microphone. "Can you see the toe of the slope from where you are? On the north side? See anything odd?"

"What am I looking for?"

"A wet spot. A trickle of water about a hundred yards up from the riverbank. Look along the seam between the natural ground and the toe of the riprap."

"I've got a clear view, but that's a quarter of a mile away. Let me put the glasses on it."

In the silence that followed, Withers drummed the side of his fist lightly against the counter top at a rate that matched his heartbeat.

He glanced at the wall clock and saw that it was ten minutes after seven. Riggs came through the control-room door and began to report on the conversation he had had with Bolen, then froze at the sound of Cooper's voice on the radio:

"A boil-out, Newt . . . Jesus God, must be five hundred or a thousand cubic feet a second. . . . We've lost her, we've lost the whole goddam thing. . . . Christ God Almighty, the dam is a goner. . . ."

III

The Failure

24

HERMAN BOLEN HAD A PAIN IN THE ASS. HE SHIFTED AROUND IN THE contoured seat of his handmade airplane to center the bulk of his weight on his left buttock. That helped the pain in his ass but intensified the pain in his neck. The heat in the cockpit remained constant. He peeled off his Eddie Rickenbacker goggles and scarf and used them to fan his perspiring face. Through the side window he gazed dully at the blanket of fog that filled the Central Valley. The sun was above the Sierra Nevadas now and the reflected light was blinding.

To take his mind off his discomfort, he tried to calculate his precise position. His ground speed was approximately two hundred and fifty miles per hour. . . . The last checkpoint was . . . The wind speed and bearing was . . . In thirty seconds he realized that his mind had dropped the numbers and equations and once again had settled on the pain in his ass. He was somewhere around Fresno, that was close enough. At least he was five thousand feet *above* Fresno and not actually down *in* Fresno, which was something to be thankful for. He was seized with the wish to be elsewhere, anywhere but in his sickeningly expensive toy five thousand feet above Fresno. Immersed in a hot tub, perhaps, while his ample belly was kneaded by the jets of a Jacuzzi, or spread-eagled on a nude beach in Brazil.

Five years—five years!—he had spent designing and building a personal airplane with the help of friends who were engineers, mechanics, orthopedists, and pilots, and still it wasn't right. It was, in fact, a torture chamber. The chair, the cockpit, the whole plane had been designed around the size, shape, and weight of his body— that's where the dream broke down. The plane was perfect, but his body had failed to adhere to its original specifications. You can let the seams out of a suit, but not a plane. The plane was tailor-made for a Herman Bolen who no longer existed. The seat was a precision fit for a memory.

"Aircraft N nine seven three zero seven, this is Oakland Center. Can you read me?"

Bolen was so lost in thought that the voice on the radio didn't register. His mind wandered over the thousands of hours he had spent in his home workshop fussing with Posa injectors, chromemoly tubing, cadmium-plated tie rods, and the custom-built power plant that could hurl the plane through the sky at two hundred and ninety miles an hour. Never mind maneuverability, he wanted *speed*. Of course it couldn't reach two hundred and ninety now because the weight of his own body had drifted so far beyond the design assumptions.

"N nine seven three zero seven, Oakland Center. Can you read? Over."

Maybe he should start over. Use an Emeraude fuselage with slotted Frise ailerons and Fowler flaps. That would catch the eyes of the ladies at the meets and rallies. If only his *own* fuselage looked a little racier and had a lower fat content. Any flashing female eyes his plane attracted tended to be turned away by the pear-shaped blob that struggled out of the cockpit. Cosmetic surgery was a possibility. He would look into it. Maybe he could find a quack who did tummy tucks on a truly gigantic scale.

Something in the back of Bolen's mind nagged him. He picked up his microphone. "Excuse me, Oakland Center. Did you say N nine seven three zero seven? I read you."

"We have a call from Sierra Canyon Dam."

"Can you patch through a direct line?"

"No, but I can relay both sides of a conversation."

Bolen hesitated. If there was an emergency, did he want everyone at Oakland Center to know about it as well as all the ham operators who happened to be tuned in? Withers was such an idiot he probably wouldn't have the sense to speak indirectly. "Tell him to call me on the telephone through the mobile operator."

"Do they have your number?"

"I don't want to give it out on the air. Tell him it's listed in the company directory under my name."

Bolen looked at his watch, wondering if the message had to do with Jeffers, Kramer, or the dam itself. It had to be something serious if they couldn't wait another forty-five minutes for him to get there. His sweep second hand made four revolutions. At exactly five minutes before seven a buzzer sounded on his instrument panel.

"Herman Bolen here."

"This is Burt Riggs, Mr. Bolen, one of the maintenance engineers at Sierra Canyon. We seem to—"

"Did you find Jeffers? Did you check Gallery D?"

"We couldn't reach Gallery D. Water is flowing out of the access tunnel into the turbine wells. It may be that the lower galleries are flooded. Jeffers might have got caught down there."

As he listened to the description of the incoming water, the inoperative meters, and the plant shutdown, the goggles and scarf slipped from his hand to the floor. Before Riggs finished, Bolen cut him off.

"Have you told the police Sutterton has to be evacuated?"

"No, we thought we'd better let you decide that."

"Jesus Christ, man, how much evidence do you need? Can't you see how everything ties together? I think the core block has been breached. Listen to me. What you do in the next few minutes could save a thousand lives. Call the police, the Sheriff, the county disaster headquarters, and the State Office of Emergency Services—the numbers are on the wall—and tell them there's a possibility we could lose the dam. Bypass as much water as you can around the turbines from the penstocks directly into the outlet works. Drop the spillway gates."

"Withers says that will cause pretty heavy flooding—"

"I don't care what Withers says! Do what I tell you!"

"Yes, sir. Mr. Bolen, I can see the television monitors from where I'm sitting and it looks like a crew from Mitchell Brothers has arrived in the parking lot with pumps."

"If you can get rid of the water faster than it's coming in, fine—that will let you into the tunnels to find the source. Maybe we'll get some good luck and find a leak that can be plugged. A quick-setting chemical grout might work. . . . Get Mitchell's opinion. But if the embankment is breached it's probably all over. Are you listen-

ing? Put at least six men on the downstream face to look for signs
of water. If a boil-out occurs, I want everybody out of the tunnels.
If you have to abandon the powerhouse, take every monitoring record with you that you can find, because when this is over we're
going to have to figure out what went wrong."

Bolen made Riggs repeat the instructions, then broke the connection. He gazed once more through the side window. The fog below
him looked soft and firm enough to lie down on and go to sleep. In
the far distance to the northwest he could make out the rounded
tops of Mount Hamilton and Mount Diablo; to the right was the
snow-covered backbone of the Sierra Nevadas. The vault of blue
sky that arched from horizon to horizon was cloudless and clear. It
was a magnificent spectacle, but cold and remote, like the view of a
planet from an orbiting spacecraft. The steady roar of the engine
was comforting; it was an engine so finely tuned it brought a glow
of appreciation to the face of every mechanic who heard it. At the
controls of his handcrafted machine Bolen felt isolated from the
concerns of the human race, which at this altitude seemed not to
exist, and he wished he could stay there forever.

Dapper Dr. Dulotte eased his station wagon around the huge
truck that was inexplicably parked on top of the dam. Before reaching the far side he had to slow down again, this time to follow the
hand signals of a policeman. A wrecker was extracting a police car
from a pile of gravel.

"What happened, Officer?" he said, rolling down a window.

"No stopping," the policeman replied curtly, waving him on.

The road left the dam and gained several hundred feet in elevation before joining the county road at a T intersection. Dulotte nodded in satisfaction when he saw the arrows and signs marking the
entrance of the trail into the woods. The Route Committee had
done its jobs well. Only the most thickheaded and delirious runners
would lose their way. He parked. It was 7:20. The race would start
at 8:00, and about an hour or so after that, if everything went according to plan, his boy, Kent Spain, would be the first to cross the
dam and disappear into the woods. He'd be reeling and ready to
quit, Dulotte imagined, but the scent of money would drive him on.

From the back of the station wagon he dragged a three-wheeled
pushcart called the Dulotte Trail-Barrow, the rights to which he
was close to selling to the State Department of Parks and Recrea-

tion, not to mention the Forest Service and the Bureau of Mines. Into it he loaded a collapsible table, a director's chair, four five-gallon bottles of water, a clipboard, a pad of record-keeping forms, a stopwatch, a first aid kit, a crate of oranges, and a lunch bucket. Ten minutes later he was striding briskly through the woods on the wide, well-defined trail, the cart rolling along ahead of him. He smiled appreciatively at the pines, the moss on the rocks, and the wild flowers on the open slopes. Drifting to his ears from the distance were the meaningless sounds of sirens and church bells.

The T-shirt was still on the branch. Behind it the bicycle was ready to go. Dulotte strode on, humming "The Impossible Dream." Even though the trail was level and the cart offered little resistance, he was soon panting. He pinched the flab around his middle and shook his head. He really should start working out.

In Stockton, a hundred miles south of the dam, Emil Hasset admired himself in the mirror before leaving for work. He tugged at the visor of his cap until it was square on his head, straightened the tie around his short thick neck, and patted his holstered gun. Behind him in one of the twin beds, his son Freddy watched sullenly. Emil turned around and spread his arms. "How do I look?"

"Same as ever," said his son. "Stupid."

Emil laughed. "Is that any way to talk to your father?"

Freddy Hasset rolled and faced the wall, the gray sheets falling away from his mottled back. "Valley Transfer uniforms make everybody look stupid. That's what you always say. Loomis guards look snappy, which is something else you always say. I think they look just as stupid. Why anybody would work as a cop or a guard is beyond me."

"The need to eat drives people to do crazy things. You'll find out when you stop sponging off me." He put his hand on the doorknob, looking at the bed. "Shouldn't you be getting ready to go to the airport? To warm up the plane and so on?"

"Plenty of time."

"Don't talk with a blanket in your mouth. How many times have I told you that? I'd feel better if you were up and showing a little pep. This is a big day for us."

"Lay off, Pop. I said I'd go through with it and I will. My word is good."

"That's a change for the better. Okay, see you later. In the wild blue yonder."

Phil Kramer clamped his hands around the bars of his cell door. A short distance away, Night Sergeant Jim Martinez sat at his desk doing paperwork, a task which, judging from his expression, left him less than thrilled.

"Let me out of here," Phil shouted, rattling the door. "This is an emergency! Let us all out! Every minute counts!"

"Shut up," somebody said behind him.

Phil looked over his shoulder. There were four cots in the cell, three of them filled with blanket-covered lumps. From one extended a bare leg so scrawny and wizened it looked like a stick of beef jerky. "I will not shut up," he said, addressing the cots. "I am trying to save your necks as well as mine." He turned to Martinez. "Maybe you weren't paying attention to what I was saying when I was dragged in here, so I will run through it again. I am a worldrenowned authority on dam failures. Ask anybody. I have just finished inspecting Sierra Canyon Dam. That's the one you can see out the window, Sergeant, if you'd care to look."

"Shut up," the voice behind him said again. Similar sentiments could be heard from other cells.

"Listen to what I'm saying, everybody," Phil said, rattling the door again. "The dam is failing. Tunnels inside of it are filling with water. . . . I saw it happening with my own eyes. A leak has started on the downstream face. You know what that means? It means that a great big lake is going to come crashing down on our heads, because once water finds its way through an embankment you can kiss it goodbye."

"Hey, we're trying to get some sleep," a gravelly voice said.

From an adjoining cell: "Pipe down, would you please?"

A third voice: "But what if the dam did break? We'd be trapped in here like rats." To which somebody replied, "Don't call me a rat, you motherfucker."

"Exactly," Phil said. "We'd be trapped in here like rats. The water is going to keep boring a bigger and bigger hole until it cuts a slot all the way to the top. Then *splooey!* That's what happened to Baldwin Hills in 1963 and Teton in 1976."

At the door of the cell opposite Phil's, a prisoner appeared dressed in a business suit decorated with dried vomit. "Hey, Martinez," he said with an air of exasperation, "can't you do something about this guy? There are people here with some very serious hangovers."

Sergeant Martinez sighed, put down his pencil, and got to his feet. He walked down the corridor and studied Phil, standing just beyond arm's reach. "This is an emergency," Phil said to him. "You've got to get us out of here and yourself as well. Turn us loose on the street if you have to—otherwise we're dead ducks."

There was a crash that made him turn around. A giant of a man with a protruding belly and a tangle of long blond hair had gotten out of one of the cots, knocking it over along with a cardboard box that served as a bedside table. He took two strides and dropped a huge hand on Phil's chest, gathered the front of his coveralls into a fist, and lifted him off the floor. His breath smelled of garlic, tobacco, chocolate, marijuana, whiskey, beer, stale air, and feedlots. "I thought I told you to shut up," he said.

"Put him down, Haystack," Martinez said. "I'll handle this."

The man called Haystack glared at Phil from a distance of two inches, then released him. He righted his cot and fell on it, almost instantly snoring.

"Kramer, you got to knock off this crap about the dam," Martinez said. "Everybody is getting all excited. We could have a riot."

"Good! That might help. I'm trying to save our skins."

"There are several things I could do," Martinez said thoughtfully. "I could transfer you over to the county jail where they got isolation cells. I could knock you out with a club. I could have Haystack force-feed you some little pills we keep on hand for troublemakers."

The phone on Martinez's desk rang.

"The dam is failing," Phil said.

"The dam is not failing. If the dam was failing, I would hear about it."

"The dam is failing," Phil said.

"I'm going to answer the phone," Martinez said. "When I get back, unless you have stopped talking and let these good people go back to sleep, I'm going to say a certain code word that makes Haystack go wild. Think about it."

Haystack stopped snoring and sat up on the edge of his cot. He needed a shave and his eyes weren't in focus. "If I strangled the turd," he said, "it would be justifiable homicide. The Governor would invite me to brunch."

Martinez walked back to his desk and picked up the phone. Phil watched the expression on his face change as he said, "Yeah? It is? Now? We are? No bull? You mean everybody? Are you sure? Right. Okay. Christ." He hung up slowly.

"What is it?" Phil shouted. "What's happening?"

Martinez ran his fingers through his hair and shook his head. "They think the dam might go out," he said. "A school bus is on its way to pick us all up." He pushed a button that set off an ear-shattering alarm bell.

Phil grinned at his cellmate. "Pack your bags, Haystack, we're getting out of this joint."

25

THE BEGINNING OF THE MOTHER LODE MARATHON WAS AN ELBOW-TO-elbow melee. At the crack of the starter's pistol, nearly fifteen hundred people surged forward, a fantastic, colorful swarm of arms, legs, and bobbing heads. Kent Spain was in the group of fifty top seeds who were given priority positions at the front, but once the race was under way he felt just as engulfed by humanity as he would have in the rear with the weekenders, school kids, geriatrics, and maniacs in wheelchairs. He hated the dilettantes, even though he knew they were the reason Dr. Dulotte could pay so handsomely for corruption. The sheer weight of their numbers, added to their clumsiness, ignorance, and enthusiasm, was a threat to the serious runner's life and limb. You never knew when one of the goddam fools was going to collapse under your feet or run up the back of your legs. Once early in his career, Kent Spain lost three minutes by absentmindedly following some creep off the marked course into a weed patch where the guy stopped, squatted, and took a shit.

The first couple of miles was more like a steeplechase than a cross-country run, a process of jumping over barking dogs, dodging dropouts who were walking back to their cars with ashen faces, and watching for chances to pass the scores of puffing laggards. For several hundred yards he matched strides with a long-legged, black-haired young woman who had the number 38 pinned to her bulging shirt. He reluctantly gave up the view by passing her. "Is the thirty-eight a measurement of anything?" he asked as he went by.

"Yeah," she answered without looking at him, "it's the caliber of the gun I carry."

At the two-mile mark, where the course left the highway and entered an expanse of grazing land below towering outcroppings of rock, the runners were strung out in single file about fifteen feet apart. Kent was never able to catch sight of all those ahead of him, but he guessed there were at least a dozen. In the next thirteen miles he would have to pass every one of them, for if Dulotte's plan was to work he would have to be first across the dam. Most of the competition would probably fold on Cardiac Hill at the ten-mile mark, if not before. Only two runners figured to be trouble—Tom Ryan, immediately ahead of him, and Nabih Yousri of Ethiopia, a world-class marathoner who had entered at the last minute. If Yousri was following his usual strategy, Kent thought, he was probably already in the lead, his bald black head glistening in the sun like a polished eight ball and his sinewy legs flicking back and forth like licorice whips. His policy was to start fast and hang on at the end to win. Passing him would take a maximum effort.

Ryan was a different kind of runner, a crafty calculator with a great finishing kick. Trailing Ryan and letting him set the pace was a sure way of getting a good time, but it was no way to win, because in the last thousand yards nobody in the world could keep up with him, much less pass him.

With steady effort, Kent pulled to within five feet of Ryan. After half a mile of lockstep, he pulled up on his heels and said, "Honk, honk."

Ryan, unworried, moved to the left edge of the trail and glanced at Spain as he went by. "What's the hurry? Still early in the day."

"Gotta catch a plane."

"Crazy. You know better. You'll burn out."

"Maybe."

In the next seven miles Kent passed ten runners, none of whom he knew, who were showing the effects of the blistering early pace. It was a pace far faster than he had ever taken himself, and he felt twinges in his calves and an ominous tightness in his midsection. He should have trained harder, especially at the fifteen-mile distance. What he had to do in this race was expend ninety-five percent of his strength over a course eleven miles shorter than he was accustomed to. Only if he succeeded would he reach the bicycle first.

Cardiac Hill was a mile-long grade that led to a ridge overlooking Warren Lake. It was the best place to catch Yousri, for at the top, where the trail curved right, there was a two-mile level stretch that was ideal for the Ethiopian. Yousri wouldn't expect to be challenged on the most punishing section of the course.

Kent spent a few seconds at the ten-mile checkpoint and aid station at the bottom of the grade. As he sponged off his face and neck with cold water, he asked the man behind the table how many were ahead of him.

"Four," the man answered, handing him a paper cup. "Yousri's in the lead, about a minute and a half ahead of you."

"I'm going to catch him." He drained the paper cup, then spat out a mouthful of green liquid. "God, Gatorade! Don't dish out that sweet shit this early . . . gimme some water." He drank the water while picking up speed and entering the shade of the woods. The trail rose cruelly through tall evergreens. He felt a definite soreness in his calves. The tightness he had noticed earlier in his stomach was becoming a palpable knot. He drove his legs hard, setting his internal metronome to a tempo better suited to a sprint than to a marathon.

"You can do it, old buddy," he said, addressing his body in a strained whisper. "Come through for me one more time, just one more time. I know it's tough, oh, it's tough, then we'll take a long rest, just the two of us. No, don't tell me to stop, no, no, no. Think of the money. Money, money, money. Push, push, push, push . . ." He timed the words to the impact of his shoes on the ground.

Five hundred yards from the top of the slope he had passed everybody but Yousri, who was still not in sight. The first runner he went by was sitting on a rock gasping; the second fought him briefly, stride for stride, before yielding and falling back; the third was almost standing still, taking tiny, shuffling steps. Kent put Yousri out of his mind temporarily while he concentrated on breaking through "the wall," that half-physical, half-psychological barrier that stood in the way of a peak performance. Never before had he encountered the wall so early in a race. His calves were red-hot pokers and his stomach a mass of cables stretched to the breaking point. It was the worst he had ever experienced, and the thought came to him that if he didn't pull up and walk for a while, he might hurt himself seriously, possibly even die of a heart attack. He kept on going, refusing to listen to his body. The secret was to ignore the pain and keep on ignoring it until the body gave up sending pain signals and unlocked its secret stores of energy.

"Push, push, push," he muttered, his teeth and fists clenched, "money, money, money, money."

Behind him he heard footsteps getting closer and closer. He turned for a quick backward glance and saw a blond teenager approaching at what seemed to be fifty miles an hour, with legs working effortlessly and only a faint trace of sweat on his arms and face. On his chest was the number 1027, which meant that he was unrated. Kent lowered his head and drove himself forward, trying to find something extra to beat off the threat of a goddam kid who looked like he was running after somebody who stole his surfboard. The kid sailed past him, then eased up and let Kent draw even.

"Excuse me, sir," 1027 said, scarcely breathing hard, "where's Cardiac Hill?"

Kent Spain's face was a mixture of agony and loathing. "At the top . . . of this slope . . . the trail swings left," he said in a desperate effort to rid himself of a new menace, "through a field of ferns. Half a mile more . . . you'll see an International House of Pancakes. That's the start of Cardiac Hill." It was hard to talk. He couldn't seem to get enough air in his lungs.

"Thanks a lot," the teenager said, pulling away. He looked back with sympathy and added, "Hang in there, old-timer, you'll make it."

Two minutes later Kent labored to the narrow, tree-studded grassland on the top of the ridge and followed the trail to the right. The area called Fern Gardens was on his left, and on a hillside beyond it he could see number 1027 striding powerfully along a path that Kent knew led only to an abandoned ranger station.

Feeling pleasure for the first time since the race began, Kent let out his own stride. Through the trees and below he caught glimpses of the lake. Rounding a curve, he almost stumbled over Nabih Yousri, who was down on one knee tying his shoe. The African jumped up and bounded away like a frightened jackrabbit, his legs showing the springiness for which they were famous. Kent smiled grimly and shifted into his highest gear. He didn't have a devastating kick, but he could sustain a fast pace for a short distance, especially at twelve miles out rather than twenty-six. Lashing himself with the fury of a madman, he gradually closed the gap.

Yousri wouldn't yield the right-of-way. When Kent tried to pass on the right, Yousri moved to the right. When Kent moved left, Yousri moved left.

"Let me pass, goddammit. . . ."

"No pass," Yousri said. "Not right for you. You poop out."

"Let me by!"

"No. Stay back. You thank me later."

"Move over, you goddam freak foreigner fag!"

The black man's reply was to quicken his pace and try to draw away. Kent Spain, teeth clenched and a maniacal look on his face, matched him step for step. For two hundred yards they ran in synchrony within three feet of each other. It was a draining duel witnessed only by the passing trees and shrubs, and both men knew that if they kept it up for very long they would collapse and be passed by the trailing herd. Kent fastened his eyes on the shoes ahead of him that were snapping back and forth like the pendulum of a high-speed clock. Timing his move nicely, he leaned forward and slapped one sideways so that it caught on the back of the opposite ankle. The great Nabih Yousri, a well-oiled running machine feared throughout the world, crashed to the ground in an explosion of twigs, pebbles, and incomprehensible curses.

At last, at mile thirteen, Kent Spain was in the lead. He was running downhill now through a hillside of scrub oak and manzanita toward the crest of the dam. In a few minutes he would emerge from the woods at the right overlook . . . provided he hadn't overexerted himself. He felt dizzy. The ground was undulating like the floor of a fun house. A roaring filled his ears. His mouth was hanging open and he was sucking and blowing air like a steam locomotive.

A persistent knocking woke Theodore Roshek, who had fallen asleep in the chair beside his bed. The door opened and Mrs. Bolen put her head into the room. "Theodore? There's a call for you from Sierra Canyon. A Mr. Withers. You can take it on the bedside phone."

Roshek listened to Withers with disbelief and rising alarm, and he pressed him for details. "How much water is coming through? Have you seen it yourself?"

"No, but I just got a radio report from one of our maintenance engineers who estimates it at five hundred or a thousand second-feet." Withers hesitated, then added, "He thinks the dam is lost. I thought I better call you. Your wife told me where you were."

Roshek exploded. "Are you bulldozing rock into the breach upstream and down? Have you dropped the spillway gates? Have you told the police?"

"We've dropped the gates and the police are evacuating the town, but as for bulldozers—well, there just isn't anybody here yet who knows exactly what to do. Mr. Bolen is on his way, but Mr. Jeffers is, we think—well, dead."

"Where's Kramer?"

"Who?"

"Kramer! The engineer who's been trying to tell us something was wrong. . . ."

"In jail. Locked up."

"Unlock him."

"Unlock him?"

"Who else around there knows more about what's going on than he does? Maybe he has some more smart ideas."

Roshek hung up and dialed Creekwood. Eleanor was in danger. If the unthinkable happened and the dam . . . was it possible? Images of well-engineered dams that had failed crowded into his mind—St. Francis and Baldwin Hills in California alone, Malpassant in France, Vega de Tera in Spain, Teton in Idaho. In 1963 a landslide into the reservoir formed by Vaiont Dam in Italy sent a wave of such size down the valley that the town of Longarone was destroyed with a loss of twenty-five hundred lives. The catastrophes were as vivid to him as the anguish suffered by the responsible engineers, many of whom were his friends. "Acts of God," "standard industry practice," "inescapable unknowns"—phrases like these came up over and over in the inquiries that followed every disaster. Certainly it was impossible to eliminate every unknown and pin down every variable; certainly nature was capable of dreadful surprises, and yet . . . Roshek couldn't help feeling that if a man paid enough attention to detail, if he had enough strength of character to resist compromise, then— A busy signal told him that the phone was still off the hook. Eleanor was either asleep or had forgotten to hang up the phone when she arose.

Could Sierra Canyon Dam fail? Was the secret contempt he held for designers of inadequate structures to be turned around and applied to himself? Perhaps the extent of the downstream leak was exaggerated. It was hard to estimate turbulent flow. Maybe it was in the order of a hundred second-feet instead of a thousand, in which case it might be possible to stop the unraveling of the embankment. If it wasn't, then no force on earth could stop the inevitable, and the name of Theodore Roshek would be attached forever not to dreams but to nightmares.

With the dam destroyed, Eleanor would be even more important to him than she was now. Her beauty, her ability to create beauty, and the sweetness of her affection for him, these things and these alone would make life worth living. He would go to her and warn her of the danger. When she saw that he went to her before the dam, that he put her above the technical achievement that in many ways defined his life, her affection would surely turn to love.

He dialed the number of Carlos Hallon, the corporation's pilot. There was enough time to reach Creekwood even in the worst possible case. Most of the ten miles of canyon between the dam and the house was rough and twisting. The water would be carrying a heavy load of silt and debris and would advance at no more than ten to fifteen miles an hour. If the dam held out for at least an hour and a half—a conservative estimate in view of the density of the embankment and the presence of the massive concrete core block—then he could reach Eleanor well before—

"Carlos? Theodore. We've got an emergency in northern California and you've got to get me there as fast as possible. Is the Lear ready to go? I'm leaving for the airport immediately. It'll take me longer than you, so I want you to arrange for a helicopter to meet us at the Yuba City airport. . . ."

Roshek slipped from the chair to the floor and, by using his hands, scuttled across the room to the closet. He pulled on his trousers while lying on his back.

"Marilyn," he called to Bolen's wife, "get dressed. You've got to take me to the airport. . . ."

26

PLUMP, GRAY-HAIRED, AND SWEET-FACED, GIVEN TO GRANNY GLASSES and sensible shoes, Elizabeth Lehmann looked more like a spokesperson for a line of frozen pies than Caspar County Disaster Control Officer, but such she was and proud of it. She threw off the robe she was wearing when the call came from the Sheriff, and hurriedly put on the black slacks, the blue blouse with the bow, and the black jacket with the wide lapels. All dark colors that never looked soiled, all half polyester to hold a crease. If the dam did fail, she might not get back home for days and she didn't want to look like a frump. Getting men to accept orders from a woman was as much a matter of *looking* as it was *acting* businesslike and professional.

In the bathroom she attacked her hair and face with a deft efficiency born to forty years' experience, then swept everything on the counter into an overnight bag. Her mind raced as she ran to the kitchen for last-second fortifications from the refrigerator. Now she would find out if all those practice sessions paid off. Once a month she forced grumbling local officials to spend an afternoon in the Operations Room of the Disaster Office reacting to hypothetical atomic explosions, chemical spills, earthquakes, hurricanes, prison breakouts, train wrecks, riots, and terrorist attacks. Every unpleasantness she could think of was proposed to make sure everybody knew what kinds of things had to be done and who had to do them. Of course it was impossible to have a detailed plan for every conceivable calamity, but at least general procedures could be established, resources identified, and priorities agreed upon.

While finishing a cup of coffee, she tried to anticipate the problems that would arise if the entire valley below the dam had to be evacuated, problems of communication and transportation that she had never found the time to work out fully. Time was short because Elizabeth Lehmann was Caspar County Disaster Control Officer only in the mornings. Afternoons she was Chief Stenographer in Purchasing. Some California counties had as many as half a dozen people working full time on it; others, like Caspar, complacent and penny-pinching, relied on a part-timer from the steno pool. Planning for disasters was a waste of county money, in the opinion of the Board, because God in his wisdom doesn't announce which disaster among the hundreds at his disposal he is going to unleash or which parcel or parcels of land he is going to unleash it against. Or when. Not to mention plague and pestilence.

A failure of Sierra Canyon Dam was certainly something God might be considering, in Elizabeth Lehmann's opinion, and she had spent a lot of time preparing for it. One serious inconvenience would crop up right off the bat. The County Disaster Control Office was located in the basement of the building housing the Sheriff's Department where it had always been, six blocks from the center of Sutterton. When the Board of Supervisors was reminded of this fact, a ruling was made that since it would cost X amount of dollars to move it to higher ground, let's not do it now. Thus the disaster most likely to befall the town would give the people trying to cope with it the handicap of being under five hundred feet of water.

While relocating her office was voted down monthly, Elizabeth, through two years of raising hell, had managed to get enough money to put the county's radio equipment into a van. Now the nerve center could be moved quickly to wherever it could function most efficiently. She was proud of her command car, which was equipped with a powerful two-way radio, medical supplies, road flares, and, most important, a "resource file" that listed the location of everything from doctors to sandbags and included checklists for setting up field kitchens, medical centers, and refugee camps. It was a rolling Pentagon from which she could supervise the county's response to almost any upheaval.

"Thank God this is happening on a weekend," she said to herself as she ran down the porch steps, pushing a piece of toast into her mouth. "No school kids to contend with, at least."

In the darkness of the garage she reached for the door of her command car. It wasn't there. The garage was empty and so was the driveway. Nothing was parked at the curb. She clutched her head when she remembered that the car was at the office. The previous week, the Board of Supervisors, faced with declining income year by year since the passage of Proposition 13, decided that employees could no longer take county vehicles home with them, a prohibition that included the Disaster Control Officer. In other words, from now on disasters would have to occur during regular office hours.

Cursing Howard Jarvis, Elizabeth ran into the street and looked both ways for help. Next to an abandoned kitchen stove in a weedy yard two doors away knelt Norman Kingwell polishing his motorcycle. Kingwell was a teenage good-for-nothing whose main function in life seemed to be revving his engine. She had not spoken to him or his rotten parents for two years, not since the day he turned fifteen and removed his muffler. She ran toward him, waving. "Crank that beauty up, Norm baby," she called, "you are taking me for a ride."

South of Monterey in the depths of Los Padres National Forest, a man looking absurdly out of place in a business suit hurried along a leafy pathway in the Zen Center at Tassajara Hot Springs. Across a lovely Japanese bridge he went, startling a black-robed acolyte, and down a series of stone steps to the open-air enclosures of the mineral baths. He dropped to one knee and peered into the steam rising from the surface of the murky water.

He found what he was looking for—a thin, naked man, submerged except for his eyes, nose, and mouth. The wan face was reminiscent of the image of Christ on the Shroud of Turin.

"You're going to have to leave," the kneeling man said in an urgent whisper. "There's an emergency in Caspar County."

The Governor of California lifted his head, blinking and blowing water from his lips. "*Caspar* County?"

"Sierra Canyon Dam has sprung a leak. It looks bad."

"Can't they plug it?"

"Apparently not. Sutterton is being evacuated."

"Hard to believe a state as big as this that spends so much

money on the university system doesn't have people who know how to plug a leak."

The Executive Assistant to the Governor shrugged. "I'm just relaying the news. If you leave right now, you can get there for at least the tail end of what promises to be a first-rate catastrophe."

"Okay," the Governor said with a sigh of resignation, pulling himself out of the water. "I'll get dressed, and you see if you can get the Plymouth started."

"A helicopter is coming to take you. You'll do a flyover, declare a couple of counties disaster areas, and talk to the press. You can bet the press will be there in battalion strength."

The Governor put on a terry-cloth robe and stepped into a pair of sandals, dabbing at his face with a towel. "What tack should I take with the press—corporate greed, ecological insult, the Big Energy boys, spaceship earth, or what? Can we blame it on the Republicans?"

"The dam was built during your father's administration."

The Governor smiled slightly, which was the most he ever smiled. "He'll kill me if I mention that. God, do you suppose all our dams are going to start falling apart on us right and left? We've got a big enough P.R. problem as it is."

"Hardly. With the press, stick to concern for people who are dead and homeless. Show that you care about them and that the state government cares."

"And that the state government will do all it can to help, within fiscal and statutory limits. Yes, that's good. How about an attack on dams? Might be a good chance to work in a plug for solar and wind, how smaller is better, breaking the grip of foreign oil, and all that."

The two men climbed the steps, walking quickly.

"Simple concern for suffering is the ticket for the first day or two," the Executive Assistant insisted. "You are deeply moved as a person, see what I mean? You are a feeling, caring human being. Don't get technical. Display some basic, heartfelt emotion."

"You're right," the Governor said after some thought. "I'll go with that. In fact, I like it."

Two yanks of the cord and the outboard came to life. With one hand on the tiller, Chuck Duncan guided his small, flat-bottomed boat out of the secluded inlet where he kept it tied. There was little wind so early in the morning and the surface of the water was smooth. Duncan set a course for the widest part of the lake, five miles above the dam. When he got there, he would cut the motor and begin a lazy day of drinking beer, listening to soft rock, salivating over the photographs in *Oui*, fishing, and working on his suntan. Next to his teeth, in his opinion, his worst feature was his complexion. A suntan helped a lot, and this summer he intended to invest whatever time it took to get a good one.

He leaned back, turned his face to the sky, and closed his eyes. The sun wasn't warm enough yet to do much good, but he was tired and wanted to relax. He had a hangover. His muscles ached. He had spent most of the night wrestling with Carla—God, she was strong—trying and failing to get her clothes off. She giggled through the whole session as if it was some sort of goddam game. Maybe next time she would tire out. Now he looked forward to getting smashed on beer and catching up on his sleep, drifting wherever the current took him.

27

THE FOUR STEEL TRUSSES CROSSED THE RIVER ON PIERS OF QUARRIED
granite. At the approach closest to the town was a concrete monument on which was inscribed:

Main Street Bridge
Sutterton
Erected A.D. 1933

Never had the structure been put under such stress, not even in
the Great Flood of 1956, when the water crept to within three feet
of the roadway. It was within two feet now and rising, a broad,
swift tide.

A yellow school bus filled with prisoners from the city jail
groaned to a stop beside the monument. "Holy Toledo," said the
driver, "look at the river! Think it's safe to cross?"

Beside him was a guard carrying a shotgun, who stooped to see
through the windshield. "I don't think so, but I'm not a goddam engineer."

"I'm a goddam engineer," said Phil Kramer, coming down the
aisle in his white coveralls and rubber boots, "and I don't think so,
either. Look how fast the water's coming up. Soon as it hits those
horizontal stringers, the bridge has had it."

"Siddown," said the guard.

The other prisoners, squeezed into the undersized seats, craned their necks and looked around worriedly. Haystack was stretched out at the back of the bus snoring like a foghorn.

"Fuck," said the driver, striking the steering wheel with the heels of his hands.

Two police cars arrived. One knifed in front of the bus to block its access to the bridge, the other stopped alongside. Suddenly policemen were everywhere, setting up barricades across the approach and redirecting the cars that were lining up behind. The air was filled with flashing lights and radio static. Wilson Hartley emerged from one car and waited for the bus driver to open his window.

"Where to now, Chief?"

"The high-school gym in Sterling City. Take 191. Don't go back up Main—too much traffic and people running around. You got Phil Kramer in there?"

The driver twisted in his seat. "Is one of you guys—"

"I'm Kramer," Phil said, pushing his way to the front.

The door folded open and the guard stepped aside to let Phil pass, then pointed the shotgun menacingly at the other passengers, some of whom were half out of their seats with notions of following.

Phil was uneasy when he saw Officer Lee Simon waiting for him. He extended his hand. "I want to apologize again for—"

Simon grabbed him by the wrist and armpit and walked him on his tiptoes around the front of the bus. "Hey, what is this?" Phil protested. Before he could say anything further, he found himself shaking hands with a silver-haired policeman with a powerful grip and a familiar voice.

"Wilson Hartley, Chief of Police. We should have listened to you last night."

"Well, I—"

"All charges against you are dropped. We need your help."

"You do?"

"They tell me that until the bigwigs get here you know more about what's going on than anybody."

"Well, I—"

"For starters we need an estimate on how long the dam is going to hold."

Phil shook his head in amazement, then tried to adopt a professional manner. "I'll have to see how much worse the leak has gotten.

Can you take me somewhere where I can see it? How about the powerhouse parking lot?"

He was interrupted by a loud popping and grinding noise from the river. All eyes turned. The water had reached the underside of the bridge roadway, and the force had broken the connection between the two center spans and the pier on which they rested. The roadway bowed left and the entire bridge began shuddering. At that moment a motorcycle hurtled onto the far end.

"Look at that crazy bastard!" someone shouted. "He'll never make it!"

Several inches of water were flowing across the pavement of the second span. The motorcycle crossed it like a speedboat, sending waves to each side. The bridge lurched downstream a foot when the bike reached the fourth span, almost upending it, but with a sudden thrust of his leg the driver managed to keep his balance. When he reached solid ground, he swerved to a stop, knocking over a barricade.

"You goddam fool!" Hartley shouted. "Didn't you see the roadblock on the other side? Are you out of your fucking mind?"

Norman Kingwell looked at the Chief with a half smile. "The devil made me do it," he said, jabbing a thumb over his shoulder.

Behind Kingwell, the Caspar County Disaster Control Officer climbed off the seat. "Whew!" she said. "That was invigorating!"

"Mrs. Lehmann!"

"It's okay, Wilson. I ordered him to take me across. Everything I need is in my car and I've got to get to it. There goes the bridge. . . ."

Water was piling up against the roadway from one abutment to the other, boiling over the railing and sidewalk. With a deep wrenching sound, the two center spans began to slip off their supports. The venerable old bridge seemed to make a final effort to hang on, but yielded when struck by a mass of floating trees and debris. The center spans folded together in slow motion, pulling the side spans after them and rolling under the water. Within one minute everything was out of sight, and the only indications that a bridge had once been there were the three equally spaced rapids formed by the tops of the piers.

Elizabeth Lehmann got back on the motorcycle behind her teenage chauffeur. "I've got to move the radio van to high ground," she said to Hartley. "Would the right overlook be safe?"

Hartley looked at Phil, who assured them both that the right overlook, being on solid rock, was perfect.

Mrs. Lehmann turned her attention to Phil for the first time, eying his coveralls and boots. "And you are?"

"For the time being," Hartley said, answering the question for her, "he's the technical expert in charge of this event. Anything he says goes."

"The right overlook it is, then. Let's go, Norman, we've got work to do."

Kingwell kicked his motorcycle to life and revved the engine noisily as the woman behind him threw her arms around his waist. He took off with a roar, smiling and giving the finger to one and all. It was the first time in his life he had had any function or status.

The Cessna rose quickly from the highway, banking right. "I'll go west out of town," Freddy Hasset said, "to throw off anybody who might be watching, then swing around the foothills."

On the low side of the plane, his father pointed through the open doorway at the armored truck he had abandoned on the shoulder of the highway. "The truck sure looks little," he said. "Like a bug that's been blasted with Raid." He smiled, unveiling a row of square, cigar-stained teeth. "Lookit, not a car anywhere! Nobody chased me. Got away as clean as a whistle!" He chuckled. "You shoulda seen Lloyd when I drove away and left him on the dock! I told him I had to run an errand and would be back in a minute. Oh, God! I watched him in the rearview mirror running a few steps this way and a few steps that way, wondering whether to shit or go blind! Then he just stood there with his feet apart and his arms spread as if he was getting ready to catch a sack of potatoes. Jesus, it was funny! I was laughing so hard people on the sidewalk were staring at me. I betcha that dumb bastard is still waiting for me to get back from the Laundromat or wherever the hell he thinks I went with a truck full of money." He turned in his seat and patted the two gray canvas sacks he had brought aboard with him. "Must be a hundred thousand in there, Freddy, my boy, maybe more, most of it in twenties and smaller." He broke into song, never coming close to a right note:

"I'm in the money! I'm in the money!

"Excuse me, Freddy, that should be

"We're in the money! We're in the money!

"How does the rest of it go? And what's that other one?

"It's a great day for chasing the blues,
It's a great day for drinking the booze."

He slapped his son on the knee. Freddy wasn't sharing his father's joy. He kept his hands on the controls and his eyes straight ahead.

"What's the matter? You should be as happy as I am. We're rich! We made it! We're in the clear!"

"We're not in the clear, not by a long shot," Freddy said grimly. "We still gotta find the goddam cabin from the air, we gotta get you to the ground in one piece, we gotta hope the plane flies by itself for a hundred miles at least, we gotta hope nobody sees the parachutes and comes around asking questions, then we gotta live together for months without killing each other. You think we're in the clear? Shit."

"Aw, cheer up. Everything is going to be terrific. Don't worry about me being hard to live with, because I'm a new man. Money does that to people. Now that I'm rich I love everybody, even you, my own son, who never gave me anything but trouble. Ha, ha! *Sure* I slapped you around a little in the old days, but you deserved it! Let's see a smile! Okay, then, don't smile. You're not gonna spoil my day. You know what, Freddy? I've never been so happy in my whole goddam life. That's the truth! It's not the money so much as it is the fucking I'm giving the company. Oh, that feels good!"

Emil Hasset tore open his collar and broke out again in an approximation of song:

"Happy days are here again,
The sky is full of beer again,
Let us eat a box of Cheer again,
Happy days are here again.

"God, I wish I knew the words to those great old songs, 'cause I sure feel like singing."

The plane completed a long turn to the east and leveled off toward the morning sun. The pilot's eyes were narrow and his hands were tight on the wheel.

* * *

Phil Kramer stood with a group of men at the corner of the powerhouse parking lot scanning the lower reaches of the dam with binoculars. The boil-out was easier to find than when Mort Cooper had stood on the same spot an hour earlier. It was a torrent now, flowing from a hole thirty feet in diameter and scouring a ditch down the hillside to the river. Phil adjusted the focusing knob. "A couple of hours ago it was hardly more than a mud puddle, now look at it. Must be thousands of cubic feet a second coming out of there."

"How long have we got till the whole thing blows?" Lee Simon wanted to know.

Phil handed the glasses to the man next to him, contractor Leonard Mitchell. "No way to tell for sure. Dams are as different as people, as Roshek put it in his textbook."

"I talked to Roshek a little while ago," Newt Withers offered. "He said maybe the flow could be pinched off by dumping rock on it."

Phil dismissed the suggestion with a shake of his head. "Too late for that. Maybe three or four hours ago, before piping started. Dumping stuff on the upstream side might slow it down a little, but the dam is going to fail no matter what we do."

"There must be something—"

"There's nothing."

"How long have we got?" Simon asked again. "That's all I want to know. We've got a town to evacuate."

"If the water is going *under* the core block," Phil said, thinking out loud, "through the foundation rock and grout curtain, that's one thing. If it's coming *over* the core block—"

"How long in minutes?" Simon insisted.

"The embankment is three-quarters of a mile thick at the base, so it's going to take a while. The hole is going to keep caving in until a notch is cut all the way to the crest. That's when the lake will come shouldering through in a big wave."

"How long have we got, goddammit!" Simon was losing his temper and turning red.

"I'd just be guessing. I've seen films of dams failing, but—"

"Take a guess, then!"

Withers put an arm across the policeman's chest. "Cool it, Lee," he said. "He's not God."

"He can take a guess, can't he? His guess would be better than mine, wouldn't it? Or yours? He's written a fucking *book* on the subject, hasn't he?"

Phil raised a hand. "A doctoral thesis. I'll take a guess. Where we're standing now could be under hundreds of feet of water in as little as forty-five minutes."

Simon threw Withers's arm aside. *"Forty-five minutes!"*

"Might take two or three times longer than that. Forty-five is minimum. At Baldwin Hills, for instance—"

"Shit, with forty-five minutes we'll never be able to knock on every door in town, which is what we're trying to do now. We'll be lucky to cover the side streets with a sound truck. . . ." He reached through the window of his car for the radio microphone.

"Suppose I keep an eye on the breach and keep giving you updated estimates?"

"Good idea. We'll put you on the right overlook where the radio van will be."

"I'll take you in my pickup," Mitchell said to Phil.

Riggs, Cooper, Withers, and a group of men from the Combined Water Districts ran for the powerhouse to complete the job of removing files and records that might later reveal the cause of the failure.

Minutes later, Mitchell swung off the county road onto the top of the dam. Ahead, the crest road stretched across the valley like a taut white ribbon. "Jesus," Mitchell said, pointing through the windshield, "look at that! Some fool is trying to land a plane on the dam."

Phil followed the contractor's gaze and saw a small plane approaching in the distance pursued by a police car. Several other cars had pulled over to the curbings and stopped to give the plane as much room as possible. The plane lost altitude rapidly, rose to clear the truck Phil had abandoned in the middle of the night, then touched down smoothly.

"I hope he sees the gravel," Phil said.

"What gravel?"

"I stole one of your trucks last night, and to slow down the pursuit I dumped a load of gravel on the road."

Mitchell squinted at his passenger. "You stole one of my trucks?"

"Well, I borrowed it."

The plane, a small sport model painted a bright red and decorated with racing stripes and painted flames, was taxiing rapidly toward them when the landing gear hit the gravel. The tail flipped upward, the fuselage balanced on its nose for a second, then toppled over on its back.

By the time Phil and Mitchell got there, two highway patrolmen were cutting the pilot out of his seat belt, from which he was suspended upside down. "I'm all right," said the pilot, a heavy, balding man, but clearly he wasn't. A contusion the size of a fist showed where his forehead had hit the windshield. "I'm all right," the pilot said again as he was revolved into a sitting position. His lips were drawn away from his teeth in pain and his eyes were tightly shut.

"Can't take him to the hospital downtown," one patrolman said. "That's being evacuated."

"How about the right overlook?" the other patrolman suggested. "Old lady Lehmann's setting up a medical tent there."

When the pilot was right side up, Phil recognized him. "Mr. Bolen! My God, it's Mr. Bolen!" He clambered out of the truck.

"Who?"

"Herman Bolen of Roshek, Bolen & Benedetz, one of the people who designed the dam. Oh, man, Mr. Bolen, am I glad to see you!"

Bolen forced an eye open and looked at Phil's boots, coveralls, and face. "Do I know you from somewhere?"

"I'm Phil Kramer. Roshek fired me yesterday, remember?"

Bolen closed his eye. "That was a mistake," he said, wincing. "We need you in London." He tried to get up, then sat down quickly. "Maybe I'm not all right."

"We'll see that you get first aid," a patrolman said. "If you're still not all right in thirty minutes, we'll run you over to the hospital in Chico for X-rays. You could have a skull fracture."

More cars had arrived and a circle of onlookers had formed. The patrolman asked if anyone was willing to take Bolen to the right overlook.

A man behind the wheel of a van volunteered. Phil and Mitchell helped Bolen to his feet and walked him slowly across the highway. He was handed a gauze pad to hold against the wound on his forehead.

"Kramer," Bolen said, "I'll apologize later for yesterday. Right now you've got to listen. Block this road except for emergency vehicles. When the breach reaches elevation seven five five, get everybody off the dam because it will go fast from there."

The rear doors of the van were opened and the two men helped Bolen inside. He sat against the wall with his legs extended in front of him, pressing the gauze against his head.

"Get everybody out of the powerhouse," Bolen went on in a strained voice. "Close the access tunnel door and brace it with trucks on both sides. It might hold."

Mitchell's eyes went back and forth between Bolen and Phil. "Then you think the dam is definitely going to let go?"

Bolen rolled his head toward the front of the van to hide the tears that were leaking from his eyes. "The dam is lost."

"There must be some way to save it," Mitchell insisted. "Suppose we dump rock in the lake over the point the water's getting in? I've got a loaded barge tied up at the quarry dock that I could have towed into position in half an hour. . . ."

"Useless," Bolen said, "even with a bull's-eye. In about half an hour a whirlpool will be forming. You'll lose the barge and everybody on it, all for nothing. Too late now. Too late, too late."

A patrolman closed one of the doors.

"We'll drag your plane off the dam," Phil said. "We'll save that at least."

Bolen lifted his hand weakly. "Forget the plane. I'm too old to fly. Dump it over the side to clear the road." He motioned for Phil to lean close. "If Roshek shows up, keep an eye on him. This may be more than he can take."

Phil nodded. "I'll do that."

"You still work for us," Bolen said. "You'll get a raise. Enough to buy some decent clothes. Did he say a fractured skull? I may pass out."

The second door was closed and Phil watched the van depart. He climbed into the pickup. Now there were tears in *his* eyes.

28

THE HELICOPTER SKIMMED THE TREETOPS AT THE BOTTOM OF THE VALLEY
ten miles below the dam. Roshek spotted the green lawn surrounding Creekwood and pointed. With a nod the pilot made a slight
course correction.

The river didn't look good . . . already out of its banks and dotted with driftwood. Roshek hoped Eleanor had heard the news and
was already gone. If not, he was prepared to sacrifice himself for
her. He would tell the pilot to lift her to safety, then come back. If
the wave arrived in the meantime, too bad. Better she survive than
him, if it came down to a choice. He was an old man physically,
and fast falling apart. His career, which just days before was on
the verge of reaching unprecedented heights, was falling apart as
well. Not that there was much chance that he would have to sacrifice himself. He could see several miles up the canyon and there
was no sign of a wave. The helicopter could easily make two trips
to high ground.

The house came into view. There was a car in the driveway and
it wasn't Eleanor's. If he was not mistaken, it belonged to Russell
Stone, the dancer she was living with when Roshek came into her
life.

Good Lord, Roshek thought, surely they aren't in the house together, not after she had sworn she was through with him. Stone
had come alone—yes, that was it—and she had loaned him the key.

"Set her down?" the pilot shouted as he approached the lawn
below the house.

"Hover," Roshek shouted in return.

The front door opened. A slim, well-muscled young man wearing
shorts stepped onto the porch and shielded his eyes. It was Stone,
all right, Roshek was sure, and he felt a rush of anger. He didn't
like the idea of a rival spending the night at Creekwood even with
Eleanor's permission . . . especially with Eleanor's permission.

A woman appeared in the shadowed doorway. "Don't let it be
Eleanor," Roshek whispered, "please, please . . ."

But it was Eleanor, dressed in the silk pajamas he had given her
for Christmas. She glided into the sunlight and slipped an arm
around Stone's waist. He put an arm around her shoulder and
pulled her close as they stared at the helicopter together. Roshek
saw her hand move to shield her eyes like a bird rising to a limb.
Even her simplest gestures were so graceful and elegant that he—

"Up," he said to the pilot abruptly, pointing upward, "take her
up."

As the helicopter soared up, Roshek was seized by convulsive
sobs. He buried his face in a handkerchief and struggled to regain
his composure.

"Hey," the pilot said, "you all right?"

Roshek nodded, blew his nose noisily, and took several deep
breaths.

When the helicopter reached an elevation of fifteen hundred feet,
it tilted slightly and swooped forward on a level course toward the
northeast. In the distance was the shining surface of Warren Lake.
The lake tapered to a narrow finger above Sutterton, where a tiny
brown patch that was the dam held it back like a cork in a bottle.

The right overlook was a two-acre flat area paved with asphalt
and lined on the canyon side with coin-operated telescopes. It was
a hundred feet above the crest of the dam, and on summer weekends was filled with the cars of as many as two hundred sightseers.
Phil, equipped with a two-way radio and a pair of binoculars, established himself at the outermost point where two reaches of
guardrail met atop a rock outcropping that was shaped like a ship's
prow. It was a spectacular vantage point. To his left the deep green
water swept smoothly over the lowered gates into the spillway,
which angled downward directly below. At the bottom, far to his

right, the torrent dissolved into a continuous explosion of spray as it struck a field of massive concrete blocks—energy dissipaters designed to pass the discharge into the river shorn of its capacity to gouge and tear.

At the far side of the river was the electrical switchyard and the powerhouse parking lot, empty now except for Phil's battered and nearly inoperable Mustang, which he had decided to abandon. As Bolen had suggested, the powerhouse had been evacuated and a protective wall of trucks set up in front of the access tunnel door in an effort to spare the generators from the costly indignity of total immersion.

Near the bottom of the dam embankment just beyond the spillway was a circular area a hundred yards in diameter that was glistening with moisture and looked soft and spongy. The lower edge was a ragged gash thirty yards long from which a powerful flow of brown water was pouring steadily and cascading down the hill.

Holding his radio close to his mouth so his words would be heard over the roar of the water, Phil reported on the progress of the failure: "Upper edge of breach now at elevation five hundred. Volume of flow has doubled in the last five minutes. Saturated area is growing and may erupt at any time. Now estimate main collapse in thirty-five minutes."

In the right distance was Sutterton, the lower sections of which were being nibbled away by the rising river. Three brick warehouses dating from the gold rush that had withstood countless floods had been pushed over and submerged. Through binoculars Phil watched a dozen wood-frame houses twisted off their foundations, upended, and smashed to pieces. A large white building with a cupola on top was magically lifted off its moorings and carried downstream without a sign of listing or turning, a grand Victorian excursion boat embarking on a leisurely tour of the Thames. At the turn the river made south of town, the cupola dropped straight down as the building collapsed in on itself and quickly sank.

Phil felt like a spotter in a war relaying battle information to generals at a field headquarters behind the lines. Field headquarters in this case was just a few feet away, for the overlook had been transformed into a kind of alternate seat of government. One of the first to arrive was Mrs. Lehmann, driving a car so loaded with equipment that it almost dragged on the ground, followed by a van that bristled with radio antennas. Next came cars carrying the Sheriff,

the Chief of Police, the Fire Chief, and the head of the local Red
Cross. Highway patrolmen kept one area clear for helicopters
bringing in officials from Sacramento, though the first helicopter to
arrive carried a television news crew.

Mrs. Lehmann set up shop on a card table behind the radio van,
with maps and lists spread out before her. She kept a steady stream
of information flowing to communities downstream, relaying reports on traffic conditions as soon as she received them from the
Highway Patrol. She made sure city and county officers knew
where the refugee centers were being set up and that they were
being staffed with appropriate personnel. Her voice had a hard
edge to it, and Phil could hear almost every word she said over the
cacophony of roaring water, vehicle engines, shouts, and loudspeaker static. She was obviously well prepared and was attacking
her job with tremendous energy and effectiveness. To a remark
from Wilson Hartley that she seemed almost to be enjoying what
she was doing, Phil heard her reply: "I'll cry if it will help any."

The idea spread that Phil not only had predicted the catastrophe
but that he was the greatest authority on dam failures in the world.
He was deferred to and treated as the ultimate authority. It was to
him, for example, that the television reporter and his cameraman
were drawn.

Hearing a well-modulated baritone voice behind him, Phil turned
and found himself looking into the lens of a television minicamera.
Next to the cameraman was a man in a butterscotch sport jacket
speaking earnestly into a microphone: "On your screen is Bill or
Phil Kramer, the heroic young engineer who spent the night sounding the alarm and who is now providing on police wavelengths a
minute-by-minute account of the dissolution of the mighty Goliath
that for ten years has tamed the once-rampaging Sierra Canyon
River, and which, or so it seems, will rampage again, this time with
a vengeance and worse, and who is credited with giving officials
enough warning time so that the cost of the disaster, if and when it
comes, will be greatly minimized, at least in terms of wasted lives."
He thrust the microphone in Phil's face and asked him to give the
viewers "an up-to-the-minute update."

Phil waved him away in irritation. "Jesus, mister, would you
mind? I'm awful busy. We've got a dam failing here."

"Gradually, as I understand it," the reporter said. "Water will
come out faster and faster until the valley is flooded, is that it?"

"No. In about half an hour the dam is going to get washed out and a wall of water will go down the valley like a bulldozer."

"A bulldozer how high?"

"Depends on the width of the valley. Five hundred feet high in narrow spots, a hundred in wide spots."

"Traveling fifty or a hundred miles an hour? What a spectacle that will be for our strategically placed cameras."

"It might go a hundred down a straight concrete canal, but this is a valley with twists and turns. Turbulence and the load the water will pick up will cut the speed down to ten or fifteen miles an hour. Now if you'll excuse me . . ."

"I'm told you spent some time in jail last night. How did you feel about that?"

Phil was rescued by Mrs. Lehmann, who shouted shrilly at two policemen: "Get those clowns away from Kramer!"

He turned and scanned the lake through binoculars. "Looks like all boats have made it to shore," he said into his radio. "Wait, I think I see one about a quarter mile from the spillway. He must have missed the warnings. Is there a helicopter or powerboat that can get out there? No sign of a whirlpool forming yet."

He swung the glasses down the valley. "On the rim of the canyon, below town, where the river bends, I see half a dozen people. They should be removed from that area. When the wave hits the hillside, it might surge all the way to the top."

Wilson Hartley put his hand on Phil's shoulder. "Did I hear you say the flood would only move at ten or fifteen miles an hour?"

"Just a guess, but I can't imagine it going much faster. There's a couple of narrow spots and some sharp turns."

"Shit, a man could drive down the canyon a lot faster than that. Make sure everybody has been moved out."

"Yes, I suppose—"

"Not the kind of risk I'd want to order a man to take, though. I'll do it myself. I'll take our best car, the one we use to track down speeders."

Phil stared at the policeman in disbelief. "Are you serious? I don't know for *sure* how fast the water will go. It might—"

Hartley turned away. "You just keep talking into that microphone so I know how much time I've got left. . . ."

A clap of thunder pulled Phil's attention to the dam. A tremendous upwelling had blown out the circular saturated area. A geyser

exploded upward and fell back, and viscous brown water gushed out like blood from a wound.

"A major blowout," Phil reported excitedly. "Flow coming through for the first time at what looks like full pressure. Spurting out like a fountain. Cave-ins on upper side of breach to about six seventy-five. The breach is now about fifty yards wide and a hundred long. Won't be long now, maybe twenty minutes. If anybody's still in town, they should get out now and fast."

On the surface of the lake three hundred yards from the spillway, a column of bubbles broke the surface and a circle of water began to revolve slowly around it.

From Roshek's helicopter, the town, the lake, and the dam presented a scene of picture-postcard splendor. Sutterton looked as sleepy and peaceful as any New England village, and only by close observation was it possible to see the lines of cars fleeing it on every available road. The lake sparkled in the sun, and the foothills rolled away from it toward the snowy high country like a rumpled green blanket. Looming ever larger as the helicopter approached was the dam, a colossal wall that swept from one side of the valley to the other. On the left side, like a silver bracelet on a suntanned arm, was the spillway, and beside it, half as high and twice as wide, was an ugly, seething mass of brown water. Roshek stared at the rupture as he might at a beautiful woman whose face was scarred, or at a painting ripped by a madman's knife. Minutes before, he had felt overwhelmed by sorrow and pain at the discovery of Eleanor's treachery and his eyes were still stinging from the tears. The tears came again at the sight of Sierra Canyon Dam in its death throes. The great structure that was as much a part of him as his heart or his brain was sprawled beneath him, broken and bleeding.

Roshek lifted his eyes and stared unseeingly at the horizon. He wanted to return to the Lear waiting for him at the Yuba City airport—what was the point of watching something you loved die at close range?—but he found himself unable to give the command. He couldn't speak or make a sound or lift a hand.

He was aware by the forces on his body that the helicopter was landing, but when it came to rest and the rotor stopped he did not move. Words spoken by the pilot came to him as from a great distance and he couldn't focus his mind on their meaning.

The door opened and he felt himself being lifted to the ground. Men surrounded him whose faces were familiar but whose names and functions he could not place. He put his arms automatically into his crutches and walked at the center of a small group. He felt a wind, and he paused to pull his hat down close to his ears.

Men were standing shoulder to shoulder at a guardrail. They parted to make room for him and said things to him he didn't hear. He looked over the edge. A powerful tide of water, green and glassy, was surging in from the lake across the lowered spillway gates and hurtling down the smooth concrete channel in perfect laminar flow, gradually changing to white turbulence exactly as the hydraulic formulas and scale model tests predicted it would. It was beautiful and hypnotic the way the power of the water was guided and controlled by the precisely calculated angles and curves of the spillway walls. It was a photograph in an engineering textbook.

Beyond the spillway, where there should have been nothing but the smooth, tawny flank of the embankment being warmed by the sun, was a raging brown beast from a nightmare, savage and roaring and gnawing a fatal cavity in one of the man-made wonders of the world. The gusher heaved and spouted, lashing like the tail of a crazed animal that was trying to back out of a hole. When it did succeed in wrenching itself free, it would be submerged immediately in a flood of unimaginable proportions.

It was all wrong, Roshek thought, shaking his head while tears streamed down his cheeks. Sierra Canyon Dam was designed in part to lift the spirit and nourish the soul. To superimpose a hideous eruption on it was insane, it was a crime, it was a grotesque contradiction. He remembered with sudden clarity the rage and frustration he had felt as a young engineer when a paper he had written was botched by a technical journal. An intricate analysis had ended with a single equation, the result of thousands of observations made in the field, and somehow it had been hopelessly mangled. Because of the stupidity of people he had never even met, an insight of great value had been transformed into something ridiculous. He had wanted to go to New York and strangle the editors with his bare hands. He felt the same urge now.

Through no fault of his, Sierra Canyon Dam was unraveling before his eyes. The smooth skin was being ripped apart. Forces of nature were at work. Since there was nothing he could do to stop them, there was nothing to be gained by becoming emotionally in-

volved. He withdrew to an infinite remoteness and watched as he
would a film from a soundproof booth. The hands of an insolent
young ballet dancer with a nearly perfect body were caressing
Eleanor James and she was smiling in response, but what was that
to him? Eleanor was out of his life now and soon the dam would be
as well. He had done his work as best he could and others had
wrecked it. She was not the Eleanor he had loved and this was not
his dam. He had worshipped perfection. The Sierra Canyon Dam
he designed and built would not cave in like a sand castle to provide entertainment for a gathering of ghouls.

Wind tugged at his clothes. His hat was snatched from his head
and catapulted into the air like a clay pigeon. Roshek watched it
soar high in the sky, then fall in a long arc, spinning, shrinking in
size until it became a hard-to-follow dot. After what seemed like
minutes it disappeared against the background of the river that was
cascading down the face of the dam.

He relaxed his hands and let his crutches clatter to the ground.
To keep from falling, he closed his fingers around the cold steel
pipe that formed the top railing of the fence. If it weren't for his
withered legs, he could have hurdled it in an instant. He became
aware then of a voice that sounded somehow familiar, and he
turned slowly to his right. Ten feet away a man in white coveralls
peered through binoculars and held a radio to his lips. Roshek had
seen that face before. "I can see a whirlpool forming in the lake,"
the man was saying. "A definite depression in the water and a
clockwise turning about three hundred yards northeast of the spillway. That's a hundred yards closer than the mathematical model
predicted. Top of breach now at seven hundred feet."

The voice was too dispassionate. Sierra Canyon Dam was failing—
weeping was called for and screams of pain. Roshek stared, trying
to place the man. What was it about the sight of him and the sound
of his voice that stirred such feelings of hatred in his heart? He
worked his way along the guardrail to get closer, sliding his hands
along the railing and ignoring the men who had to step back to
make way.

"Main break only ten minutes or so away," the man said into his
radio. "I still see people standing on the ridge below town. They
may be goners if they stay there."

The man turned, lowering the radio and binoculars. "Mr. Roshek!" he said in astonishment. "Oh, Jesus! God, I'm so *sorry*. . . ." He gestured toward the dam. "It's . . . it's a great structure, a magnificent structure. There was nothing wrong with the design. . . . The studies will prove that, I'm sure. . . ."

"It's Kramer, isn't it," Roshek said, pulling himself close. "Yes . . ."

The younger man drew back slightly, as if afraid he was about to be spat upon or struck.

"You were lucky," Roshek said in a quavering voice, "incredibly lucky. It was a chance in a billion that the dam would fail and you would blunder in when you did." The roar of the water was so loud he had to raise his voice to be heard. "Your idiotic computer program had nothing to do with it. . . . Sheer stupid luck." He let go of the railing and took hold of Kramer's shoulder. "Before you came, there was no problem. You made this happen, yes, somehow you let the water through—don't deny it! Sabotage . . . to prove your crazy theory, to attract attention to yourself, to tear me down . . ." Roshek was shouting to make himself heard over the surrounding din, but his voice was thin and cracking. He had a powerful urge to try to wrestle Kramer over the edge and fall with him into the flood below, but he forced himself not to yield to it, knowing that the effort would fail. The boy was strong and young and would fight him off and would be helped by the men who were crowding close. An assault would do nothing but provide still another spectacle for the jackals who were watching.

Roshek felt a strong hand on his arm. He turned and saw a man with his head wrapped in bandages who was shouting his name. "Can't you hear me?" he was saying. "Don't you recognize me?"

It was Herman Bolen. Roshek evaluated the situation coldly. If I don't answer him, he reasoned, he will think I've lost my mind. I must put him at his ease. . . .

"Of course I can hear you, Herman. What happened to your head?"

"I tried to break the windshield of my plane with it. I just got out of the medical tent. Took six stitches. For a while there I was bleeding like a stuck pig."

"Like the dam," Roshek said. "You'll kill yourself eventually with your driving and flying."

There was a deep, rolling thunder from the dam. A great triangular block of the embankment near the top gave way and sank into the river of water surging beneath it. The lake seemed to leap forward into the slot that now reached from the bottom of the slope to within a few yards of the crest, fighting its way through with an awesome frenzy. Directly above the breach, the crest roadway began to show a noticeable sag.

Roshek turned away. He leaned his back against the guardrail and held out his hands. "Where are my crutches?" When they were handed to him, he swung himself between the cars and trucks toward his helicopter. "I don't want to watch," he said to Bolen, who had to hurry to keep pace. "I'm not a masochist. I'm going back to Los Angeles. Carlos is waiting for me in Yuba City with the Lear."

Bolen helped him climb into the passenger's seat. "Wouldn't it be better, Theodore, if you stayed till this was over? The press is here and they want to talk to you. We should agree on some sort of statement."

"A crippled old man crying," Roshek said, buckling his seat belt. "That would make a nice thirty-second spot on the noon news, wouldn't it? No, thanks. You talk to them. Say whatever you want."

Bolen wouldn't let him close the door. "Are you sure you are . . . will you be . . ."

"I'm perfectly all right, Herman. Stop worrying. I got a little . . . well, unhinged when I first saw the dam and Kramer, but I'm okay now. Everything is under control, believe me. We'll have a talk when you get back to Los Angeles. Especially about Kramer. The press is going to make a hero out of him, I'm sure you realize. We have to think of a way to turn that into a gain for the company."

Roshek concentrated on speaking rationally and on presenting himself as a man who had been subjected to crushing pressure but who had enough strength of character to recover from it. He smiled and nodded reassuringly as he lifted Bolen's hand off the door.

Bolen hesitated, then backed away.

The helicopter lifted off vertically. When it was above the tops of the surrounding trees, it tilted and veered away toward the southwest. Roshek watched Bolen looking up at him and saw him almost bumped into by a jogger, who appeared from the woods with no apparent idea of where he was going. He twisted in his seat for a last glimpse of the ravaged dam. The breach now dwarfed the spillway and the final breakup was obviously near. Tens of thousands of tons of water per second were pouring through in a flood that was like a slice of Niagara Falls and three times higher. He watched in spite of himself, and he watched until a mountainside mercifully obstructed his view.

29

THREE TIMES DUNCAN PULLED THE CORD AND THREE TIMES THE MOTOR
failed to start. "Shit," he said. The boat had drifted much more
quickly than usual toward the dam, which was now only a quarter
of a mile away. He decided that the spillway gates must have been
lowered during the night . . . the pull wouldn't be so strong with
only two feet going over the top. Not that he was in any danger.
There were trash racks on the lake side of the gates—large steel
grilles—designed to retain debris so that it wouldn't damage the
spillway, and a hundred feet from the dam was a long string of logs
chained together that prevented private boats from running
aground on the upstream slope of the embankment. But Duncan
didn't like being so close to the dam. He saw enough of it during
the week, and fishing was better farther upstream.

He tried again to start the motor—this time it caught. He swung
the boat around and set a course for the center of the lake. Tilting
his head back, he drained the last drops from a can of beer, then
held it over the side until it filled with water. He dropped it and
leaned over the edge to watch it sink. Usually he could follow a can
fifteen or twenty feet down, sometimes farther. The water in the
lake was mostly melted snow and extremely clear, but this time the
can faded from view after a few feet. Weird. He had never seen the
water so murky in this part of the lake, where it was eight hundred
feet deep. Something must be stirring up the sediment.

He sat up and looked around. There was a man standing on the

crest of the dam waving his arms. Was he waving at *him?* Duncan
waved back. The right overlook was full of cars and trucks. What
was that all about? Maybe something to do with the marathon. He
noticed that he was even closer to the right side of the dam than he
had been before. "Well, for Christ sakes," he said aloud, moving
the throttle to full open and redirecting the propeller thrust. He
kept his eyes on a fixed onshore point to check his progress—he was
still losing ground.

He shifted in his seat and looked toward the spillway. If the current was so strong, maybe the best way to escape was to run with
it, angling slightly to the side so that he would reach the shore at
the right abutment. From there he could surely make his way back
upstream by sticking close to the canyon wall. He pointed the boat
toward the spillway, and for the first time became aware of a
muffled roar. Usually on the lake it wasn't possible to hear the
sound of the water at the bottom of the spillway, because the dam
acted as a sound barrier. They must be spilling the whole twenty-
two feet, he thought, otherwise I'd never be able to hear that noise.
He had visions of his boat being drawn against the trash racks and
held there like a stick of wood on a sewer grating. If that happened, he and the boat would have to be lifted out with a crane.

He saw a helicopter leave the overlook and disappear to the
southwest. A minute later another helicopter rose from the same
point and headed directly toward him. His boat was picking up
speed and the tiller angle had no effect on his direction. First he
was drawn toward the dam, then parallel to it, and now he was
being swung in a broad arc *away* from it. He noticed then a depression in the surface of the water about a hundred yards away, a
depression around which a large section of the lake was revolving.
"Jesus," Duncan said, "I'm caught in some kind of goddam
eddy. . . ." He managed to turn the boat so that it was facing
away from the depression, and watched with rising fear as he was
swung in a wide circle, returning to the same point a minute later
but ten yards closer to the center. His outboard motor was useless
against the speed and power of the quickening spiral current. After
two more revolutions, he was within fifty feet of the center and his
boat was angled steeply downward. It was as if the surface of the
water were a rubber membrane that was being pinched and pulled
downward from below.

Whirlpool! The word dropped into his mind like a snake. In a panic he saw that he had been drawn so far beneath the surrounding surface of the lake that he could no longer see the dam or the shore. The boat spun in ever-tightening circles until it was so close to the deepening spout of the funnel that Duncan could have pitched an oar into it. The helicopter appeared above him, descending, the pilot half out of the door gesturing for him to try to grab one of the landing runners. The helicopter hovered in a fixed position as the boat made two twisting passes beneath it. Both times Duncan, kneeling on the seat, reached as high as he could but missed making the connection. As the boat careened around the banked curve for a third approach, Duncan rose unsteadily to a crouching position, trying not to lose his balance and capsize the boat. This time, he vowed, he would catch hold even if he had to leap upward to do it.

He never got the chance. Striking a half-submerged log, the boat was upended and Duncan was pitched into the center of the vortex, where he was instantly sucked out of sight.

The helicopter lingered, turning slowly, before lifting away.

Kent Spain wondered how much longer he could last. Staggering out of the woods onto the right overlook, he ran into the side of a parked police car. Rebounding, he nearly knocked over a fat man with a bandaged head. As he threaded his way through sawhorse barricades that were so ineptly placed they hindered his progress rather than guided it, he felt both nauseous and dizzy. There were a lot of spectators, but for some reason they didn't greet him with the spontaneous cheer usually given to the runner in the lead. Several people shouted congratulations of some sort when they saw him, others were looking in the wrong direction.

Reaching the pavement of the road across the dam and ducking under a chain that somebody had stupidly stretched across it, he saw a cop waiting for him with a hand extended. Spain had no intention of stopping for a handshake. The cop, apparently not wanting to be denied, lunged at him as he passed. The runner sidestepped and slipped out of his grasp with a shrugging motion of his shoulder. Now the cop was chasing him and shouting words he couldn't hear because of the head-splitting roar that filled his ears. The dumb bastard probably wants me to stop and give him an autograph, Kent thought, marveling at the general thickheadedness of the human race. Legs churning, he increased his speed as much as his remaining strength would allow, which was enough to leave the cop behind.

A few minutes earlier, as he had come down the hillside to the dam, the trees shimmered and the ground undulated like a flag in the wind. He had heard roaring then, too, but it was nothing like the thunder that filled his skull now. The road here was not so much undulating as it was quivering and at one point seemed to sink beneath his feet so that he had to run downhill into a trough and up the other side. Stop for a minute, an inner voice told him; sit on the curbing and wait for the roaring and quivering to go away. No! He would keep going if it killed him. Perseverance was the mark of a champion. He would not allow his body or his brain to talk him into taking a rest. The only thing that would bring him to a halt was if his body came unhinged at the joints and fell into a pile of separate parts.

There were people at the other end of the dam, too, clutching at him as he ran by and shouting things at him he couldn't decipher. The sign marking the point where the trail left the road and entered the woods had been knocked down. Good. That might delay runners who didn't know the route.

Soon Kent was alone again among the trees, jogging determinedly along a trail that followed the contours of a side canyon. At the end of a long switchback Dulotte would be waiting. He was beginning to feel a little better and he kept his eyes open for the white cloth that marked the hidden bicycle. His breathing was not as ragged as it had been coming across the dam. The roar had diminished and the ground had almost come to rest. Then his legs failed. They simply turned to rubber. In the space of five strides he was transformed from a man running to a man face down in the dirt. He clutched the ground as he would a life raft and gasped like a beached fish.

It's all over now, he thought; I've blown it. Yousri will come flying by first, maybe stopping to kick dirt in my eyes, then Ryan, then the panting, sweating, salivating herd. If I don't roll over into the weeds, I'll be trampled to death.

After several minutes of lying still, strength seeped back into his limbs. He sat up. It was eerily silent. Nobody was coming down the trail. He must have had a bigger lead than he realized. With some effort he got to his feet and brushed himself off. A few cuts and bruises. His left kneecap was bleeding slightly. He walked for a while. A cool breeze felt good and he began to jog, tentatively at first, then with a trace of vigor.

He stopped when he saw a Center for Holistic Fitness T-shirt dangling from a limb. Still there was nobody on the trail. "Christ," he said as he parted the bushes, "I must have left those assholes miles behind." The bike was there, gleaming and beautiful. He dragged it into the open and bounced it several times before climbing aboard.

When Dulotte saw the bike coming, he stepped from behind his table and held out his hands. Kent skidded to a stop.

"Not so fast," Dulotte said with a smile. "At this rate you'll break the world record by ten minutes. How are you holding up?"

"A few minutes ago I thought I was dead, now I feel terrific. How far ahead of the field am I?"

"I don't know. Back in this canyon there's nothing but static on the radio. Did you make use of the pedometer-watch, the Pulsometer, the—"

"No. All that shit broke down a couple of miles out. And the way my crotch feels, I think the Jog-Tech Living Jock died, too."

"Well, nobody will ever know. Leave the bike here and jog the rest of the way. Your time has to be in the realm of reason."

Kent got off the bike and gave it a push into the weeds. "Anything you say, Doc." He drained a cup of water and helped himself to a peeled orange. As he trotted away, he looked over his shoulder and waved. "So long," he said, "see you Monday at the Bank of America."

Officer John Colla sped through the side streets of Sutterton with his siren wailing, stopping at every third house to tell anybody he could find to head for high ground after first warning the neighbors. When he heard Kramer's radio report that the major break would come in as little as twenty minutes, he realized that at his present rate he was never going to be able to cover the section assigned to him. He switched to stopping at every fifth house. Most of the houses were already empty, thanks in part to a plane equipped with a public-address system that had spent forty-five minutes flying a low crisscrossing pattern over the town broadcasting the evacuation order. The plane was from Sutter County. Mrs.

Lehmann, bless her heart, had obviously talked somebody into releasing it.

Colla found one man who didn't want to leave because the baseball game he was watching on television looked headed for extra innings. Colla argued with him only briefly before running back to his patrol car. As he made a U-turn in the street, he saw the man come out his front door and head for his garage. "I'm leaving," he shouted to the policeman. "Power failure. Lost the picture."

When the break was estimated at five minutes away, Colla abandoned his efforts and took one of the roads leading to the tablelands above the town. On the way he stopped to tell Mr. and Mrs. Orvis, who were trying to tie an upholstered chair to the roof of their car, to give up and clear out. Colla was satisfied, based on what he had seen himself and reports he heard on the radio, that Sutterton was almost entirely empty. He would be surprised if more than a dozen people out of the population of 6,500 were unaccounted for when the flood was over.

At the edge of town, where the road turned sharply uphill, he stepped on his brakes. Two kids not more than ten years old were sitting quietly in a tree.

"What the hell are you kids doing?" he shouted out of his window.

"The dam is breaking," one of them called down. "We can watch the water come out from here."

Colla got out of his car and ordered them down, telling them they'd drown if they stayed where they were. "Where are your mom and dad? In the house?"

"Dad's divorced," the older of the two boys said, working his way to the ground. "Mom's upstairs fixing her nails."

"Hasn't she heard the sirens and the bells and people shouting and the airplanes?"

"She said it was awful noisy today."

"Get in the car."

"Really?"

Colla fired two shots in the air. A woman's face appeared in an upstairs window. When she saw what looked like an arrest of her babies, she started screaming.

"The dam is failing!" Colla shouted. "I'll wait thirty seconds for you, then I'm getting the boys out of here."

The woman raised her eyes and looked across the rooftops toward the dam. What she saw made her mouth fall open. She was running down the front walk twenty seconds later, a cat under each arm, a fur coat over one shoulder, and purses swinging from both elbows. She was a good-looking woman, Colla noticed as he helped her into the car, even without makeup and wearing a housecoat. He filed away a mental note to look her up when it was all over.

"Look out," an excited voice on the radio was saying, "here it comes. . . ."

From Phil's vantage point it looked like the end of the world. With deep-throated booms and crashes, great chunks of the dam fell into the breach until a ragged V-shaped notch had been opened all the way to the top. A section of the crest roadway hung like a suspension bridge over the torrent before dropping, seemingly in slow motion, as a single piece. The lake, sensing that it had an unobstructed path to a level a thousand feet lower, pushed forward like a suddenly energized green glacier. The lower section of the breach, where brown water was still erupting like lava from a volcano, was obliterated by hundreds of thousands of tons of white water landing on it from above. The massive tide quickly blasted a wider and wider path for itself as the once stubborn dam seemed to lose its will to resist. The concrete spillway was undermined, sagged sideways, and was torn apart from the top down, one ponderous block after another. Phil took several steps backward instinctively, fearing that the solid rock abutment on which he was standing might be the next to go. He had intended to continue describing the scene before him, but his radio was no longer working—it was soaked with water, as were his clothes. He had lost the power to speak anyway, so stunned was he by the way the unleashed reservoir smashed through the dam. He had seen films of other dams failing, smaller dams impounding smaller reservoirs, but there was nothing in his experience or his imagination to prepare him for a display of destruction like this. It was like watching a mountain range breaking up or California sinking into the sea.

The ground beneath his feet shuddered as it would in an earthquake when a section of the dam a thousand feet wide and four thousand feet thick at the base detached itself from the rest of the embankment. A crack appeared halfway between the breach and the far end of the dam, revealing itself by a new eruption of water. Fully a third of the dam, a mass containing at least thirty million cubic yards of material, began to edge downstream as a unit, unable any longer to hold back the weight of the water pushing against it. As it moved, it slumped until water was sweeping over the crest and down the face as well as boiling around the sides, and when that happened it slowly lost its shape, sinking and spreading like a pile of mud.

A river wider than the Columbia pushed through the opening, sloping downward as it streamed to a new, lower level a quarter mile downstream. The widening flood fan from the first break was overtaken and overwhelmed by an avalanche of new water hundreds of feet deeper. In minutes Sutterton was crushed and obliterated by a fury that would scour the valley down to bedrock from one end to the other.

The main wall of water, unobstructed, rolled over the town at fifty miles an hour. When it struck the hillside below the town where the river and the canyon turned right, a mighty sheet of water surged up the slope like the crash of surf against a seawall. It was a splash of death. When the wave fell back into the main flood, the slope had been swept clean of trees, topsoil, houses . . . and sightseers.

30

KENT SPAIN WAS FEELING FINE, STRIDING LONG, AND BREATHING FREE. And smiling. Only a mile more to the steps of the Sutterton City Hall, where he would break the tape for a stunning new Mother Lode Marathon record. After coming so close to dropping out, the big bucks, the fame, the cars, the clothes, the women, and the food would be his after all. Downhill the rest of the way, along a lane on a hill above the town, to the fairgrounds, down a steep gravel road to the city limits, then up the length of Main Street waving to the cheering throngs.

A helicopter clattered overhead, the fourth he had seen since crossing the dam. Sure a lot of hoopla for a relatively obscure cross-country run. The sport was getting too big for its own good. Rounding a corner, he saw people standing with their backs toward him. They were in the pathway, on the grassy slope above the path-way, and on the ridge in the distance, people with suitcases and laundry bags and boxes, people in clusters with their arms around each other. Children were crying.

"Keep this lane clear!" he shouted, sidestepping his way through the strangely silent crowd. "There's a race going on! Let me through. . . ."

"Stupid goddam fool," he heard a man say.

Responding with curses of his own, Kent left the path and picked his way along the hillside to get around the congestion. When he saw what they were looking at, he stopped in confusion. He was on the edge of an inland sea. Where he expected to find the gravel road that descended into town, there was only water, water that stretched to the hills on the opposite side of the valley a mile and a half away.

"Where am I?" he shouted, bouncing up and down on the balls of his feet to keep his circulation going. "I must have made a wrong turn. Where's Sutterton? Which way do I go? What the hell is wrong with you people? What's going on? Are you deaf? Which way to City Hall?"

A woman raised her arm and pointed toward the center of the lake, where floating debris revealed a swift current. "There is Sutterton," she said in a small voice, "under the water. The dam broke. Everything is gone."

Kent stopped bouncing. He turned in a slow circle as the truth of the woman's words sank into his brain like a deadening gas. The desolation on the faces of the people around him made it clear that the loss he had suffered was trivial compared to theirs.

Sitting on the grass next to him were a man and a woman and three children, all sobbing quietly. Beginning to sob himself, he sat down beside them and lowered his face into his hands. Sitting was bad for the lumbar, but Kent Spain didn't care anymore.

Freddy banked the plane to give his father a view of the clearing. "There it is," he said. "You jump first. When you're on the ground and out of your chute, I'll drop the moneybags to you, point the plane toward Mexico, and jump myself."

"You gotta be kidding," Emil Hasset said with a smile that was threatening to become permanent. "Me jump before the money? No way."

"You think I'll head for Vegas or someplace without you, is that it? What'd I tell you? We ain't even out of the plane yet and already we're at each other's fucking throats."

"Who's at anybody's fucking throat? Not me. I'm happy. I feel like a million bucks. But when I go out that door, the million bucks is going with me, one sack under each arm. Leaving you up here with all the loot is just not good business, with all due respect."

"Pop, you can't jump with the money. When your chute opens, you'll get a jolt and you'll drop the bags in the trees or the river and we might never find them. If you did manage to hang on, you'd be so heavy your legs would break like pretzels when you hit."

"I'm not leaving you with the loot, period. It's a temptation even the Virgin Mary would snap at. I know you, Freddy! You once tried to split my forehead with a pool cue." He took off his cap. "Lookit, I still have the scar."

Freddy sighed. "That was ten years ago. Okay, here's another idea. I circle low and we drop the sacks close to the cottage. Then I go up to about fifteen hundred feet and you bail out. I'll jump from two thousand because I got to make sure the plane clears the ridge."

"Ain't fifteen hundred a little low for me? I'm just a beginner."

"Plenty high. Can't take you higher because you don't know how to steer. If a wind comes up, you might land in Minnesota or some fucking place."

Emil fingered the harness on his chest. "How does this work, anyway?"

"Simple. That thing there's the ripcord. Soon as you're outta the plane, pull it. When you hit the ground, don't try to keep your feet. Go limp. Crumple up and roll with the punch."

"Sounds easy enough. Let's get it over with." Emil put a hand on his son's shoulder. "Look, kid, I'm sorry if it sounded like I don't trust you. It's just that I—"

"You don't trust me," Freddy snapped, pushing his father's hand away. "So what? That's nothing new. Always you think I'm going to fuck you over in some fucking way."

"Maybe because you *have* so many times. I know I haven't been the greatest dad a kid ever had, but in the next couple of months you're going to see a new man. You'll see I'm not such a bad guy. Maybe when the heat is off, you and I can—"

"Oh, bullshit. You're in this for yourself and for the money, and the same goes for me. When the heat's off, I'm splitting. Forget the family stuff. I don't want to hear that shit."

"Okay, okay," Emil said, raising his hands. "Calm down. Sure, I'm in this mainly for myself. That doesn't mean we can't forget the old days and all that ancient history. Why can't we start over?"

Freddy refused to continue the conversation. Instead he pointed at the moneybags and told his father to move them into position in the open doorway. Freddy's aim with the bags was excellent. When he said "Now," his father pushed them out of the plane and they landed within twenty feet of the cottage. His aim with his father was just as good. Emil Hasset, struggling to open a parachute pack that had been sealed shut with a few twists of a pliers, dropped like a rock into a clump of small trees at the edge of the clearing where his body would be out of sight and yet easy to find.

Freddy banked in a wide circle, then straightened out for another jump run. Adjusting the controls carefully, he trimmed the plane for straight, level flight. Floating under his canopy thirty seconds later, Freddy watched the Cessna, climbing gently in response to its reduced weight, disappear over the ridge. It would go two hundred miles south at least, maybe twice that far, with any luck at all. It looked as though luck was finally running with Frederick N. Hasset.

He guided himself to a patch of ground free of rocks, tumbling expertly on impact. Regaining his feet, he unbuckled and slipped out of the parachute harness, gathered the billowing folds into a ball, and carried it to the cottage. The keys were where they had left them—under a coffee can on the porch. After throwing the chute inside he paused, looking and listening. There was nobody around. No nosy fishermen, hunters, hikers, wardens, or neighbors. A clockwork heist. The newspapers would be talking about criminal masterminds.

He retrieved the canvas sacks, dragging them into the small front room and leaning them against the sofa. They were heavier than he thought they would be and he was anxious to count the contents. No time for that now, though. He had to conduct a simple, nonreligious burial service.

The garden tools were in a storage crib outside. He selected a spade and carried it to the clump of trees at the low side of the clearing. The ground was wet and soft, and his father's body was pressed into it face down like some kind of broken swastika, the arms and legs protruding awkwardly. There was blood oozing from the collar and cuffs of the guard's uniform.

Freddy worked quickly, digging a shallow grave. When it was long and deep enough, he used the point of the spade to turn the body into it. In returning dirt to the hole, he started at the head end in order to cover the grin that was frozen on his father's face.

As he worked, he became aware of a distant rumble, like that of a train crossing a bridge. There was no railroad in the valley. The sound grew steadily louder. Freddy straightened and rested his hands and chin on the top of the shovel handle. He had heard a sound like that once before at an air show at Travis Air Force Base

near Sacramento when a squadron of World War II bombers was
approaching from behind a hill.

An odd wind sprang up in the trees, odd because it was without
gusts . . . just a steady stream of air from the northeast moving at
about fifteen miles an hour and carrying with it a suggestion of
moisture, like a breeze off the sea. It didn't smell like the sea,
though. The smell was more like the San Joaquin River at flood
stage, a combination of fish, sewers, and fresh-cut grass.

The wind grew stronger. A hundred birds rose from the trees and
headed down the valley.

Leaving his father half uncovered, Freddy dropped the spade
and walked uphill to the side of the cottage. From there he could
see a mile upstream. More birds took to the air. A rabbit dashed
crazily across the clearing.

The horizon was formed by the tops of the hills where the valley
narrowed to nearly vertical cliffs that followed the river around a
sharp bend. The sky was clear and blue, but rising from somewhere
beyond the bend was an enormous black cloud of dust. An avalanche was the only explanation Freddy could think of. A mountain
had caved in and frightened the animals. But that growing
roar . . .

The wall of water flashed into view, coming around the turn in
the canyon like the head of a snake with scales that reflected blacks
and browns and silvers. It collided against the outside of the turn,
rising high on the cliffs before folding back on itself. The roar increased a thousandfold and Freddy was hit by a blast of wind so
strong that he was almost knocked backward off his feet. He
dropped to all fours and stared at the apparition the way a dog that
was frozen with fear might stare at an approaching locomotive. He
was in the grip of a terror so great he was unable to move or
breathe. A seething mass of water hundreds of feet high was hurtling toward him like a fantastic wall of surf, boiling with debris, a
great, rolling wall of water that nearly filled the canyon to
overflowing, ponderous, thundering, impossibly huge, a monster
from a psychotic nightmare, leaping, writhing, roaring, crashing,
every part in motion, always falling forward.

Freddy managed to get to his feet in the face of a gale-force
wind that filled the air with dust, pine needles, and the branches of
trees. He staggered up the slope, unable to tear his eyes from the
mountain of moving water that now filled half the sky and resem-

bled a constantly collapsing building that was being pushed forward from behind. He ran into a tree and threw his arms around it,
embracing it with all his strength, knowing he would be engulfed
so quickly that trying to reach high ground was utterly useless.

The flood was so close now he could pick out details—a billboard,
the side of a house, entire trees, a truck trailer—all of it boiling with
a million other pieces of debris, sliding down the face of a towering
waterfall only to be revolved back to the top and thrown down
again. Freddy could see the trees on the floor of the valley being
knocked over toward him in great rows like weeds before a scythe,
partly by the down-crashing water and partly by a great mass of
debris that was being pushed ahead like a rolling windrow of trash
in a bulldozer blade. He tightened his grip on the tree and closed
his eyes. His heart stopped beating. Just before he was hit, he did
the only thing he could think of, and that was to hope that the
roughness of the bark against his hands and cheek was the real
world while the world that was exploding around him was
madness.

Forty-five minutes after the destruction of Sutterton, Police Chief
Wilson Hartley was ten miles below the dam, careening down the
county road in his police cruiser, stopping at every campgrounds
and dwelling that didn't require a side trip. He had managed to
pound on the doors of at least thirty cottages, house trailers, and
camper trucks, almost half of which were occupied by people who
hadn't heard a thing about the approaching flood. He had sent
three fishermen and a dozen members of a Sierra Club hiking party
scampering up hillsides to safety. No telling how many unseen
campers and hikers had heeded the warning he broadcast over
and over on the car's public-address loudspeaker. To make sure one
house was empty, he had to shoot an attacking German shepherd
that had been abandoned by its owners in their haste to flee.

The advance of the water was being monitored from planes and
relayed to the communications van. Hartley heard Mrs. Lehmann's
voice, cut by static, report that the wave had just hit the fish hatchery at Castle Rock. The hatchery was a mile and a half upstream.

He braked to a stop at the driveway leading to Creekwood, Roshek's imposing summer home. He debated with himself whether
he had enough time to check it out . . . he was between five and
eight minutes ahead of the wave. He had seen Roshek arrive and

leave the overlook in a helicopter, so chances were the old man himself had made sure there was nobody at the house, but still . . . Hartley had been at Creekwood only once, when Roshek had hosted a stiff and proper lawn party on the day of the dam dedication. The driveway was about a quarter of a mile long, he remembered, and fairly straight. It would only take twenty seconds each way, and when he got back to the main road he would still have at least four minutes to spare. From there to the mouth of the canyon it was a straight shot he could take at top speed, putting some breathing room between himself and disaster. Two miles downstream, just across the bridge, were three different roads he could take to high ground. With his siren turned to high, he turned into the Creekwood driveway.

From the top of the massive stone chimney curled a peaceful column of smoke. A man and a woman who obviously had heard him coming were watching him from the porch. Hartley was relieved to see that they were young and healthy; otherwise he would have had to take them with him. He wanted as much room in his car as possible to pick up stragglers he might meet in his final sprint to safety.

"The dam has broken!" Hartley shouted, stopping at the bottom of the porch steps and waving his arm. "A flood hundreds of feet deep will be here in minutes. . . . Go up the hill all the way to the top . . . right now, get going. . . ."

The couple looked at each other in amazement, then back at Hartley.

"The dam has broken!" Hartley shouted again, cutting the siren to make sure his words were understood. "You've got to climb the hill as fast as you can." With the siren off it was possible to hear a distant rumble, so faint it was hardly more than a whisper. Hartley pointed upstream. "Hear that noise? That's the flood coming down the canyon. . . . Look, you can see the dust it's raising. Run up the hill, run as hard as you can and keep running. . . . It's your best chance . . . good luck!"

Hartley made a hard U-turn on the lawn, the tires cutting black gashes. He paused for a few seconds to watch the frightened pair running up the grassy slope behind the house. They bounded forward like gazelles and were plainly in remarkable physical condition. Probably athletes of some kind. There was no question that they would make it to the top. He floored the accelerator and shot down the driveway, confident that he had saved two more lives; now he would concentrate on saving his own.

The two miles between Creekwood and the mouth of the canyon he took at seventy miles an hour. Just before the road crossed the river and intersected with a state highway he had to slam on the brakes. Four cars were stopped ahead of him. The Sierra Canyon River, out of its banks and carrying a heavy load of flotsam, had taken out the bridge. Hartley got slowly out of his car and collapsed against it with his arms on the roof, staring at the gap in the road where the bridge had been. There was no way he could climb to safety on foot, for this part of the valley was lined with nearly vertical cliffs. The drivers and passengers from the other cars ran to him and surrounded him. A screaming woman clutched at his uniform and pointed at the river. Her husband restrained her, explaining in a voice broken by sobs that the bridge had collapsed just minutes earlier and that in a car that had been swept away with it were their daughter, their son-in-law, and two grandchildren. Any notions Hartley might have had about bursting into tears himself or falling to his knees in prayer had to be set aside. Ten people close to hysteria were crowding around him, shouting questions and expecting him to give them answers. They wanted to be told what to do. More than once in his career he had managed to calm people down simply by adopting an authoritative pose. Doctors did the same thing when they pretended to know more than they possibly could. He raised his hand and asked for silence. "There's a Forest Service fire road a half mile upstream!" he shouted. "Get in your cars and follow me."

Driving back up the canyon in the face of a steady head wind, Hartley saw in his rear view mirror the caravan of cars following him. What he saw through the windshield made it plain that they were all on a journey of futility. Above the trees was a cloud of boiling dust that turned the morning brightness into a deepening and ominous gloom.

The fire road was little more than a wide dirt path, rutted from spring runoff and blocked to bikers and hotrodders by a horizontal steel beam that was hinged to a post at one end and padlocked at the other. Hartley ran to the barricade and shattered the lock with two shots from his service revolver. As he climbed back into the car, wind whipped his clothes and hurled dirt and pine needles at him with such force that he had to close his eyes to keep from being blinded. A continuous and growing roar told him that the wave was no more than half a mile away.

The car lurched forward, weaving from side to side as the wheels spun in the dirt, bouncing over the ruts and scattered rocks. He eased up on the accelerator until the tires achieved traction, then gradually pressed it to the floor. The high-powered V-8 engine, capable of sending the car down a freeway at a hundred miles an hour, enabled Hartley to leave the other vehicles far behind, but he wasn't thinking about them. He didn't risk taking his eyes off the treacherous roadway to glance in the mirror. He didn't look over his shoulder, either, afraid that he might see the source of the thunder that had grown so loud it blotted out every other sound. He jerked the wheel right and left to avoid the worst gullies and boulders, smashing through fallen limbs and hoping that he wouldn't find the way blocked by a ditch or an upended tree. A light splash of water struck the windshield, instinctively he flicked on the wipers.

The fire road followed a sidehill course, rising at a constant grade of twelve percent. For a full minute Hartley plunged recklessly ahead, gaining at least two hundred feet in elevation. Even though one tire had gone flat and the oil pan had been lost to rocks, he kept the accelerator floored. The feeling came over him that he was going to make it after all. One more minute, that's all he needed, just one more minute.

The road, always pitched steeply upward, curved to the right and entered a crease between two mountain shoulders. Hartley was traveling directly away from the river now. To his left was the steep mountainside on the other side of the draw, brown in color from a layer of humus and decayed needles and dotted with widely spaced pines and rock outcroppings. Looking left and upward, Hartley could see far above him on the opposite slope a diagonal line—that, he knew, was the fire road after it had rounded the switchback at the end of the side canyon. If he could reach that elevation, he would be safe.

With stunning speed, the brown slope turned white. A sheet of foam swept over it from left to right as if a bucket of soapy water had been dashed against a wall. At the same time, a river of water several feet deep surged uphill around and under the car, sliding it ahead and causing the rear wheels to lose their grip. The engine died. Within seconds a powerful backwash streamed over the hood and roof, turning the car until it was facing downhill and pinning it against the slope on the high side of the road. Water boiled over the windows.

Hartley set the emergency brake and waited, hanging tightly on to the wheel. The car was totally submerged and water was squirting through crevices in the floor, the dashboard, and the doors. He wondered if this was the worst of it. Maybe the flood would subside before the car filled with water, maybe . . . He felt a current dislodge the car and give it several gentle shoves along the ground, like a box being nudged by a giant paw. He realized then that he was sobbing, not from fear of pain or death but because of his utter helplessness. There was absolutely nothing he could do but grip the wheel and hope for the best. As a policeman, he had long ago come to terms with the possibility that he would die before his time, but he had always assumed that if it happened to him it would be swiftly, most likely by gunfire—not this way, not trapped in a car under water, my God, not by drowning.

A tremendous force lifted the car, revolved it slowly end over end, and dropped it on its side to the ground. Hartley was dazed when his head struck the doorpost, but he clung to consciousness. His reasoning powers continued to function with eerie coolness. Two windows were broken and water was jetting against him. He moved a hand toward the buckle of his seat belt. An air bubble will form near the rear window, he told himself. If the car stays where it is, I can last for an hour and maybe more. The water will have dropped by then. No bones broken. If I run out of air, I'll push myself through a window and swim to the surface.

The car was picked up again and pulled swiftly in a long arc out of the draw and into the main canyon. With a profound sense of hopelessness, Hartley realized that he was caught up in the flood's main current. The force of acceleration was so great it pressed him against the seat. The car was rolling over and over and was quickly filling with water. When Hartley felt the coldness on his face, he held his breath. There was no sense of panic. He was simply a boy again on a carnival ride. He was being drawn with delicious anticipation to the top of the roller coaster, ready for the big plunge that would make the girls scream and the boys hang on to their caps. Suddenly the car was hit by a counterforce that sent it straight down. He braced himself the way a man would in an elevator that was dropping in a free-fall toward the bottom of a shaft.

Along with a thousand other pieces of debris, the car was hurled against the canyon floor from a height of two hundred feet, crushed to no more than a fourth of its original size, then rolled along the ground like a wad of paper on a windswept street. Again the car was drawn upward by circular currents in the flood wave, this time almost to the surface, and propelled downstream in a broad sweep through the mouth of the canyon. The second time the car dropped, it was driven like a stake into the loam that lined the Sacramento River. In the following three hours, as the tide rolled over it with decreasing energy, it was buried under thirty feet of silt.

31

IT WAS TWELVE MILES FROM THE DAM TO THE MOUTH OF THE CANYON, where the Sierra Canyon River emerged from the foothills and followed a meandering course through the flatlands of the upper Central Valley to a confluence with the Sacramento River at the town of Omohundro. The flood fought its way down the twisting canyon like a thing alive, a lengthening serpent, surging from one side to another and gathering into itself everything that wasn't solid rock. The sides and bottom of the flow, retarded by the rough surfaces presented by the indented hills, rock palisades, and side canyons, and the work of scouring and uprooting, advanced more slowly than the main mass of water, which was constantly flowing downward from above and pounding the valley floor with an endless series of hammer blows. In the hour it took the flood to reach the canyon mouth, it picked up so much debris that only half of it was water—the rest was dam embankment material, topsoil, river gravel, trees, logs, telephone poles, structures ranging from houses to bridges, farm animals, and at least fifty miles of wiring and fences.

Those who saw the advance of the wave from hilltops and planes were later to describe it in a variety of ways.

"The first thing I saw was the dust cloud," said Kitty Sprague, a Forest Service trail worker. "I thought it was smoke, and radioed that a huge fire had broken out. A few minutes later I saw the flood, which was like a rolling mountain of water pushing a city dump. The front of it was half hidden by mist, but I could see a fantastic squirming, with whole houses being tossed around."

An orchard handyman named Knox Burger had a narrow escape. "I was running up the hill as fast as I could. Behind me was my brother Kurt carrying his three-year-old boy. The wind was so fierce it near ripped my shirt off, and I saw a barn get flattened as if somebody stepped on it. When I looked down below, I couldn't believe my eyes—a monster as big as the valley was sliding along making a noise like World War III. We thought we were high enough to be safe, but a splash of water landed on us and tried to drag us down. I grabbed a tree and kept my feet, but the boy was torn out of Kurt's arms. He let out a bellow and jumped in the water, and that was the last I saw of either of them."

Evelyn Frances Hayes, state assemblywoman from Sausalito, was camping with a group of Girl Scouts on McFarland Peak above the mouth of the canyon. "The odd thing was that it was such a beautiful day," she told the Sacramento *Bee*. "One would expect the end of the world to come with the sky full of thunderclouds and lightning flashes. That's what I thought, that Armageddon had arrived. All of nature's destructive forces seemed turned loose. God was destroying the world without giving anybody time to pray. It never occurred to me that a dam had failed, because the devastation was taking place on such an enormous scale that it seemed beyond anything human beings could be responsible for. I gathered the girls into a group and we all put our arms around each other. We watched the flood come out the canyon and fan out across the orchards and rice fields like a stain growing on a piece of cloth. When it reached Omohundro, the houses got pushed together as if somebody was sweeping toys into a pile. Then they got folded under and we couldn't see them anymore."

Tim Hanson, an operatic tenor who lived in Omohundro, told his story several times on national television hookups from his hospital bed in Chico. What viewers saw and heard on their screens was a man whose face, hands, and arms were covered with bandages, whose gestures seemed intended for audiences in the upper balcony, and whose voice was full of dramatic tension. "I didn't hear the warnings because I was in a soundproof booth I built in my bedroom so I can rehearse without the neighbors calling the police. I was working on the role of Lindoro in Rossini's *The Italian Girl in*

Algiers, which I'm doing next month in San Francisco for Pippen's Pocket Opera.

"When I felt the house shaking, I left the booth and looked out the window. Three blocks away a tumbling wall of rubbish was coming toward me knocking down trees and houses. I didn't see any water at all, just a churning mass of trash and trees and pieces of buildings. A couple of miles away, though, I could see water—it was pouring from Sierra Canyon like syrup from a pitcher.

"I ran up the stairs to the attic and climbed through a skylight to the top of the roof. I sat with my arms around the chimney and watched the houses down the street get crunched one after the other. When my house got hit, it stayed in one piece and started rolling over. It must have rolled over three or four times before it broke up, with me climbing to stay on the high side like lumberjacks do on logs in a river. The noise was terrific, the roll of a thousand drums with the sound of trees and boards splitting. I ended up getting swirled downstream hanging on to a piece of an outside wall. A woman I know who works at the bank came floating by on a barrel. I called her name and she turned and nodded as if nothing unusual was happening. She sailed by as if she knew exactly where she was going, and I never saw her again.

"Where I was going was down the Sacramento River. I didn't know where I would end up, but I had visions of eventually going right under the Golden Gate Bridge. Finally I got snagged in some bushes and people with ropes helped me get to solid ground. I was covered with cuts and bruises and was taken here to the hospital. I'm going to sing in that opera even if I have to dress like *The Return of the Mummy.*"

The San Francisco *Chronicle* in its coverage quoted a retired army colonel named Tom Stewart, who had witnessed the destruction of Sutterton. "When the water subsided, the town had disappeared without a trace. The valley was nothing but wet bedrock. Everything had been shaved off clean as a whistle, including building foundations. I got in my car and drove north along what used to be the edge of the lake. I was in a daze. I think I was *looking* for the town, expecting to see it around every turn. All I saw were mud flats and boats on their sides. In some places the lake had dropped so fast fish were trapped in puddles. Hundreds of them were flopping around. I saw two kids going after them with sacks."

*   *   *

Roshek was seen leaving the overlook in a helicopter and he was seen at the Yuba City airport boarding his company's private jet. When he landed in Los Angeles, the press was waiting. Jim Oliver was appalled by both the size and the bad manners of the crowd. He had thought he might have to compete with three or four people at the most, not a swarming pack of thirty. Reporters and cameramen surrounded the wheelchair like pigs at a trough, extending microphones, firing flashbulbs, and shouting questions. Oliver jotted a line in his notebook about the change in the engineer's appearance. His face was as hawklike as ever and his heavily browed eyes just as intense, but his chin was close to his chest instead of defiantly thrust forward. His body didn't seem to fill up his clothes. He looked like a man returning from a long stay in a hospital.

At curbside, when Roshek was being helped into his limousine, he showed a flash of his old personality. With a sudden thrust of a crutch he knocked a camera to the sidewalk.

"You son of a bitch," a photographer said, stooping to pick up the pieces.

"Sue me," Roshek said. "My attorney needs the money."

Before the door was closed, Oliver managed to elbow his way to the front. "I'm Jim Oliver," he said through the clamor. "I interviewed you five years ago when an earthquake hit close to the dam. Remember? The Los Angeles *Times*. Could I call you for an appointment?"

Roshek didn't look at him. "I read the Anaheim *Shopper* myself. Now there is a hell of a paper."

Oliver straightened up and stepped back. Roshek had said something similar to him five years before, and he had included it in his article. It wasn't the same this time. The line was delivered now mechanically, as if Roshek were playing a role that was expected of him. He was impersonating himself. Oliver made another entry in his notebook.

The limousine rolled ten feet down the street and stopped. The front door opened and the driver got out. "Jim Oliver of the Los Angeles *Times?*"

Oliver raised his hand. The driver motioned him inside the car and held a rear door open for him.

"Thanks very much for singling me out like that," Oliver said when the limousine was under way again. "I can certainly understand why you might not want to talk to the press right now."

Roshek waved his hand to indicate that pleasantries were unnecessary. Oliver noticed that his business suit was flecked with mud, that his collar was starched and one size too big, that his skin was as white as typing paper, and that he wasn't wearing his hat.

"I singled you out because I remember that last article you wrote about dams. It was one of the least ridiculous pieces ever to appear in a newspaper on an engineering subject. Why do papers have science editors and not engineering editors? People are touched by engineering every minute of the day. Cars, television, frozen food, plastics—these things are more the artifacts of engineering than science. Newspapers should—"

"Did you see the dam fail?" The question stopped Roshek. His mouth closed and his eyes drifted into the distance. "Could you tell me how it made you feel?"

"Imagine," Roshek said in a quiet, unemotional voice, "looking into a mirror and seeing brown water gushing from a socket where one of your eyes had been. Imagine looking at your stomach and seeing it slowly split open and your guts spill out on the floor."

Oliver swallowed. His pencil was momentarily paralyzed.

"My feelings aren't important," Roshek went on in the same voice. "If you are intending to write a so-called human interest story featuring my feelings, you can get out of the car right now."

"Your feelings *are* important. I don't intend to feature them, but I would like to ask a few questions about—"

"I don't care about your questions. I have a message to give to the American people. That's why you're here."

"I see. The American people. The American people are going to want to know why the dam failed."

Roshek was stopped again, and a shadow of pain crossed his face. He covered his eyes for a moment before answering. "The dam failed because of me. Because I thought it couldn't. I believed that nothing I designed could fail. I still believe that, but only if I stay with the structure to make sure it is properly cared for. Because I thought the dam was invulnerable, I turned it over to others who didn't recognize the dangers and who didn't keep on top of the details, as I would have. As the saying goes, if you want something done right, do it yourself. The world is in a hell of a mess today, wouldn't you say, Oliver? You know why? Because God sent his only begotten son to earth to save the human race and the job was botched. He should have gone himself. See the parallel? God's mistake was that he sent a boy to do a man's job."

Oliver eyed the man who was slumped in the corner of the seat, wondering if he was losing his grip on reality. He certainly looked broken physically. Maybe his mind was going as well.

"I don't mean to compare myself to God," Roshek said, "if that's how that sounded. I was a creator—small 'c.' I accept part of the blame for what happened. At the same time, though, God is partly to blame, if you want to use that term. In designing the dam, I applied the mathematics as perfectly as God could have done it himself. God is to blame for providing misleading geophysical data."

"I'm afraid I—"

"I didn't know the fault was there. The one that caused the earthquake five years ago. We had brown water coming into the lower drainage galleries on that occasion, too, did you know that? No, because we managed to keep it quiet. We didn't want the public to get excited over nothing. We thought the problem was minor and we corrected it. It's obvious now we were wrong. You are probably looking for a villain to make your story easier to write. An incompetent designer, a contractor using substandard materials, a corrupt politician pushing through a pork-barrel dam project that made no sense. It's not that simple. The dam made a lot of sense. If there is a villain, it is the unknown, which we can never eliminate entirely. What we knew and what we were able to find out, we took into account. What we didn't know destroyed us."

Oliver looked up from his notebook. "Let me see if I have this straight. You say an earthquake weakened the foundation. You thought you fixed it. The weakness reappeared five years later and wasn't noticed because . . . Why wasn't it noticed? Aren't there instruments in the dam that—"

"It wasn't noticed because of an incredible string of human and mechanical breakdowns," Roshek said, gesturing, his voice getting louder. "Instruments failed, instruments gave wrong readings, instruments weren't read, instruments were ignored by a chief inspector who was suffering from what can only be called terminal optimism. When we knew something was wrong, we sent him below, when the dam still could have been saved, and he died of a heart attack or some goddam thing. As if that wasn't enough, we had a nincompoop of a control-room operator who didn't grasp what was happening until it was too late." Roshek's eyes were flashing, and he was opening and closing his fists in frustration. "The timing was another thing. The state was due at the site today to take a look . . . today! Yesterday and the whole mess wouldn't have happened. Another terrible thing is that this happened in California, which has the best system of dam safety regulations in the world, regulations I fought for years to get adopted. . . ."

Roshek turned his face to the window. Oliver spent five minutes catching up on his notes, then asked the engineer if it was true that a young employee of his sensed something was wrong and spent the night fruitlessly trying to sound an alarm.

"If you can't have a villain, you want a hero—is that it?"

"I'm only trying to verify rumors I've heard."

"A young employee," Roshek said with distaste, "tried to sound an alarm that would have been sounded anyway."

"But not as soon. Because of him a couple of hours were gained, isn't that so?"

"Five minutes is more like it. No, I take that back. Just because I detest Kramer doesn't mean I should run him down. What he did was remarkable. Maybe two hours is fair. Ask somebody else. I can't be objective."

"Is it true you fired him for telling you the dam was in trouble and that you had him jailed for trying to prove he was right?"

Roshek's response was so explosive spittle flew from his lips. "It's also true I had him released from jail when I knew he was right. I ordered him put in charge. And when I saw him a few hours ago I had the urge to kill him. Why? Because the whole thing was so goddam unfair I couldn't stand it. The greatest engineering structure ever built was failing, a structure that was as much a part of me as . . . as these goddam crutches. Because it was failing, an arrogant young puppy who still doesn't realize how incredibly lucky he was and who has contributed *nothing* to the building of this nation—absolutely nothing!—is to be idolized, while I . . . My life and my career are wrecked. My . . ." He clapped a hand over his eyes and bared his teeth as if trying to withstand a terrible pain without crying out. He fell back into the corner of the seat. The driver of the limousine turned around with an expression of concern, lifting his foot from the accelerator, but Roshek with irritation told him to keep going, that he was all right.

The limousine swung off the Harbor Freeway at the Wilshire exit. When Roshek spoke again, he was calm. "Just because a man

is a hero doesn't necessarily mean he is likable. Kramer is still with
our firm and we have big plans for him. He puts the lie to the impression the public has of engineers as mechanical men without
hearts."

"I don't imagine you want me to write that you had an urge to
kill him."

"Write what you want about me. If you want to trivialize your
story by dealing with personalities, go ahead. Gossip may be what
the American people want, but it's not what they need."

"What is it that they need? What is it you want me to tell them?
Assuming I can get their attention."

Roshek leaned toward Oliver and spoke with great earnestness.
"The American people need safe dams. There are nine thousand
dams in this country that would cause extensive damage if they
failed, and a third of them don't meet modern safety standards. It's
like having three thousand bombs waiting to go off. One survey
concluded that it was between a hundred and a thousand times
more likely that a dam would fail and kill a thousand people than
that a nuclear accident would do it. Unbelievable as it seems, there
are states where a real-estate developer or a farmer can build a
dam without even applying for a permit! Without hiring an engineer to design it! When it's built and forgotten about, there is no
requirement for periodic safety inspections. Not more than thirty
states have even a half-assed set of rules and regulations on the
books backed up by an adequate enforcement. How many people
are going to have to be killed?"

The limousine pulled up in front of Roshek's office building.

"I care about dams, you see," Roshek said. "When one fails, it is
a reflection on engineering, on engineers, and on the whole idea of
dams. That this country tolerates unsafe dams is because of politics,
not engineering. Engineers know what has to be done, but politicians won't give us the green light or the money to do it. That's
where you come in, Oliver. There will be a big clamor now about
dam safety, but it will die down the way it did after the failure of
Teton and Taccoa. Don't let it fade! Keep beating the drums! Make
the states face up to their responsibilities before there's an even
worse disaster than the one we just suffered through. If the states
won't act, make the federal government step in."

"That's a big order. I'm just a reporter and feature writer."

"Promise me you'll do what you can."

"I'll do what I can. It sounds like a worthy campaign. I can't imagine that things are quite as bad as you say."

"They are far worse, as you'll find out."

On the sidewalk, Roshek made a show of being his old self, sitting erectly in his wheelchair and shaking the reporter's hand with vigor and decisiveness. Oliver watched through the building's glass doors as Roshek wheeled himself across the lobby to the elevators. He was surprised to realize that he liked the sharp-edged old man. He felt he almost understood him. He felt something else as well—that he would never see him again.

32

PHIL KRAMER TOOK A LAST LOOK. DOWNSTREAM FROM WHERE THE DAM had stood, the valley was denuded. Above the damsite were deeply fissured beds of sediment through which a placid Sierra Canyon River meandered, sparkling in the noon sunshine. On the far side of the canyon was the apparently undamaged intake tower, rising from the mud like an elevator shaft without its skyscraper. All that was left of the dam was a section of the embankment extending about a thousand feet from the opposite abutment. Phil could see Herman Bolen's airplane on the crest roadway, still lying upside down where it had been left.

He turned when he heard his name, and saw the television reporter in the butterscotch sport coat. "Mrs. Lehmann says it's okay to talk to you now," he said. "Everybody agrees you are the key to this story, so we'd like an interview. Maybe in depth."

Phil walked slowly away from the railing and sat down on the front bumper of a truck. "I don't want to be interviewed. I need a couple of days of sleep." He hung his head and closed his eyes. "My legs are killing me. My back is killing me. I feel sick. My car is gone. I'm hungry. I want to go home, but I don't have my clothes or my shoes or my billfold."

"If you could just tell me how you got arrested, and then how you got *un*arrested. . . . Hello? Are you asleep?"

Phil raised his head. "Say, are you the guys with the helicopter?"

"Yes. We call it the Telecopter."

"Tell you what. I'll give you an interview, in depth or any other way, if you'll do me a favor."

"What kind of favor?"

"See that thing sticking up out of the mud that looks like the world's tallest silo? That's the intake tower. It's eight hundred and forty-five feet high. My shoes and watch and clothes and billfold are up there in a neat little pile."

The reporter eyed him narrowly. "On top of the tower? How did they get there?"

"That will emerge during the interview. I also want you to take me to a phone so I can call Santa Monica and ask a certain special someone for a date, whose name will also emerge during the interview."

"Mr. Kramer, I don't know if you're joking or not, but I do know I can't give you a ride in the Telecopter. Crew only. No outsiders under any conditions. I could lose my job."

Phil shrugged. "Okay. I'll give the interview to someone else. Why not channel seven? I see some guys over there with sevens on their jackets."

The reporter cursed under his breath. He pointed at the helicopter. "Get in," he said.

The phone call to Janet was made from a booth in Chico. Phil sat on the sidewalk holding the folding door open with his shoulder. A group of television and newspaper reporters waited nearby, anxious to resume questioning him.

"Phil, is that you?" Janet answered before the first ring was completed. "I'm so glad to hear your voice! I saw you on television a few minutes ago and you looked . . . well, exhausted."

"That's probably because I'm exhausted. I feel like a washrag that's been wrung out and thrown in a corner. All I want to do is collapse in a bed. Preferably yours. Jesus, Janet, what I've been through in the last twenty-four hours has been . . . I can't find words. I'll say this, though, I don't think I'll ever smile again."

"I'll make you smile . . . with my magic fingers."

"I'm smiling again."

"I'm so proud of you! What you did was absolutely fantastic!"

"You weren't so bad yourself. The guys in the control room said they got phone calls from all kinds of agencies asking about a crazy woman in Santa Monica."

"I had to act crazy to get anybody to take me seriously. When I acted serious, they thought I was crazy. The problem, I think, and I'm embarrassed to admit it now, is that I was afraid I was making a fool of myself. I was only three-fourths sure you weren't hallucinating. When you woke me up and said you were surrounded by cops, you sounded—well, overwrought."

"I was overwrought, all right. Whatever you did worked, because you sure stirred everybody up. God, I'm so tired! I'm totally knocked out. I can hardly hold the phone."

"What are you going to do now? When am I going to see you?"

"Soon as I get a few hours' sleep, I'm going to get on the first plane headed in your direction. I'm going to wrap my arms and legs around you and stay that way for about a month. After that, I don't know. According to the network nerds who have been following me around, I could spend the rest of my life appearing on talk shows. I don't want that. I can't see myself as a star of stage and screen. Give me a desk somewhere and let me sit in peace adding and subtracting numbers."

"For Roshek, Bolen & Benedetz?"

Phil laughed dryly. "No, not for Roshek, Bolen & Benedetz. Bolen says I still have my job, but I don't want it as long as Roshek is running the company. He's not only weird, he hates my guts. I can't help feeling sorry for the poor bastard, though. It must have been the shits for him to see the dam getting wiped out. I'm not thinking about a job right now. I'm thinking about sleep and I'm thinking about you. I don't ever want to be more than five minutes away from you again. Excuse me for going all mushy, but that's how I feel."

"You're a sweetheart, you know that? Do you mind if I call you sweetheart? And darling? And honey?"

"Music to my ears."

When Janet was off the line, Phil didn't bother hanging up. He let the receiver slip out of his hand. Dangling from its cord, it swung away and rattled against the sides of the booth. He waved at the newsmen and told them to get lost. Then he rolled face down and fell asleep on the sidewalk.

"I came in as soon as I heard the news."

"Thank you, Margaret," Roshek said. "I knew I could count on

you." It looked to him as if his secretary had powdered her face to
cover the traces of tears.

"Some of the men are here, too. Mr. Filippi is downstairs. Shall I
tell him that—"

"No, I don't want to be disturbed."

"You have a ton of messages. Everybody under the sun has been
trying to reach you, including your wife."

"Tell them I'm in a meeting."

Roshek locked his office door behind him, got two white towels
from the bathroom, and shifted himself into the swivel chair behind
his desk. He gave his wheelchair a push and watched it roll silently
across the rug and bump into the wall fifteen feet away. He
wouldn't be needing it again.

A touch of a button turned on the television set next to the
door. The three network channels were presenting flood coverage,
and he lingered for a minute or two on each one. The Sacramento
River was out of its banks and the capital was bracing itself for a
water level at least five feet above flood stage. No serious threat
was posed to the Rancho Seco nuclear plant. Ranchers in the delta
region were sandbagging levees even though state officials were as-
suring them that that far downstream the effects of the flood would
hardly be noticeable. Suisun Bay, San Pablo Bay, and the northern
half of San Francisco Bay were expected to turn brown for a day or
two, but marine biologists did not foresee a major fish kill. The
towns of Sutterton and Omohundro were thought to have been
evacuated in time. Most homes and summer cottages in Sierra Canyon were also emptied, thanks in part to a still-unidentified and
still-missing policeman who raced down the valley one step ahead
of the wave. Property damage would go over a billion dollars.
Fifty-six people were known dead and twice that many missing.
The Governor credited the amazingly low death toll to the well-or-
ganized emergency service programs in the affected counties,
which were set up with state assistance and coordinated with disaster control offices at the state level.

The Governor is right about something for a change, Roshek
thought as he turned off the set. In any other state thousands of
people might have been killed. Eleanor . . . had she survived? To
reach her, the daredevil policeman would have had to go quite a
distance off the main road. Well, it didn't make any difference.

He turned on his recorder and dictated a long memo to Herman

Bolen, giving him suggestions on how to act as president of the corporation and giving him his thoughts on the firm's most important contracts. Because of insinuations that might be made by certain rival engineering firms, Roshek warned his colleague, clients should be assured that the failure of the dam had nothing to do with design deficiencies. Roshek advised that Bolen and Filippi should immediately pay a personal visit to every major client, particularly those with whom contract negotiations were under way.

"With regard to Kramer," Roshek said, speaking crisply into the microphone, "it is absolutely essential that he remain with the firm. For him to join a competitor would have a devastating effect on our image. During the next few weeks, he is going to get a great deal of media attention, and it should not be surprising to you if he is invited to appear on the popular talk shows to narrate film clips of the failure. By giving him a promotion—say, to the head of a new department of dam safety investigation—any acclaim he gets can be shared by the corporation. Keeping him is the key. Offer him fifty thousand a year if you have to.

"As you know, Herman, I regard Kramer as a presumptuous young twerp who just happened to be in the right place at the right time. Seeing him in a position of prestige and seeing him honored by the engineering societies would make me sick. Fortunately, I'm leaving.

"You're a good man, Herman, all things considered. Best wishes."

Roshek picked up his fountain pen. On a sheet of company stationery he wrote: "I, Theodore Roshek, president of Roshek, Bolen & Benedetz, Inc., being of sound mind, as unlikely as that may seem to some, declare this to be my Last Will and Testament, written in my own hand, and hereby revoke all other Wills and Codicils previously made by me. I direct that my just debts be paid and all that sort of thing and that my body be cremated and disposed of without participation of the clergy. I direct that my entire estate be given to my faithful wife, Stella, who deserved better treatment from me than she got in the last few years.

"I do not wish any part of my estate to go to Eleanor James of San Francisco, who in my previous Will was provided for so generously and foolishly. Let me phrase that another way to make sure there is no misunderstanding: I want my wife to get everything and I want Miss James to get nothing. If Miss James gets so much as one dime of my money, I will come back from the grave and make those who let it happen so miserable they will wish they were dead instead of me.

"To my wife I want to say I'm sorry.

"As far as bequests to individuals and institutions are concerned, my wife, if she chooses, can follow the directions I gave in the last Will we prepared together."

Roshek signed and dated the sheet and added a line for his secretary to sign as a witness. Next he dictated a letter to his attorney.

"Dear Jules: Enclosed with this letter is a handwritten Will. I trust you will make sure the terms are carried out and that my previous Will, which was drawn up against your advice, is junked. I don't know if Eleanor survived the flood or not. If she did, she may contest my cutting her off by claiming that I am not mentally competent, as evidenced by my suicide. I assure you I know exactly what I am doing and am not off my rocker by any reasonable definition. On the contrary, taking my life now proves my sanity. It will save everybody a lot of grief and pain, including especially myself, and will, I suspect, add to the sum total of human happiness. My body is giving me more and more trouble and would not last more than four or five years in any case at the rate it is deteriorating. I am not going to spend my declining years in courtrooms testifying in the endless damage suits that even now are being concocted in offices like your own.

"Should you be called upon to *prove* my sanity on this day, you can put the Will into evidence. Note the strong, smooth handwriting. Not that of a crazy person, is it? Or play the tapes I have just recorded. Experts will find nothing in my voice that suggests tension or strain. It's my normal speaking voice. Not the voice of a man who is desperate or distraught. Far from it. Knowing the end is near, I'm almost happy.

"It's been nice knowing you, Jules. If you want to remember me, insult somebody who deserves it."

Roshek turned the television set on again and changed channels until he found a newscaster who resembled an actual human being. While listening to "updates on the disaster situation," he spread one towel on his desk and folded the other one into eighths. He removed the gun from the drawer and checked to make sure it was loaded and the safety was off. There were only five bullets. Five would be enough.

"Coming in the next hour," the newscaster said, "will be an ex-

clusive interview with Philip Kramer, the heroic engineer who is
being credited at this hour with saving the population of Sutterton,
the stories of an opera singer and two ballet dancers who had close
calls but lived to tell about it, and a replay of some of the most incredible film footage ever taken. Right now we take you live to the
campus of Cal Tech, where our Linda Fong is in the office of engineering professor Clark Kirchner. Linda?"

Roshek arranged every article on his desk so that the edges were
parallel with each other. A photo of Eleanor went into the waste-
basket, a photo of Stella was turned face down.

A mustachioed man on the television screen was holding forth on
the design of Sierra Canyon Dam. "I maintained then and I main-
tain now that it should have been able to resist a quake of six point
five at four miles rather than five miles. The slope of the upstream
face, considering the materials used, was at least ten percent too
steep. This was the highest embankment dam in the world, remember, and should not have been used to test so-called progres-
sive design theories that—"

The bullet entered the center of the screen, which imploded with
a vacuum pop and a shower of silvery glass needles. The next bullet shattered the glass that covered a painting of the dam.

Roshek heard Margaret scream. She was a dignified woman who
had been his secretary for twenty years. He had never heard her
scream before. He looked with respect at the weapon in his hand. A
remarkable invention, the gun. It gave a man the godlike ability to
hurl lightning bolts, like Thor, and its sound was the sound of
thunder.

On the right side of the office was a framed cross-sectional view
of the underground powerhouse. The third bullet smashed its glass
into a thousand pieces. Men were shouting and trying to force the
door open. Roshek could imagine Margaret, having found her key,
running to unlock it. No matter. They would never get to him in
time. The glass display case that housed the scale model of the dam
collapsed with a satisfying crash.

One bullet left. Roshek picked up the padded towel and held it
against the left side of his head, leaning forward over the towel
that was spread on his desk. He positioned the muzzle solidly
against his right temple, adjusting the angle so that the bullet
would strike squarely. He didn't want to graze his brain and turn

himself into a vegetable. This had to be a suicide, not an attempted suicide, and it had to be neat, clean, and efficient. No more failures. Sierra Canyon Dam was enough for one life.

When he was sure the gun was close to perpendicular to the side of his head, he pulled the trigger without hesitation.

Author's Note

I am deeply grateful for the help I received from J. Barry Cooke and his miracle-working daughter and office manager, Bonnie. Cooke has served as a consulting engineer on the siting, design, construction, and operation of nearly a thousand dams worldwide. Discussions with him and access to his remarkable library are in large part responsible for whatever air of technical authenticity the text projects.

I am grateful, too, for the friendly cooperation of Dr. Bruce Tschantz, Chief of Dam Safety for the Federal Emergency Management Agency and professor of civil engineering at the University of Tennessee; James J. Watkins of the California Office of Emergency Services; Charles Von Berg of the California Department of Water Resources, Oroville Field Division; Thomas Struthers, Butte County (California) Civil Disaster Coordinator; Larry Gillick, Sheriff-Coroner of Butte County; Richard Stenberg, Undersheriff of Butte County; and Paul Girard, Pacific Gas & Electric Co. The drawings were made by Mark Mikulich of Windsor, California.

For reading parts of the manuscript and making many valuable suggestions, I wish to thank Leonard Tong, Don McGinnis, Bob Jewett, Janice Davis, Mark Van Liere, Gooch Ryan, David Parry, Julia Reisz, Sally Culley, Kent Bolter, and Madeleine Bouchard.

None of the above-named is in any way to blame for the plot of this novel, for the characters, or for the views the characters express, which were entirely of my own devising. The characters are not patterned after anybody I ever knew or heard of.

Sierra Canyon Dam, which does not exist, shares a few design features with Oroville Dam, which does. The similarities were adopted for convenience and are not intended to imply anything about anything. Oroville Dam is as safe as it can be.

Not all of America's fifty thousand dams are as safe as they can be. In 1981 the Corps of Engineers will complete a four-year survey of the nine thousand nonfederal dams that would cause the most damage if they failed. Results so far are alarming: a third of the dams are unsafe. In West Virginia, South Carolina, Tennessee, Georgia, and Missouri, according to figures in the Corps study, more dams are unsafe than safe. Nobody wants to pay the cost of repairs.

Existing dams are one problem, future dams are another. Amazingly, in most parts of the country there is little to impede construction of still more hazardous dams. Very few states have adopted anything resembling the design, construction, and inspection regulations urged by the United States Committee on Large Dams. Readers who don't like catastrophic man-made floods should write to their legislators and demand action.

Robert Byrne
San Rafael, California